Ruth Meyer has once again crafted a gripping story that doesn't shy away from the hard and the messy of life. Our favorite characters have returned, a bit more mature and as real as ever, and they've brought with them some great additions. Come join Meyer again in her world of love, loss, growth, and above all, Christian life together.

Sarah Baughman
Author of *A Flame in the Dark: A Novel About Luther's Reformation*
Houston, Texas

I have been addicted to this series since starting Grace Alone! With each book I become more engrossed with the characters and their ever-changing lives. In this book there is major growth for several of the characters and relationships are strengthened even through many hardships. I love the sincerity and authenticity of the characters and feel as though I truly know them and can connect with them. The scripture woven throughout the text of the book reminds me that during good and even hard times there is His promising word to look to and hold on to. The characters stand up for their beliefs even if that means they must "stand alone." This is a great read and Ruth is brilliant in her writing because she will have you laughing and crying for this admirable family! I pray there is more to come because I am eager to find out what will happen next!

Esther Marz
Registered nurse, proud mother, avid reader
St. Louis, Missouri

I was hooked into this series from the first book, and the story continues to get better. The characters are extremely relatable and they encounter a variety of situations that make them question, but ultimately strengthen, their faith in God. In Stand Alone, *we get an inside look into Jackson's life. I thought it was extremely interesting given the fact that I've "watched" him grow up in the last couple of books. Every time Ruth publishes another book in this series, I just feel like I'm going back into my comfort zone with a family that I keep rooting for.*

Melissa Kwiatkowski
High School Teacher at International Academy
Bloomfield Hills, MI

When I pick up a book by Ruth Meyer, her characters draw me into their hearts and homes. I love following members of the Neunaber family and their friends through the joys and struggles in life. Through her books, Ruth has connected readers with characters of all ages. In Stand Alone, *we walk through the excitement and temptations that Jackson experiences as he transitions to college life. This book provides encouragement for all families to look to God and His unchanging Word for love and forgiveness. It is refreshing to see how a family can live their Christian faith out loud and be witnesses for Christ in all situations. Share this book with a friend!*

Deb Margrett
Lutheran Preschool Teacher and School Librarian
Milwaukee, Wisconsin

For my own Sam,

that you may always stand up for the truth

STAND ALONE

A NOVEL BY RUTH E. MEYER

THE SOLA SERIES

TruthNotes Press

On Christ, the solid rock, I stand;

All other ground is sinking sand.

—Edward Mote, 1797-1874

CHAPTER

1

From the very start, the game was neck and neck. The undefeated Franklin Cougars had met their match against the Mapleport Chargers in the football semifinals. Whenever one team scored a touchdown, the other team answered in kind. Grace's stomach was in knots the entire game, especially whenever Jackson had the ball. The stakes were higher for this game than for most, and not just because it was the semifinals. Rumor had it that a few college scouts were in attendance, with their eyes on two players from Franklin as well as the star receiver of the Chargers. It was nerve racking to know they were here to watch her son's performance.

As the final seconds approached, Mapleport was down by three with the ball. There was just enough time left for two plays if they could stop the clock after the first. The center snapped the ball to the quarterback, who faked a long pass before slipping it to Jackson. He snuck around behind the line and made a breakaway, running for all he was worth, two opposing players hot on his heels. He made it to the forty-yard line... the thirty...

"Go, Jackson! You can do it!" Katie cheered for her brother, jumping up and down.

He passed the twenty-yard line. "We're gonna win!" Freddie shouted next to Katie. "He's gonna score!"

Jackson had just crossed the ten-yard line when one of his pursuers decided to make a last-ditch effort to stop him. Mid-stride, he leaped at Jackson and managed to grab his leg. Jackson stumbled, and the sudden change caused the other Franklin player to trip as well, stepping on Jackson's leg as all three of them fell. Jackson's other leg was stretching out for the next step, and he looked like he was doing the splits as he went down. Before long, the rest of the players on the field reached them and piled on top.

"Did he make it?" yelled a lady near Jackson's family. Grace realized she was crossing her fingers, willing Jackson across the goal line.

As the players started detangling themselves, they got up one by one until only Jackson was left. The ball was inches from the end zone. He hadn't scored. The crowd groaned in disappointment.

But Jackson didn't get up. He rolled into a fetal position, grabbing his leg. Grace clutched David's arm tightly, the blood draining from her face. "I'm going down to him," she said, but her husband restrained her.

"Hang on," he urged. "The coach and athletic trainer are coming out. Let them check on him first. You know Jackson would be humiliated if his mom ran onto the field for a pulled muscle."

It quickly became apparent that it wasn't just a pulled muscle, though. Jackson's cries of pain echoed through the otherwise eerily silent stadium. He wasn't one to put on a show or fake an injury. This was for real.

Grace's heart all but stopped as the athletic trainer summoned the paramedics on duty. When they brought the stretcher onto the field, Grace turned and fled down the bleacher steps, desperate to reach her son. David didn't stop her this time. He was right behind her.

When they reached the field, they both broke into a jog to follow Jackson as he was wheeled toward the waiting ambulance that attended every game as a precaution. The crowd clapped as a show of support for the wounded player, but Grace barely heard it.

"Jackson!" she shrieked as she approached. He looked over at her, grimacing in pain as the paramedic put a knee immobilizer on him. They had taken off his helmet and his face was deathly white, covered in beads of perspiration.

"Sorry, Mom," he gasped through clenched teeth. "I didn't make it."

Tears sprang to her eyes. "Oh, Jackson," she sniffled, reaching out to grasp his hand. "Don't even worry about the game! What happened?"

"My leg..." groaned Jackson. "I've never been in this much pain before. It's really bad."

"Is it his ACL?" David asked the paramedic, who was prepping things to take Jackson in the ambulance.

The paramedic's face was grim. "Looks like a broken leg," he said quietly. "But until they get x-rays, it's impossible to know exactly what happened."

Grace cried openly as she smoothed back Jackson's sweaty brown hair. "My poor baby," she wailed.

"I'm sorry, ma'am, but we need to get him to the hospital," the paramedic said. "Only one of you can ride with him."

"You go," David insisted. "I'll check with Liv and Andy about taking the kids so I can meet you at the hospital. Text or call with updates."

Mutely, Grace nodded and followed her son into the ambulance, feeling detached. She was aware of the fact that the coaches were conferring with the refs on the field, but she couldn't care less about the game anymore. Her son was on his way to the hospital.

And Jackson Williams was not coming back.

X-rays at the local community hospital showed that Jackson had a high femoral break. Looking at the images on the film, Grace cringed. The bone had actually been broken in two places, as if a triangular chip had been cut out. Due to the severity of the break, the doctor on duty told Grace that the injury would require surgery. They had already consulted with an orthopedic pediatric surgeon at the children's hospital an hour away, and he recommended they do the surgery as soon as possible. Thus, Grace found herself once more in an ambulance with Jackson, this time on their way to surgery.

David met her at the children's hospital shortly after they arrived, and together they met with the orthopedic surgeon, who explained that he would insert a metal plate along the length of Jackson's femur. There would be two incisions in his leg, and the plate would be screwed to the bone for support.

"Treatment for broken femurs has come a long way," Dr. Kahn informed them. "When I first started practicing, standard procedure was to put the patient in traction. Imagine having his leg in a big cast and not being able to move it at all for an entire month. It was dreadfully cumbersome. With his metal plate, Jackson will still be able to go to school, provided he can navigate with his wheelchair at first. He should be able to get around with crutches after a week or so. He's much more mobile this way."

Their consultation over, Grace and David shook the doctor's hand, hugged Jackson, and watched the nurses wheel him toward the operating room. Another nurse led them kindly to the waiting room and left them there with blankets in case they got chilly. When she left, the doors shut behind her with a dull thud that seemed to accentuate the fact that they were completely alone in the deserted waiting room. It was already one thirty in the morning, well past normal hospital hours. Only emergency surgeries took place at this time.

Grace fought waves of panic as the strain of the last number of hours caught up to her. David pulled her into a hug and sank down onto a plastic couch with her.

"He'll be okay," David assured. "He'll be in a lot of pain for a while, but his leg will heal."

"I know," Grace said in a tiny little voice. "But being back here again brings back all the memories of Katie's surgery three years ago. And then Faith's health scare and surgery a few months later. I was hoping we were done with hospital visits."

"I know. Me too."

"Besides, David," continued Grace, "my son is on an operating table in there, and I am completely powerless to do anything to help him."

"Actually, that's not true," David contradicted gently. "We can pray."

Grace looked at him with tears in her eyes, and together they petitioned their Heavenly Father on behalf of Jackson, Dr. Kahn, and the other medical staff in the operating room that night.

The next three hours passed slowly, and Grace dozed off in David's lap a few times, the hospital-issued blanket slung over her shoulders. When the nurse finally came in to inform them that the surgery was over and the doctor would be in shortly,

Grace could see David looked as bleary-eyed as she felt.

Dr. Kahn arrived half an hour later, assuring them that everything went well, and still half an hour later, another nurse came to tell them Jackson was waking from the anesthesia. She led them to the recovery room to see Jackson, who was loopy from the anesthesia and couldn't really carry on a conversation. By the time they got to the hospital room and officially checked in, it was five forty-five in the morning.

Grace knew David was every bit as exhausted as she was, but there was only one tiny couch in the room. It pulled out into a bed of sorts, and David insisted she sleep on it while he piled pillows and blankets on the floor next to her. It was by far one of the least comfortable ways to sleep, but they were so tired they both fell asleep immediately for a few fitful hours of sleep.

With the seven o'clock shift change, the new nurse on duty came into the room cheerfully to check Jackson's vitals and meet her charge. Grace was groggy as her eyes adjusted to the light the nurse turned on. She had a terrible headache, her eyes felt like they had sand in them, and she was feeling pretty sorry for herself and her son, who would now require help for even the most basic functions like making it to the bathroom. The last thing she needed was one more dependent person in the household.

Once the nurse left, David suggested, "Why don't you go down to the cafeteria and get some coffee and breakfast? The coffee will help put you in a better frame of mind. Bring me a cup too. I'll stay here with Jackson in case the doctor comes to discuss things with us."

Nodding weakly, she kissed him on the forehead, squeezed Jackson's hand, and grabbed her purse before she left the room. For once, she was grateful for her thick, curly hair, which generally looked the same whether she combed it or not. She ran her fingers through her dark locks a few times and decided it was good enough.

Upon reaching the cafeteria, she got in line behind a drawn-looking man at the grill. He ordered an omelet, and the cook asked, "How is she today?" The man shrugged and smiled a sad smile, at which the cook nodded sympathetically. He busied himself with the omelet, and when he handed it to the stranger ahead of Grace, he said, "God be with you."

Wondering slightly at the exchange, Grace placed an order for an omelet as well, and four minutes later she was pulling out a chair in the cafeteria, a hot breakfast and two cups of coffee on her tray. While she ate, she answered texts and updated her sister and mom about Jackson's situation. Setting down her phone at last, she took a swallow of her coffee.

And that's when she saw them.

The man who had been ahead of her in line was sitting in the corner with a little girl. The girl was in a wheelchair, hooked up to a rolling IV cart. Even from the back, Grace could tell she was quite sick. Grace's eyes clouded with tears as she watched the man feed his daughter small bites, smiling and encouraging her. He snapped a picture of her on his phone, pride and love showing on his face.

Feeling as though she were intruding on a private moment, Grace looked away, trying desperately to blink back her tears. As she glanced around the cafeteria, she saw children with bald heads, children pushing IV carts, and others being pulled in wagons, propped up with pillows. Grace knew that some of those children would never go home.

Suddenly her own situation seemed very insignificant. A broken femur was nothing to sneeze at, but Jackson's leg would heal. He would miss basketball season, but he would be okay in time for baseball. Her son would live.

Abruptly, Grace stood and walked to a small courtyard to be alone. Once there, she broke down. She cried for all the children who suffered from terminal illnesses. She cried for their families. She wept for the doctors and nurses who had to deal with these situations on a daily basis. As she wept, she prayed for them. When her tears were spent, she wiped her face and took a cleansing breath. She needed to get back to Jackson.

Walking back to her table in the cafeteria, she saved the two cups of coffee and disposed of everything else before walking to the elevators. When she got there, she was surprised to see the father and daughter who had been eating in the corner. The stranger looked at her with compassion in his eyes, perceiving she had been crying.

"How are you holding up?" he asked quietly as they boarded the elevator.

That did it. Grace's tears started anew as she sobbed, "I'm not crying for me. I'm crying for you. My son is only here for a broken femur." The words sounded ludicrous, but he seemed to understand what she meant.

"She is dying," he replied with his sad smile. There was no time to mince words.

"I know," she whispered.

"Cystic fibrosis. Her older brother already died from it. My wife and I are both carriers. I don't know if our youngest will get it or not. I don't think we can take it if she does."

Grace could only nod. She felt sick to her stomach.

By now they had reached his floor, and as he pushed his daughter off the elevator, he said, "God be with you, ma'am. Go give your son a hug."

"I'm praying for you," she called, just as the doors shut

behind him. Her words fell flat even to her own ears. A complete stranger had just shared his heartbreaking story in less than a minute, and she gave a stock, pithy answer?

As the elevator rose to her floor, Grace had an overwhelming urge to do just what the man had suggested—give her son a hug. She'd never thought she would be grateful for a broken femur.

CHAPTER

2

When her sister and brother-in-law arrived around noon, Grace welcomed the distraction. Olivia and Andy McNeal were sure to get her mind off the doctor's visits and the father and daughter she'd met earlier. She only hoped Jackson was up for their exuberance.

"Hey, man, what were you thinking?" Andy greeted Jackson heartily.

"Seriously!" Olivia seconded. "I mean, I get that you like being the center of attention, but *this*? A bit drastic, don't you think?"

Jackson chuckled halfheartedly through his pain. The nurse had just given him more painkillers, but they hadn't kicked in quite yet. The poor kid looked bad.

"Did we at least win?" he asked. "David didn't even watch the last play." He glanced reproachfully at his stepfather as he gingerly shifted to better face his visitors.

"They put up a good fight," said Andy gravely.

"Oh, man, we *lost*?" groaned Jackson. "After all that?"

"So Josh fakes a handoff to Garrett—" Olivia began, but her

husband interrupted.

"Garrett barrels through the defensive line, making like he has the ball—"

"While in fact Josh kept the ball to run it in himself!"

Andy took up the story. "And the Cougars realized it and piled on top of him right at the goal line…"

"Same deal as your tackle—everyone gets up one by one until only Josh is left there with the ball," Olivia added, before both fell uncharacteristically silent.

"And…?" prompted Jackson. "Did he score or not?"

"Touchdown!" they both shouted exuberantly. The entire floor could probably hear them.

"*Yes!*" Jackson pumped his fist in the air. "We're off to State!" Then his face fell. "Well, *they're* off to State," he said dejectedly. "Without me, I don't know how good they'll do."

"How *well*," corrected David as the adults chuckled. Grace exchanged a smile with her husband. At least Jackson's ego was still intact. It was refreshing to see some of his usual spunk.

"Besides, you can be, like, their mascot or something," Andy encouraged. "With you sitting on the sidelines in a wheelchair, they'll play extra hard for you. Maybe you can still motivate them to win!"

Jackson's chest swelled. "That's true," he agreed. "They'll rally behind their captain."

Everyone laughed again, and the McNeals peppered Jackson with questions about his surgery, but a few minutes later he started to yawn.

"That's our cue," Olivia said. "Come on, Andy. We need to let this guy rest." She turned to Grace. "Will he be released today?"

"Probably not," answered Grace. "He needs a wheelchair before they'll discharge him, and the medical equipment place is unpredictable on weekends. They've been calling and faxing the order from here, but it looks like it won't be delivered till the morning."

"Probably better that way," Andy said. "Gives this tough guy one more day of recuperating before going home to a full house and all those younger siblings. Get your rest, man," he addressed Jackson. "And when you get your prescription, come to me. I'll hook you up with some good narcotics."

"Andrew McNeal!" his wife gasped. "Handing out narcotics to a teenager!"

"Trust me, nothing else will touch this kind of pain," Andy said. "We pharmacists know these things. He'll only get slightly hooked in the couple weeks he has to take them. A few withdrawal headaches will be the only side effect."

"Wonderful," Grace said dryly.

"Ah, no worries. Just some of the pros and *Kahns* of surgery," he answered with a sly grin.

David was the first to get the pun and groaned in response. "I'm sure Dr. Kahn's *never* heard that one before," he muttered with a shake of his head.

"Ooh, good one, Andy!" Olivia said with a sparkling laugh. "Dad will love that!"

"And speaking of which, we'd better get back so we can relieve your parents of childcare duties," said Andy. "David, you come with us. Leave the car for Grace and Jackson to take home tomorrow. Watching the kids one night is fine, but I'm not getting four kids ready for school tomorrow."

David chuckled. "I'm pretty sure Freddie and Katie can get themselves ready," he pointed out. Freddie was in the eighth grade, and Katie was in fifth. "The twins usually get dressed on their own too. You just have to put their hair in ponytails."

"Those days are well past for me, my friend," insisted Andy.

"Like, twenty-plus years past. I'm not used to dealing with four-year-olds anymore."

"Besides, I promised we'd bring you back for supper so you can have a decent meal," Olivia said. "Mom's making a huge pot of chili and a double batch of her famous corn muffins."

"Go ahead," Grace encouraged her husband. "You'll sleep better in our own bed. We'll be fine here."

David relented at last, gave her a kiss, clapped Jackson on the shoulder, and left with the McNeals. Jackson drifted off to sleep, and in the lull, Grace went over to the pull-out couch again. She could use a nap herself.

A soft knock on the door startled Grace out of her sleep, and she sat up in alarm. Glancing quickly at the clock, she realized she'd been asleep for nearly three hours. How had that happened?

Jackson stirred and moaned from his spot on the bed, waking as well, so Grace invited, "Come in!"

The door opened slowly, and a young female voice asked, "Jackson?"

"Yeah, I'm here," he said, fiddling with the buttons on his bed to adjust it to a more upright position.

A pretty young lady entered the room with a bouquet of balloons and a poster board. Her long blond hair was pulled up into a loose ponytail with soft tendrils escaping from the sides. She wore a tight sweater that showed off her curves to full advantage, as well as a pair of skinny jeans that might as well have been painted on. Grace's eyebrows shot up as she entered. It was an hour drive from Mapleport. Obviously, she'd made a concerted effort to visit.

When Jackson saw her, he turned deep red. "Oh, hey, Miranda," he said, trying to be casual. Grace knew she'd heard the name before, and the girl looked vaguely familiar, but she couldn't place her.

"Hey, Forty-Three," Miranda said flirtatiously, referring to Jackson's football number. "How are you doing?"

"I've been better," replied Jackson.

She giggled and handed him the poster board while setting the balloon bouquet on the rolling table next to the bed. "All the football players and cheerleaders signed it for you, and a whole bunch of other students who were at the game too. We're all rooting for you."

"Thanks," Jackson said. "That was nice of you."

"It's the least the Queen could do for her King," she replied, still in that flirty voice. Jackson flushed darker as he glanced covertly at his mother.

It finally dawned on Grace why Miranda looked so familiar. She had been voted the Homecoming Queen a month ago, while Jackson had been voted King. Miranda looked different at Homecoming, of course, wearing a dress and sporting an elegant updo for her hair, but now that the connection was made, Grace couldn't believe she hadn't realized it sooner.

Miranda perched on the foot of the bed, avoiding Jackson's leg, and looked at Grace. "You must be Mrs. Williams," she said in a perky voice.

"Actually, I'm Mrs. Neunaber," Grace replied levelly, put off by Miranda's bold familiarity with both Jackson and herself.

"Oh! I thought you were Jackson's mom."

"I am," Grace assured her. "Jackson's father and I have been divorced for more than ten years. I remarried five years ago."

"Ah. I see."

There was an awkward lull in the conversation, and Grace figured both teenagers would be more comfortable without her in the room. Dutifully, she rose and stretched. "Jackson, I'm going to grab another cup of coffee, okay? Miranda, nice to meet you."

"Likewise! Take good care of him, okay?" She was back to using that overly-cheerful voice, and Grace inwardly rolled her eyes at the inane statement.

"I will," Grace promised in a slightly syrupy tone, hoping Miranda didn't pick up on the fact that she was mocking her.

Breathing a sigh of relief as she exited the room, Grace took her time strolling down to the cafeteria, keeping an eye out for the father and daughter she'd encountered earlier that day. Although she loitered in the cafeteria awhile, she didn't see the two, and eventually she figured she'd given Miranda and Jackson plenty of time to flirt with one another. Upon reentering the room, she was grateful to find only Jackson there.

"Did you have a nice visit with Miranda?" Grace asked as she settled herself in the chair by the built-in desk.

Jackson reddened and answered, "I guess."

"It was awfully nice of her to come all this way to see you," she continued, hoping to elicit a more forthcoming response.

"Yep."

He wasn't making this easy on her. "Do you like her?" Grace finally prompted. She couldn't help herself. She was dying of curiosity.

"She likes me," said Jackson.

"I figured as much," Grace said. "But you didn't answer me. Do you like her?"

"She's the most popular girl in our grade. All the guys want to go out with her."

"Including you?"

Jackson squirmed. "She's super hot, yeah—I mean, *really pretty*," he amended quickly, catching her disapproving glance at the description. "Anyone with eyes can see that, but…"

"But…?"

"She's not really my type."

"Why do you say that?"

"Mom, why do you care about this so much?" Jackson sank back onto his pillows with an exasperated sigh.

"I'm just curious, that's all!"

He rolled his eyes. "Okay, fine. She's not my type because all she seems to care about is guys. She flirts too much. And she thinks because she's pretty every guy should practically worship her."

Grace considered his response. It was mature of her son to see past Miranda's outward beauty and realize she was shallow. Miranda *did* have strikingly good looks going for her, but Grace was glad that wasn't the only thing Jackson noticed.

"So is there anyone at school you *are* interested in?" Grace asked with a sly smile.

"*Mother!*" Jackson slapped his hand to his forehead. "Why do you suddenly want to talk about this? I don't want to discuss girls with you! If I start going out with someone I'll tell you, but until then, don't worry about it!"

He crossed his arms over his chest and turned his head away from her as if to go back to sleep. Grace smiled to herself and shook her head. As well as she thought she knew her children, she hadn't the first clue what kind of girl would finally catch Jackson's eye. But now she was dreadfully curious to find out.

CHAPTER

3

Jackson was restless as the afternoon dragged on. He wasn't one to sit around doing nothing, and it irked him that he was now confined to a hospital bed. The pain meds were wearing off, but he wasn't allowed another dose for half an hour. Plus, he was getting irritated with his mom hovering around trying to start a discussion.

So when Grace asked *again* if she could get him anything, he decided to send her on an errand. Even though he could easily have called the cafeteria to deliver food to his room, he asked his mom to run to McDonald's for a large fries, two Big Macs, and a shake. He figured that would keep her out of his hair for awhile.

Once she left, Jackson basked in the quietness of the room for a few minutes before he carefully eased his leg off the bed and lowered it to the floor. He knew he wasn't supposed to attempt hopping anywhere or using his crutches without someone else in the room, but he at least wanted to change his position. His entire backside was sore from lying in bed.

A knock on the door made him groan. *Now* what? He

hoped it was just a nurse. He wasn't up to facing anyone else or making small talk. When the door opened, however, he was stunned to see who was there.

"Hey, kiddo, how ya doing?" Bob drawled with a sympathetic smile.

Jackson could only stare, mute, at the man standing before him.

"Are you trying to go somewhere?" continued Bob. "Need me to help you make it to the bathroom?"

Jackson felt his face flush as a surge of anger coursed through his veins. Even if he was limited in mobility, he wasn't about to ask the father he barely knew to help him use the restroom. "What are *you* doing here?" he demanded.

"What do you think? I came to see you! Your mom told me it was a pretty bad break."

"It would appear that one of us has to be in the hospital before you come to see us," he sneered.

"Son—"

"You can stop right there," Jackson interrupted coldly. "There's only one man in this world who's earned the right to call me 'son,' and it isn't you. Depositing your DNA doesn't automatically qualify you for the position."

"Okay, okay, you're right, *Jackson*," amended Bob. "I—"

"So you're here to swoop in like the caring dad once more, huh?" he interrupted again. "Just like you came to see Faith when she was in the hospital. You think because you gave her part of your liver you're some sort of family hero now? Like that one act erases all those years of completely ignoring us? You might be Faith's hero, but you aren't mine!" Jackson crossed his arms over his chest defiantly, wishing he could storm away. Unfortunately, his dad had him more or less cornered, which made him even more upset.

"I'm not trying to be your hero, so—ah, Jackson. I just wanted to see you."

"Hmm. Seems to me you could have come any number of times. Maybe to one of my football games? I've had a few away games near Kalamazoo. That's not such a bad drive from Chicago. But no, this is more dramatic, isn't it? You look better if you come make a hospital visit."

"I know you're mad about the divorce, Jackson, but that was years ago. Faith and I have made up. I'd like to do the same with you. But you seem determined to resent me and hold on to your hard feelings no matter what I say."

"That's because you can *say* anything you want. But it's your *actions* that count. And you abandoning us speaks louder than any words you say now. It wasn't just when you left, *Dad*," he said mockingly. "What about all the times after that when you failed to be there? You never sent birthday cards or Christmas gifts. It's like you just disappeared off the face of the earth. You left when Mom was *pregnant*! And you didn't even come back to meet Katie! So, no, I don't respect you at all. Maybe you won everyone else's hearts when you donated your liver, but you didn't win mine. Now please just leave. I have nothing more to say to you." He glared at his father, who stepped back after a moment, his shoulders sagging slightly.

"I didn't mean to upset you," he said. "I'm sorry. But I hope you recover quickly."

"So do I."

Bob waited a moment longer, as if waiting for Jackson to say more or change his mind, but Jackson remained silent, still glowering at him. Bob sighed and turned toward the door. "Take care, then," he said as he walked out.

Jackson watched him go, and only when he was convinced his father wasn't going to return to the room did he allow himself to take a full breath. He was awfully glad his mom hadn't been here for the exchange. Goodness knows she would have been after him to be kinder to his dad, urging him to forgive and forget. But Jackson was nowhere near ready for that.

He grunted as he struggled to get his leg back onto the bed without causing excruciating pain. He'd pretend he was sleeping when his mom returned. She didn't need to know Bob had been there at all. The less she knew, the better.

CHAPTER

4

When Jackson was released late Monday morning, Grace brought him home, slightly apprehensive about how his limitations would affect her. Selfish as it sounded, she didn't want to be waiting on her teenager hand and foot. She'd never realized how poorly their house was designed for someone who was handicapped. The halls were too narrow for Jackson's wheelchair, the bathroom on the main floor was too small for him to fully extend his leg, and stairs were out of the question.

Since Jackson's room was in the basement, he had few options other than sitting on the couch with his leg extended in front of him. His four-year-old twin sisters constantly pestered him to play with them or read to them, and Grace found herself taking advantage of that fact, often relying on him to keep them occupied. She figured it was a good tradeoff, since he asked her for stuff from his room or snacks throughout the day.

As Andy predicted, Jackson was prescribed narcotics, and over the next few days, his pain level moderated slightly. Grace could tell the hardest thing for Jackson was sitting still for so long. He didn't feel up to navigating school yet, so she insisted he stay home for the shortened week of Thanksgiving. She'd called the high school to ask about homework, and the secretary assured her that a friend named Sam had already offered to drop off his assignments.

On Wednesday afternoon, Grace hummed to herself as she chopped tomatoes for the salad, excited for the visitors who were due to arrive any minute. When the doorbell rang, she wiped her hands on a towel and called excitedly, "That'll be Faith and Spencer with the kids!"

She hurried to the door, a smile lighting up her face. She sorely missed her oldest daughter and was itching to see her grandchildren again as well. But it wasn't the Youngs on the porch. It was a high schooler. A girl, at that.

Her wavy sandy-blond hair had a conspicuous streak of green off to one side, and she had a small diamond stud in her nose. She wore a belted denim shirt dress over leggings, complete with army boots. Looking slightly nervous, she tucked a lock of hair behind an ear and pushed her glasses up on her nose.

"Oh, hello!" Grace exclaimed in surprise.

"Hi," the girl replied shyly. "You must be Jackson's mom. I came to bring his homework. My name is Sam Lewis."

Grace gaped in amazement. She'd never even considered the possibility that Sam was a girl. Grace wondered what exactly her relationship with Jackson looked like.

Remembering her manners at last, Grace responded, "It's very nice to meet you, Sam. Thank you for bringing his homework. He'll have a lot of catching up to do, that's for sure. Right this way," she continued, leading Sam toward the living room.

When they reached the doorway, Grace said, "Someone

here to see you, Jackson."

Jackson was turned away from them, his left leg extended on the couch as he bent his head in concentration over his little sister's hand. Without looking up, he said, "Hey, sis. Glad you guys made it back okay. I don't know if Hope is old enough yet, but I can paint her nails next if you want me to. I'm almost done with Evelyn's manicure."

At the awkward silence that followed his comment, Jackson turned his head toward the door, a red nail polish brush poised in his right hand. When he saw Sam standing there, he turned the same shade as the polish. "Ohhhh..." he groaned in dismay. "I... um... I thought... I was expecting my older sister and her daughter. I'm supposed to be watching the twins, and... I mean, I don't usually paint nails for little girls..."

Charlotte bashfully walked over to the newcomer and displayed her nails. "Jackson already did mine! Don't I look pretty?"

"You sure do!" encouraged Sam, a kind smile on her face. Grace silently thanked her for the response.

"Want him to paint yours too?"

Jackson turned a shade darker. "That's a tempting offer," Sam answered, "but I just stopped by to give him his homework from school."

"Are you his girlfriend?" piped up Evelyn from the couch.

By now, Jackson was nearly purple, and Grace intervened on behalf of her son before the twins could embarrass him further. "This is Sam. She's a friend from school. It was very nice of her to bring his homework so he can work on it over the weekend. Sam, this is Charlotte and Evelyn. Jackson has been a real trouper about helping me keep an eye on his sisters while he's confined to the couch. Make yourself comfortable while he's finishing with Evelyn, and then you girls come into the kitchen for a snack so Sam can show Jackson what he has to do, okay?" She turned to Sam to ask, "Can I get you anything to drink?"

"Oh, no, ma'am. I'm fine. Thanks, though."

As Grace returned to the kitchen, Sam wandered over to the wall to look at family pictures while Jackson hurriedly slapped polish on the rest of Evelyn's nails. He was mortified that Sam had come while he was painting nails, of all things.

"Okay, Evy, you're all set," he proclaimed. "Blow on them for a while before you touch anything, though."

The girls happily bounded into the kitchen to ask for their promised snack, and the door to the backyard opened as Freddie entered. "I cleaned up all the dog poop out there," he announced to the assembly at large, "so the girls can play outside with Griffin if they want." He raised his voice to shout into the living room, "Hey, Jackson! Need me to help you go to the bathroom before Faith gets here?"

Jackson closed his eyes and prayed that Jesus would return immediately. At least Sam was facing away from him, graciously pretending not to hear as she studied David and Grace's wedding picture intently.

"Jackson has a friend in there," he heard his mother explain in a low voice to Freddie.

"His girlfriend!" Evelyn exclaimed brightly.

"Is it the chick who came to the hospital?" asked Freddie, not softly enough.

Take me now, Lord. Take me now, Jackson pleaded.

Just then there was a knock at the door before Faith's voice called, "Hello! We're here!"

Grace and Katie both squealed and ran to the entryway to greet the newcomers. Forgetting all about wet polish, Charlotte and Evelyn ran to greet their oldest sister and say hi to Griffin.

Footsteps sounded on the stairs as David ran down. "G. David! How are you, buddy?" he enthused. David was the only one who called Griffin *G. David*, to accentuate the fact that Faith had chosen the middle name in his honor. "And look at that little beauty!" he crooned. "Hi, Hope!"

Excited chatter and laughter echoed through the house, and Sam shifted uncomfortably from one foot to the other, looking dreadfully embarrassed.

Jackson offered an apologetic grimace. He didn't envy her coming when his whole family was there. This had to be overwhelming for her.

"Jackson! Good to see you, bro!" Faith exclaimed as she entered the room carrying Hope. She sailed right past Sam without noticing her due to Sam's position by the wall. "How's the leg?"

"Not good," said Jackson. "But, hey, I stopped the clock for the team! We won semis!"

Faith laughed. "All for the greater good, huh?" She handed the baby and a bottle to him. "Listen, can you do me a huge favor since you're sitting here anyhow? Can you feed her for me? I pumped some breast milk on the way here."

Jackson's face burned. Sam had to think their entire family was insane. He desperately hoped she wouldn't mention any of this at school. He'd never live it down—the star football player who painted preschoolers' nails, couldn't use the restroom without help, and conversed with his older sister about breast milk.

Faith turned to leave the room, only then noticing Sam. "Oh! I'm sorry! I didn't realize anyone else was here. Am I interrupting anything?"

"Sam stopped by to give me the assignments I missed this week," Jackson explained, willing the color to leave his face.

"Sam, this is my older sister, Faith. She and her husband and kids live in Ann Arbor. This is their baby, Hope. She's six months old."

"She's adorable," Sam said, walking over to inspect the infant, who by now was busily sucking the bottle.

"Thank you!" Faith beamed as she gazed at her daughter. "She's a really good-natured baby. And I'm telling you, Jackson is seriously awesome with babies. He's a pro. Even changes poopy diapers for me since I can't do it myself." With that, she left the room, leaving Jackson to flush deeper still. This kept getting worse and worse. His carefully cultivated image as a jock was shot in a matter of minutes, no thanks to his family.

Sam frowned in confusion. "She doesn't know how to change diapers?"

"Um, no… I mean, yeah, she does, but she's not supposed to unless she's wearing a hazmat suit. She had a liver transplant a few years ago and there's this laundry list of things she's not allowed to do. For some reason changing diapers is on the list." He couldn't believe he was talking with a classmate about poopy diapers. *Thanks for nothing, Faith,* he thought sarcastically.

"Hmm. Weird. I wonder why," she said with a shrug. "Well, I'll be quick. I didn't realize I was stopping at such a busy time here. The assignments are pretty self-explanatory, but if you need clarification, call or text me." Jackson nodded but doubted very much he'd need her help. He was half tempted not to even bother with the assignments. His teachers would be understanding, wouldn't they? After all, he'd had surgery less than a week ago.

Sam continued. "I'm really sorry about your leg too. I'm sure you're disappointed you can't play for the championship game or do basketball this year. And who knows what this will do for football in college? I know how much you want to play for U of M. But when you get back to school, if you need help getting around, I'd be happy to push your wheelchair for you or carry your books or whatever. Just let me know, okay?"

"Sure thing," Jackson replied. "I appreciate that. Thanks for coming over. I'm sorry my house is so crazy right now. It's not always like this." Then, with a devious smile, he lowered his voice to say, "It's usually worse."

He grinned at the sound of her laughter. When she turned to leave, he said, "I wish I could walk you to the door. I hate to make you fend for yourself with all of them out there. Although if you prefer, you could sneak out the back way into the yard and let yourself out through the gate. After all, Freddie cleaned up all those doggie deposits. You're safe."

Sam giggled and tucked an errant lock of hair behind her ear. "I'll be fine," she assured him. "See you at school."

There was a small commotion when Sam reached the entryway. Jackson cringed as he overheard the conversation.

"Ah! Who have we here?" David asked.

"That's Jackson's girlfriend!" exclaimed Charlotte.

"Want to come play Barbies with us tomorrow?" Evelyn asked excitedly. "Jackson promised he would be Ken!"

"Are you gonna marry Uncle Jackson?" asked Griffin.

Just leave, Sam. Jackson begged silently. The sooner she left, the better.

Grace spoke next. "This is Jackson's friend from school. Sam stopped by to drop off his assignments." She made the proper introductions to David, Spencer, and Griffin.

"Why do you have a boy's name?" Griffin asked. "And I think you got paint in your hair in art class."

"Griffin!" admonished Spencer. "That's not polite. Sam is a nickname for Samantha, and she does her hair like that on purpose. She likes it that way."

"Hey, Griffin, wanna see Jackson's scar?" Evelyn asked. "It's way up at the top of his leg. But you might see his underwear," she added with a giggle. All three pre-kindergartners snickered. Jackson wished he could disappear.

"I need to get back home," Sam said hastily, "but it was nice to meet all of you."

"Likewise, Sam," said Grace.

The adults said their goodbyes, and when Sam had left, the others joined Jackson in the living room, where he was fuming on the couch. "Can you guys be any more humiliating?" he stormed. "Seriously! What is Sam going to think of me now?"

Faith looked at him in surprise. "Why are we embarrassing?"

Was she really that clueless? "Hello! Telling Sam that I change poopy diapers!" Jackson was suddenly irritated that he was still feeding Hope. He set the bottle down and shifted her to his shoulder so he could burp her, feeling more and more annoyed with his sister. Glaring across the room at her, he asked, "Since when is that an appropriate topic of conversation?"

"We talk about it all the time," she said, carelessly shrugging one shoulder. "It's part of life with a baby." Spencer nodded as he plopped down next to her on the floor.

"And asking me to feed Hope *breast* milk! Honestly, did you need to say the word? We figured it out without you spelling it out for us!" Hope let out a well-timed burp at that moment, and Jackson gritted his teeth as a wet spot appeared on his shirt from her spit up.

"Then what's the big deal?" Faith grabbed a burp cloth from the diaper bag next to her and threw it to Jackson. "It's a completely natural process."

"Guys don't want to hear about stuff like that, Faith," admonished Freddie.

"I don't mind," said Spencer, giving Faith a wicked grin. She elbowed him and rolled her eyes.

Jackson ignored them both and turned on his brother as he wiped his shoulder with the burp cloth. "*You* certainly didn't help matters either, Freddie! Talking about dog poop and asking if I needed you to help me go to the bathroom! Seriously?"

"I didn't even know she was here!" insisted Freddie.

"So *are* you gonna marry her?" asked Griffin.

"No!" Jackson yelled. "She's not even my girlfriend. And at this rate, she never will be!" He stopped abruptly and clamped his mouth shut, busying himself with feeding Hope the rest of the bottle.

"So you *do* like her?" Faith prompted with a sly grin, flipping her long brown hair over her shoulder.

Heat rose to Jackson's face. "It's none of your business," he shot back defensively. "She's a good friend and she's really nice. We were paired up in biology for the pig dissection lab a few weeks ago, and we got to know each other better. She's different from most other girls in my class. Like, more than the color of her hair. But I don't want to scare her away because of my crazy family!"

He continued darkly. "This stupid broken leg is a pain in more ways than one. Right about now is when I'd stomp off to my room and slam the door. Only now I can't. I'm stuck here with *you* people."

"Now, Jackson, if she's as good a friend as you say, she's probably glad to see you interact with your family," said David. "Sometimes people like it *more* when they catch others with their defenses down. Need I remind you that my first impression of your mother was her singing 'Life is a Highway'? She was mortified, but I thought it was adorable. Vulnerability can be quite charming."

Faith spoke next. "Besides, you're one to talk, brother dearest. One of Spencer's first impressions of our family was courtesy of you, as I recall. We walked into the house to hear you yelling at David and slamming your bedroom door in his face. Pretty sure you even knocked a picture off the wall. Great first impression."

"I remember that day," laughed Grace. "You were so embarrassed, Faith."

"But I loved seeing a glimpse of real life in your household," insisted Spencer. "It didn't scare me away at all."

"See? We've all had less-than-favorable experiences with first impressions," David pointed out. "It's probably not as big a deal as you fear."

"It's still humiliating," Jackson mumbled.

"Well, sweetie, we're sorry," soothed Grace, although she was the one who least needed to apologize. "We'll try not to embarrass you when guests are here. But for now, who's hungry? I've got snacks in the kitchen if anyone wants something before we eat. The lasagna will be out of the oven in half an hour. Jackson, I'll get you a plate of munchies."

Everyone dispersed to the kitchen, but David lingered until the others left the room, then walked over to address Jackson quietly. "I know how it is when you're trying to impress a girl," he said. "And I'm sorry things worked out for you the way they did today. It *is* embarrassing to be caught off guard like that, and younger siblings don't always have a lot of tact."

"*Older* siblings don't either," muttered Jackson, the baby in his arms a stark reminder of that fact.

David chuckled. "If Sam is a true friend, she won't let this color her perception of you. But I'd like to share a pearl of wisdom regarding women that's taken me many years to figure out. Are you ready for it?"

Jackson raised an eyebrow dubiously.

David lowered his voice to a dramatic whisper. "Women are completely impossible to understand. The sooner you know that, the better." He gave Jackson a little punch on the shoulder before joining the others in the kitchen.

Jackson shook his head and breathed out a laugh. His stepfather was hopelessly weird, but he was trying to connect with him, and that counted for something.

He sobered as his thoughts returned to Sam. She wasn't like the girls who tried to flirt with him to get his attention, who probably *would* make fun of him for the whole debacle this afternoon. If it had been Miranda there today, he was sure the whole thing would be all over social media by now.

But Sam wasn't like that. She was a little more serious, and being the new girl in class, she was also fairy shy. She kept to herself and ignored the curious looks of other students. Jackson wouldn't have gotten to know her had it not been for that biology lab, but when they'd worked together, he found she had a sense of humor and was genuinely friendly. He'd honestly be very surprised if she teased him about this afternoon.

Jackson allowed himself to relax ever so slightly. Sam was definitely a friend worth having.

CHAPTER

5

Later that evening, Faith sat with Spencer's family in the Youngs' formal living room, enjoying the hush that had settled over the house with the kids in bed. After dinner with her family, they'd driven the four miles to Spencer's parents' house, where they stayed most of the time they came back to Mapleport. The Youngs had plenty of space, and Faith couldn't deny that their house was considerably less chaotic than her own family's was.

"How's medical school going, Spencer dear?" inquired Vivian, taking a sip of wine.

"I love it," he answered. "This first year is what they call the 'Scientific Trunk.' In-depth classes about normal versus abnormal organ functions. I especially enjoyed the unit on the liver. I was already practically an expert, thanks to Faith." He smiled at his wife as he put his arm around her.

"I still don't know why you insisted upon staying at U of M," said Mr. Young, pausing for a swallow of whiskey. "Your undergrad grades were excellent, and we easily could have afforded Harvard or Johns Hopkins."

"I didn't want to go there," Spencer said. "U of M is ranked among the top ten in the country for primary care in medical schools. Besides, we didn't want to be so far from family. We want our kids to know their grandparents."

"That must have been Faith's idea," Mr. Young said, peering over his half glasses at the two of them. "Heaven knows *you* wouldn't have cared about that. I assume it's her family you're talking about anyhow."

Faith cut in before her husband could respond. "Since Griffin and Hope are your only grandchildren, I would think you'd be glad we decided to stay in Michigan. This way we can plan our visits around times when you're home from business." It was a slightly sarcastic reply, but Faith had long since gotten used to Mr. Young's caustic comments, and wasn't afraid to answer in kind.

"And this way Faith can keep the same doctors for her checkups and bloodwork," Spencer added. "She doesn't have to start all over somewhere else."

"Especially my post-transplant coordinator," Faith said. "She's a gem, helping me take care of all my appointments and my prescription refills and everything. She's like my personal secretary. I'd be lost without her."

"How are you feeling, darling?" Vivian asked in her characteristic breathy voice. "Is everything still okay?"

"I'm fine, thank you. I only have to get bloodwork done once a month, so that's a relief. And I just had another CT scan, what? A week ago, Spencer? They said everything looks great."

"Oh, that's *wonderful*, dearest," gushed Vivian. "We're so glad to hear things are going well. You certainly gave us all a scare a few years ago."

"I still don't know that it necessitated a career change for you, though," Leonard said, casting her a semi-disapproving look. "I'm sure there are nurses out there who have had transplants. You needn't be overly cautious. You can't avoid germs forever."

"Dad! Her medication is immunosuppressant. She *has* to be careful of germs because her body can't fight them!"

"I understand that, son. Being careful is one thing, but becoming a germaphobe is quite another."

Faith felt heat creep into her cheeks. Not for the first time, she wondered why they even bothered to come when Mr. Young was home. At best, the visits were uncomfortable. Spencer's dad wasn't affectionate toward his grandchildren, and conversing with him wasn't enjoyable. More often than not, he complained or gave unwarranted advice.

"If anyone has a reason to be a germaphobe, it's Faith," Spencer answered his dad. "And she doesn't even do everything they tell her she should. Whenever she goes out in public she's supposed to wear a mask to avoid germs from other people. Give her a break. So what if she washes her hands and uses hand sanitizer a lot? She has to in order to stay healthy!"

"And all I'm saying is that she could do the same thing if she was a nurse," insisted his father, refusing to back down.

It bothered Faith that they were talking about her as if she weren't sitting right there. "My decision has less to do with germs and more to do with my experiences from my transplant," she informed Mr. Young. "You're right—there are a number of transplant patients who are nurses. I've talked to a few of them. But when I was going through the process for evaluation, then the surgery, and all my prescriptions afterward—I assure you, dealing with insurance was a nightmare. I decided to go into medical billing to help other people as they navigate the system. It's very intimidating otherwise. Patients need someone they can trust."

"You're absolutely right," Mrs. Young said. "And I think it's a fabulous idea."

"You don't *need* a degree, you know," pointed out Mr. Young. "Spencer will be making more than enough as a doctor. You don't need a second income."

"Now, Leonard, you leave her alone," scolded Vivian. "Many young people nowadays are choosing to work, and that's just fine. It's not a matter of money. She wants to get her degree, and we should support her in that."

'We *are* supporting her. Financially, at least," he replied.

"I told you you didn't have to do that," Faith reminded him in a tight voice. "There are plenty of student loans available."

"Youngs don't do loans." His voice was firm, and Faith knew the discussion was closed in his mind. It was the closest thing to a compliment she could expect from him. He at least acknowledged her as part of the family.

Mr. Young swallowed the last of his drink, then stood. "I'm going to turn in," he said. "I trust I won't be wakened by crying babies in the middle of the night?"

"Dad, even if Hope screams all night, you won't be able to hear her in your room. Why are you being so rude?" Faith could tell Spencer was trying not to lose his temper.

"Watch your tone, young man," his father warned. "I'm simply stating my desire for a good night's sleep."

"And you'll get it! We promise Hope won't bother you. If you're so concerned, maybe we *will* stay with Faith's family for the weekend! Jackson is out of the basement with his broken leg. We can stay down there."

"You will do no such thing," answered Vivian, ever the family diplomat. "You know I love having a full house. Leonard, darling, sleep well. I won't wake you when I come up either. Now come give me a kiss."

Her husband complied, walking over to her to exchange an air kiss to each cheek. Faith had never seen them give one another a real kiss. She wondered if they even knew how.

As Mr. Young left to go upstairs, Spencer tried to diffuse the tension of the last few minutes. "Dad must be getting old," he teased his mom. "It's barely nine fifteen."

"Oh, you know how hard it is on him," answered Vivian. "He travels so much that his system doesn't know what time it is. He probably has permanent jet lag."

"I have to admit, I'm pretty beat myself," confessed Faith. "Hope won't wake up the entire household, but I do have a feeling she'll be up a few times tonight in an unfamiliar setting. I think I'll go to bed too. 'Night, sweetie," she murmured to Spencer, giving him a real kiss.

She walked up the lavish curving staircase and down the hall to the guest suite, pausing to look in on a sleeping Griffin in the room across the hall.

Faith got ready for bed quietly so she wouldn't disturb Hope, and as she slid between the sheets, she wondered if she'd ever feel comfortable around Spencer's dad. She couldn't imagine how Spencer had grown up with a father like that and turned out so different from him. Maybe it was because his father had so rarely been around. Regardless, Faith breathed a prayer of thankfulness that Spencer hadn't inherited his father's disposition. He was a good daddy and a loving husband, and Faith knew she was blessed beyond measure. Before drifting off to sleep, she wondered fleetingly if Vivian Young ever felt the same way.

47

CHAPTER

6

The Saturday after Thanksgiving, Jackson met his teammates at the school for the State Championship game. An entire crowd of students and community supporters showed up to send them off, and his wheelchair was stowed away safely as his teammates helped him hop up the steps to the bus. It was an uncomfortable ride, but Jackson didn't mind. It was the championship, after all.

They faced a team from the Detroit area, and Mapleport struggled in the first half to regroup without their star receiver. From his vantage point on the bench, though, Jackson saw a weak spot in their opponent's defensive line and pointed it out to Coach Navarro, who agreed with his assessment. The second half of the game, they exploited that weak spot, but it wasn't enough to pull out a win.

Jackson was beside himself. He was sure he could have broken through the seemingly impenetrable line of defense that stonewalled his teammates. The rest of the weekend he brooded about the loss and about his broken leg.

Come Monday morning, Jackson was ready for a change of

pace in getting back to school, although he'd never admit it out loud. Sam was already waiting at the curb when his mother dropped him off, and Jackson grinned, thinking that a broken leg could come in handy sometimes.

His mom pulled up to the curb and lugged the wheelchair out of the trunk to unfold it on the sidewalk, making sure to lock the wheels before helping him out of the van. He hopped awkwardly on one foot, using his mother's shoulder for support as they navigated the few feet from the van to the wheelchair. Once he was situated with his broken leg extended straight in front of him, Grace hooked his backpack on the handles of the chair and turned him over to Sam.

"Thanks for agreeing to help him out," she said. "He's pretty good at wheeling himself around, but for the distances he has to go, it's much easier to have someone push him. I appreciate it."

"No problem," replied Sam. "Glad to help."

"You're sure you're okay, Jackson?" Grace asked.

"I'm *fine*, Mom," he mumbled, embarrassed by her concern.

"Okay, then. Have a good day. I'll pick you up here after school."

Jackson nodded and unlocked the wheels. He wanted to get moving. As his mom drove away, Sam started pushing him toward the entrance. "Brace yourself," she warned. "You're going to get mobbed in there. You were the main topic of conversation last week when you were gone. If you were looking to get attention, you sure accomplished that!"

Jackson laughed at her comment, and as they approached the school, he realized she was right. Students turned and stared at him as Sam clumsily tried to open the door and pull him through backward. A teacher passing by jumped into action and held the door open, making Sam's job easier. "Hey, champ! Good to see you back here!" he enthused, slapping Jackson's shoulder as he passed.

"Forty-Three!" bellowed a fellow football player. "Man, if you were gonna go down in a blaze of glory, at least you could've saved it for State, huh? We could have used you out there on the field on Saturday." Landon punched him on the arm good-naturedly and lowered his voice. "Seriously, man, good to see you back. Really sorry about the leg. It's every football player's nightmare."

As they walked to Jackson's first class, numerous students called out greetings and well wishes. Jackson felt a bit like he was parting the Red Sea as they progressed down the hall and students magically separated to make way for him. It was like he was in a parade, everyone gawking and pointing at him.

"Jackson Williams!" called a pouty female voice from behind him. Miranda caught up to them and stepped in front of the wheelchair, causing Sam to stop abruptly so as not to run into her. Miranda's mini skirt showed off her shapely legs, and her V-neck top plunged lower than Jackson's mother would deem appropriate under any circumstances. She stood her ground, crossing her arms over her chest in a mock pout. "What gives? You didn't even tell me you were coming back today? After I made the trip to visit you in the hospital and everything? Humph."

Jackson's face burned at the increased attention they were garnering in the hallway with Miranda's standoff, but she wasn't finished. Her voice changed to a condescending tone as she continued. "I guess I can't hold it against you. You have a lot on your mind. But really now, sweetie," she addressed Sam, "I'll push him. It was nice of you to offer, but don't you think the Homecoming King should have the help of his Queen?

Hmm?"

With that, she flicked her long blond hair over her shoulder and slid behind the wheelchair. Jackson turned to see her grab the handles from Sam, a triumphant gleam in her eye.

"Miranda!" he admonished, frustrated that he was in such a helpless position in the first place.

"Now, don't you worry, hon," she soothed, patting him lightly on the top of his head as she sashayed down the hall. "I've got you. Let's get to homeroom before the bell rings. We only have three minutes left."

Jackson craned his neck to look back at Sam. He saw her standing quite alone in the hallway, her face crimson. Jackson gritted his teeth. On second thought, a broken leg didn't come in handy after all.

Although Jackson looked for a chance to talk to Sam later, she kept her distance from him the rest of the day, which wasn't difficult. Other students swarmed him wherever he went, and in class he had to sit at the desk closest to the door because he couldn't navigate further into the rooms with his bulky wheelchair. For the classes they shared, Sam simply chose a seat far away and avoided eye contact. Jackson tried to get her attention, but she ignored him completely.

After the final period of the day, Miranda possessively took her place behind Jackson's wheelchair, but he'd had enough. The last thing he wanted was for his mother to see Miranda pushing him out. "I'm *fine*, Miranda!" he said sharply. "I don't want you to wheel me outside. I didn't even ask you to do this, and you were rude to Sam about it. I'll ask Tyler to push me around tomorrow. Just leave me alone."

Miranda looked at him, her eyes large. "You don't have to be so touchy about it!" she insisted in a wounded voice. "I'm just trying to help!"

"Well, you're not," he countered. "You only made things worse today." He turned his chair and wheeled down the hall as quickly as he could, which was admittedly not terribly fast. If she'd had a mind to do so, Miranda easily could have caught up to him. Fortunately, she didn't try.

Jackson had some trouble at the exit, but a passing student held the door for him while another backed him over the ridge. He scanned the area for Sam, but she was nowhere to be found. He didn't see her car there either. Groaning in disappointment, he wheeled toward his mom's van, where she helped him into the vehicle and folded up his chair to heave back into the trunk.

"How was your first day back?" Grace asked cheerfully. "And where's Sam?"

"I don't want to talk about it," Jackson said with a scowl.

Her eyes widened in surprise, but she didn't press him. Instead, she changed the subject to the neutral topic of weather. Jackson glared out the window as they drove. He didn't hear a word his mother said. All he could think about was Sam.

Since he couldn't drive himself to Sam's house to talk in person, Jackson figured the least he could do was give her a call. He knew she was hurt and embarrassed by the fiasco with Miranda that morning, and he was well aware that he should have spoken up right away to stick up for her. He had to make things right. When he got home, he insisted that Grace help him down the stairs to the privacy of his room, strictly forbidding anyone to enter.

After a few false starts, Jackson finally worked up the courage to call her. He waited with a fair amount of apprehension, secretly hoping to get her voicemail, but at the same time needing to hear her voice.

"Hey," she answered dully just before he was about to hang up.

"Oh! Hi, Sam... Um, it's me... Uh, Jackson," he fumbled, punching himself on the knee for the lame start.

"I know."

An awkward silence settled over the two of them until Jackson spoke into the void. "Look, Sam, I just want to... I mean, about this morning... I should have..."

This was going badly. *C'mon, Williams, pull yourself together!* he thought angrily.

"It's okay, Jackson," she said. "I get it. I know how it is."

What *does she get?* he wondered uneasily.

"No, but Sam, I should have spoken up back there. I don't want you to think—"

"Jackson, I have to go," she interrupted. "My dad's calling me. Don't worry about it. It's fine."

"Yeah, but—"

"Bye, Jackson. I'll see you at school." Without giving him a chance to say more, she hung up.

"Ugh!" yelled Jackson in frustration, hurling the phone into his pillow with a fair amount of force. "Curse this stupid broken leg!" He sat on his bed, silently seething at Miranda for ruining everything that morning. Things would have been just fine if it hadn't been for *her*. But as mad as he was at Miranda, he was even more upset with himself. His cowardly silence may have cost him Sam's friendship.

And he was *not* okay with that tradeoff.

CHAPTER

7

True to his word, Jackson asked Tyler to help him navigate his wheelchair the next few days at school. He was aware of the fact that both Sam and Miranda were now avoiding him. So be it. He was hardly in a position to go chasing either of them down. Not that he really cared what Miranda thought of him one way or the other, but he didn't like the recent tension between Sam and himself.

By Friday afternoon, Jackson was ready for a break. He was exhausted at the end of each day, mentally and physically, and he was tired of spending the entire school day in a wheelchair. So over the weekend he made it his sole purpose to master navigating with crutches so he could ditch the wheelchair.

He also decided he no longer needed the narcotics for pain relief. As his uncle had predicted, he got withdrawal headaches, but by Monday he was ready to go to school again, basking in his newfound independence on crutches and thankful for aspirin to help with his headache.

Naturally, the other students made a fuss over him when he arrived on the scene without his wheelchair, and as he fumbled with his locker between classes that Monday, Miranda sidled up to him.

"Looking good, Forty-Three," she murmured coyly.

"Hey, Miranda."

"Need me to carry your backpack for you?"

"Nah, I've got it. Thanks."

"Are you still mad at me for pushing you around last week?" she asked with a mock pout.

"I'm not mad at you," he said. "But you have to be careful how you come across. Sometimes you're pretty bossy."

"And that's a bad thing?" she asked coquettishly, batting her eyelashes at him.

Despite himself, Jackson grinned. Miranda was hopelessly ditzy.

She mistook his grin for an encouraging sign and leaned over to give him a little peck on the cheek. "See ya around, Forty-Three," she whispered with a wink, and then she was off, strutting down the hall as if she were a model walking down a runway, her long hair swinging behind her back.

Jackson rolled his eyes and shut his locker, adjusting his backpack and crutches to get to his next class. When he turned around, his heart plummeted. Standing a short distance away was Sam, who'd obviously seen at least the last part of the exchange between him and Miranda. She flushed deeply when he saw her and ducked her head to hurry away in the opposite direction.

He watched her go with dismay. The one-minute warning bell had just rung, and Jackson was slow as it was. There was no way he could catch up with her even if he wanted to. Clenching his jaw, he set off down the hall to his own class. Why must girls make everything so complicated?

* * *

Balancing awkwardly on his good leg, Jackson tried to pull a folder out of his backpack to put into his locker. The folder caught on the zipper, and when Jackson yanked it harder, the thing flew out of his hands and landed on the floor, scattering papers all over. He sighed deeply and wondered how to retrieve them. School was out, and he'd stayed afterward to chat with the coach, so the hallways were more or less deserted. But just then another student came around the corner.

It was Sam.

Seeing his predicament, she wordlessly stooped to pick up the errant papers, then stood and handed the folder back to him.

"Thanks," he said. "I was wondering how I'd get those."

She chuckled and replied, "No problem. See you." She started to leave, but Jackson grabbed her arm, the momentum very nearly causing him to fall flat on his face.

"Sam, wait," he said, fighting to regain his balance. "I've been meaning to talk to you for the past week. I'm really sorry about what happened that first day back with Miranda. I should have told her right away that I wanted you to help me. It was rude of me to let her get away with it, and I know it hurt your feelings. I'm sorry I was such a jerk. I would have preferred you anyway."

She colored slightly and fiddled with the zipper on her jacket. "So you guys aren't, like, dating or whatever?"

"My goodness, no!" he exclaimed without thinking.

Sam giggled. "I don't know these things," she said in her own defense. "I'm still the new girl, remember? She visited you in the hospital, and I saw her kiss you earlier."

Jackson shifted uncomfortably on his crutches. "*She* kissed *me*. I'm not interested in her."

Sam seemed pleased by his answer, and Jackson blurted out, "Hey, want to come with me to our Youth Group event for December?"

Her eyes widened at his sudden invitation, and her smile disappeared. Afraid she would say no, he hastened on. "It's still a few weeks away, but we're going to Krazy Katz for our Christmas activity. It's the day after we get out of school for break. It's always our best-attended Youth Group get-together." He needed to wrap this up or she'd think he was as crazy as the rest of his family. "I'd love to have you join me."

The smile returned to her face. "That sounds fun," she answered, pushing her glasses up. "I'm in."

Jackson beamed with pleasure. "Great! I have my one-month follow-up appointment the day before we go, and I'm hoping he'll say I can start going without crutches part of the time. Otherwise, laser tag and bowling will be kind of hard…"

They laughed together, and he walked her out of the building. He knew he'd kept his mom waiting, but when he got into the car, Grace didn't seem to mind at all. In fact, his mother didn't stop grinning the entire way home.

Krazy Katz teemed with people. The chilly weather made it impractical to do much outdoors, so instead people turned to indoor events to keep their kids occupied. It was mayhem.

Fortunately, Mr. Sanders, the Youth Group leader, had thought ahead and reserved a few bowling lanes and a slot for laser tag for the whole group. Almost everyone brought a friend or two with them, so there were twenty-seven high schoolers present. They had about an hour before laser tag, so Jackson and Sam started out with a few games of bowling along with a couple of other kids. Neither of them were very good, and they teased each other good-naturedly.

"I finally found a sport that all-star Jackson Williams hasn't mastered," Sam ribbed him after he bowled two gutter balls in a row.

"Humph," he grumped, feigning offense. "I *do* have a broken leg, you know. I'm barely off crutches. And besides, I don't want to make you feel bad. I'm being a gentleman and letting the lady win. I just didn't realize how bad you were to begin with." His devious grin belied his cruel words, and she laughed in response.

"Jackson, is that you?" a voice shrilled over the noise of pins crashing and balls rolling down the wooden lanes. Jackson froze and stared at Sam in dismay, seeing a similar expression in her eyes. Of *course* Miranda would be here today of all days.

"What a surprise to see you!" she continued as she approached with her groupies. "Are you two here... *together?*" She sounded shocked, as if this were a scandalous thing. Her group of female devotees tittered and giggled. Sam turned deep red, and Jackson felt his own face flame.

Jackson opened his mouth to respond, but Sam beat him to it. "We're just here for a Youth Group event," she explained, almost apologetically. "There's a whole bunch of us." She averted her eyes and looked at the ground.

"Oh, how cute!" Miranda said in a syrupy voice. "Then I claim a game of mini golf with you next, Jackson. I'll be at the snack bar when you're ready." She blew a kiss in his general vicinity, and flipped her hair expertly over her shoulder as she turned on her heel to walk away, her loyal clique in tow.

Jackson glanced at Sam, who looked simultaneously humiliated and crestfallen. He also noticed that she'd deflected attention away from the fact that he had asked her to join him in the first place. Apparently, she believed he would be embarrassed to be seen with her in a public setting. It was the wheelchair fiasco all over again. But Jackson was determined not to let that happen.

"Miranda!" he called after her.

She turned and flashed him a dazzling smile. "Mmm?" she prompted sweetly, tilting her head to one side.

"I'm here with Sam today. Yes, it's a Youth Group thing, but I specifically invited her to come with me. So I appreciate your offer of mini golf, but I can't. She and I have plans. And if we don't hurry, we'll miss our laser tag reservations. Come on, Sam. Let's go."

He firmly grabbed Sam's hand and limped away from their unfinished game of bowling, leaving Miranda and her gang staring after them in disbelief, scoffing indignantly.

Beside him, Sam squeezed his hand and whispered, "Thanks, Jackson."

It was a simple statement, but it spoke volumes. Sam's eyes shone the rest of the afternoon, and the look on her face was worth it all to Jackson.

CHAPTER

8

"So how'd your talk go with Coach Navarro?" Sam asked.

The two were in the food court at the mall, attempting without much success to eat Chinese food with chopsticks. It was an informal date, walking around the mall and eating lunch together over Christmas break.

"I don't know," groaned Jackson. "I'm not really sure what to think. I was more or less set to get a scholarship for the University of Michigan, but now with my leg... I mean, Sam, I've been working toward this for *years*. I've gone to all their camps to get noticed, and I've had more than a few colleges ask about me. Signing Day is in early February, and that's when I could officially get the scholarship, but now, I... I don't know if I can even play." He swallowed hard over the familiar lump of disappointment in his throat.

"If I have any chance at all, I need to work hard to get back to full strength," he continued. "I'd have to do physical therapy to help overcome my limp, and I'm not sure what I would do for my follow-up surgery. Ideally, I should get the metal plate removed over the summer or fall, but that would put me out of commission another month. I could maybe wait till after football season so I have the off season to recover and do more physical therapy, but it's dicey. Competition at the college level is brutal, and I'm a weak link right now."

Sam remained quiet, apparently mulling over his words for a few moments. When she spoke, her question surprised Jackson. "What do you want to do with your life?"

"Well... uh, I don't... I haven't really thought about it, I guess."

"Do you hope to go pro? Or maybe be a coach or something?"

"I... I don't know," he stammered. "I don't have what it takes to get to the NFL, and I really don't want to anyhow, so going pro won't happen, but... I... I just really don't know." After a brief pause, he asked, "What about you? Do you know what you want to do?"

She smiled sadly and looked at her plate, absently swirling the noodles around with her chopsticks. At last she spoke. "Want to know why I have a green streak in my hair?" she asked.

The sudden change in topic floored him. What did her hair have to do with what they were talking about?

Sam raised her eyes to look at him before she continued. "The green ribbon is for mental health awareness. No one knows this, because it's not a subject anyone cares about. You know, everyone gets that pink is for breast cancer awareness and yellow shows support for the troops, but people don't like to think about mental illness. Until it affects them."

She looked down at her plate again, blinking back tears. Jackson didn't know what to think. "So... *does* it affect you?" he prodded gently.

"Yes, it does, but not in the way you might think." She

seemed to be struggling with whether or not to say more. Finally she said quietly, "My brother has schizophrenia."

"Ah." She didn't elaborate further, so Jackson filled the silence. "I didn't even know you had a brother."

"No, I guess you wouldn't," she murmured, almost to herself. "Chris… uh… He doesn't live with us. We started noticing weird stuff about him maybe three or four years ago. Like, he thought we'd poisoned his coffee when he came to stay with us for a weekend because the water tasted different."

She glanced at him as if to gauge his reaction, like she expected him to laugh at the statement. Jackson wasn't sure what to do. Was she serious? He decided to wait her out and see what else she'd say.

"He was also worried that his neighbor was spying on him because one day the envelopes were leaning the opposite direction in the mailbox," she said. "He was convinced the neighbor had read his mail. Stuff like that. I mean, it almost sounds humorous, like stuff a kid would think, but it's completely serious. And dangerous. He wasn't able to distinguish reality from fantasy. We finally convinced him to get help, but it was a huge ordeal, and with all the HIPAA laws, we couldn't find out anything about his treatment except what he told us, and we weren't sure if that was reliable. It was really frustrating."

"Huh," was all Jackson could manage. Despite the fact that he was taking psychology this year, he couldn't for the life of him remember one thing about the schizophrenia unit. He wished he'd paid more attention.

"So I want to go into psychiatry," she said, getting back to the original topic. "I want to understand mental illness better and be able to help other families cope. It's very isolating when a close family member is diagnosed with schizophrenia. People look at and treat you differently when they know your brother is literally crazy."

Sam's voice shook, and tears filled her eyes. Jackson wanted to reach across the table to take her hand but worried she might resent it.

"Even church people act different, Jackson." She looked at him accusingly, as if he were guilty of the offensive behavior too. "No one knows what to say to you. Most people mean well, but I also know a lot of people have this misconception that if someone in your family goes insane, somehow their upbringing must have something to do with it. Mental illness is totally a taboo topic. No one wants to talk about it or acknowledge that it's out there. And there's a sort of general consensus among people that Christians shouldn't get stuff like that, or that if they do, it's because their faith is weak or something stupid like that."

She was getting worked up right there in the middle of the food court. Jackson didn't know what to say, so he wisely remained silent as she vented.

"A lot of people either ignored the topic and tried to be all perky about stupid subjects like the weather, or they gave us these sad, pitying looks." She stopped her monologue to push her bottom lip out, mimicking the expression in an obviously exaggerated way.

"And then there were the classic one-liners," she continued with an eye roll. "People would tell us, 'God never gives us more than we can handle,' or, 'You just have to trust God.' Trite statements that sound great in theory, but really aren't what a hurting and confused family wants to hear. Oh, and of course, the standard—'We're praying for you.'" Her voice was mocking, almost cruel. "You know what? I'll bet at least ninety percent of the people who told us that didn't even say one prayer for us. It sounds like such a nice thing to say, but it means *nothing*!" She slapped the table, causing Jackson to jump.

He was conscious of the fact that other people were casting curious glances their way, since Sam's voice was getting louder. Most people probably thought she was chewing him out. He wished they were in a more private setting for this conversation, but he didn't want to stop her now. She obviously needed to get this off her chest, and if she trusted him enough to open up to him, he didn't want to ruin the moment and suggest they go to the car. But he did want to diffuse her anger, so he quietly asked, "What *did* you want people to say?"

Her eyes widened as she looked at him, almost as though she'd forgotten he was there. "Honestly? Nothing. Nothing at all. The people who responded best were those who just hugged us. What we needed was a shoulder to cry on, a listening ear, someone who wouldn't judge us or offer pious platitudes."

She looked off into the distance and chewed thoughtfully on her lip before continuing. "Those were also the people who stopped by with a meal or a gift card to the grocery store or a restaurant. They knew we needed practical things too. With everything that was going on, it was great to have people help with meals so we didn't have to worry about it."

"Yeah, I bet." Even as he said the words, Jackson wondered why they'd need people to bring meals for them. Yes, it must be stressful to have a family member diagnosed with a mental illness, but that didn't mean they couldn't get dinner on the table… did it?

"Want to know something shocking, though?" Sam continued, lowering her voice. "I don't even know if I believe in God anymore."

"Oh?" He hoped she'd take that as an invitation to explain herself.

"How could He let this happen to my family?" she went on, her expression challenging him to give a satisfactory response. "You have *no* idea how much we've been through already. We were a good Christian family. We went to church together every Sunday, learned Bible verses, went through Confirmation—all that. My dad was the DCE at our church! And despite it all, *this* is what we get?" Sam threw her hands up in a gesture of futility. "What's the point of believing in God if He can't stop something like this from happening to a faithful family?"

Jackson racked his brain for a good answer to why God allowed bad things to happen to good people, but came up blank.

Sam wasn't finished. "My parents have completely changed since all this happened. My mom was ashamed to face people back home, so she withdrew from everything—church, her job, even going to the grocery store. Dad quit his job there and found a part-time one at Peace, but to make ends meet, he's working another job that barely pays more than minimum wage."

That explained why they moved into town, then, although Jackson felt like he was missing something. Did a diagnosis of schizophrenia really merit packing up and leaving town for a part-time job elsewhere?

"...Mom and Dad have been fighting all the time," he heard Sam say, and chastened himself for tuning out, even for a moment. "I hoped maybe with the move, that would change, but it's gotten worse. It's like they're blaming each other for the way things turned out. I know my dad believes God is still working through all this, but I can't see it. My parents like

Peace, and they make me go with them, but I'm really just going through the motions."

"I see," he said. His answers thus far had been practically monosyllabic. He hadn't the faintest idea how to respond to Sam. This was the deepest conversation he'd had in a long time.

"So I guess you're thinking I'm pretty messed up, huh?" she asked with a sad smile.

"No, actually I think you're pretty amazing to handle all that while you're still in high school." He was proud of himself for answering in a complete sentence.

"Only I'm *not* handling it very well," she admitted, her voice cracking.

Jackson couldn't resist this time. He reached across the table and took her hand in his own. "No one is meant to carry all their burdens by themselves," he said, knowing it was a cheesy line. His mom had made the comment before, but he never thought he'd use it himself. "I'm glad you trust me enough to tell me about your brother. And if you ever want someone to talk to, don't be afraid to tell me to shut up and listen."

"Thanks, Jackson." She gave his hand a small squeeze before releasing it to blow her nose on a napkin. "You know, when I first got here, I thought you were just a dumb jock who only cared about sports. I'm glad to know that's not *completely* true," she said with a small smile.

"I *am* mostly a dumb jock, but I have my moments," he teased back. "Just don't let word get out. It could ruin my reputation."

They laughed together, and he picked up her tray and rose from the table. "You want to walk around for awhile?"

She nodded, and as they strolled, Jackson replayed the conversation in his mind. His own woes about his injured leg

RUTH E. MEYER

seemed very insignificant in comparison with a lifelong
diagnosis of mental illness. Sam had been through a lot and
was still dealing with baggage from her brother's condition, but
she was using that to help other people by going into
psychiatry. Now his own ambitions for the future seemed
incredibly selfish.

Maybe it was time to rethink his plans.

"Do you think I'm self-centered?" Jackson asked Grace that
evening. He'd been pensive since he'd returned home from his
outing with Sam, waiting for a chance to talk to his mom
without his younger siblings hanging around. Now that the
kids were in bed, he could have a private conversation with
Grace and David.

"What brought this on?" asked Grace, turning off her
phone to give him her full attention. He noted that she was
evading the question. Truthfully, his mom probably did think
he was self-centered. If he couldn't be the best player on a
team, the sport was hardly worth playing in his opinion.

He sighed. "Sam thinks I am."

"She told you that?" Grace seemed surprised.

"Well, no, not in those words. But I could kind of tell."

"Because...?"

"We were talking about what we want to do in life, and I
realized I haven't even thought about it. I've spent so much
time focusing on getting into college sports that I haven't
looked beyond that. And now with my broken leg, I don't see a
bright future in college sports either," he finished dejectedly.

"Very few people have their life mapped out when they're in
high school," Grace pointed out.

"I guess," he said half-heartedly.

"Does Sam know what she wants to do?" she prompted.

"Yeah."

"Care to elaborate?"

"She wants to be a psychiatrist."

"That's pretty ambitious."

"She… um… she knows someone who's struggling with mental issues, so it's sort of personal for her," Jackson said vaguely.

"Hmm. Well, good for her. I've needed the help of a psychiatrist before myself. It's a worthy occupation."

"Yeah."

There was another pause until Grace spoke again. "So what are your thoughts after that conversation?" she asked. "Did that make you start thinking about your options?"

"I guess it did." Jackson sighed heavily. "I mean, Mom, I never really thought past making it to a good college football team. How shallow is that? And even if I hadn't broken my leg, and I made it to a good team, what then? Football doesn't last forever. Sam is doing something that will make a difference in the world. She wants to help other people. Me? I just want to do stuff that'll make *me* look good and be happy. It seems really lame in comparison." He looked dully at the floor, embarrassed to finally admit out loud what he'd been thinking all day.

David had been listening, and now set aside his laptop to enter the conversation. "You know, Jackson, God uses His children in many different ways. If you like football, great! Obviously you're a very talented player, and I know you've worked hard to become so, but God gave you a great deal of natural talent as well."

Scratching a non-existent itch on his knee, Jackson avoided looking at David. He was never sure how to take a compliment from his stepfather.

"Don't sell yourself short," David continued. "If you want to do something with football, God can and will use you in your chosen profession. Young men need good Christian mentors to look up to, and if you decide to go into coaching or playing, you'd be an excellent role model. Any vocation is honorable when it's done to God's glory. You may be helping people in a different way than Sam, but that doesn't mean it's less valuable."

Jackson remained silent, considering his stepfather's words. There was truth to them, certainly, but at the same time, he felt guilty that he hadn't seriously thought about his future yet. Coaching would be fun, and he'd probably be pretty good at it, but it was incredibly competitive, even at the high school level. He also knew that coaching was rarely a full-time position, at least in terms of pay. Even if he did decide to coach, he'd need something else on top of that.

He sighed again. His future, which had once seemed so promising, now looked rather bleak indeed.

CHAPTER

9

The sound of the doorbell was barely audible over the low roar in the Neunabers' living room and kitchen. It was New Year's Eve, time for the Monopoly marathon that was a tradition for David's family. Although in the past they'd done so at David's parents' house, they'd changed that after the twins were born. With both sides of the family there, the result was nothing short of chaos.

"I'll get it!" Evelyn exclaimed brightly when she heard the doorbell. She and Charlotte had long since tired of the board game and were looking for any distraction they could find. She bounded off to the front door and came back a minute later, tugging on the hand of a decidedly uncomfortable-looking Sam.

"Jackson's girlfriend is here!" she chirped in a perky voice.

There were very few things that could have effectively quieted the crowd as quickly as Evelyn's announcement. Sam blushed mightily at the sudden void as every eye in the room turned to her. Jackson's face burned as well. He was certain they both matched the Christmas decorations still hanging in the living room.

"Why, Sam Lewis!" Olivia broke the silence. "Is that you?"

"Hi, Mr. and Mrs. McNeal. Yes, it's me." Poor Sam was still fire-engine red.

"Jackson, why didn't you tell us you were dating this young lady?" Olivia asked reproachfully. "She goes to our church, you know."

Jackson didn't miss the look David and Grace exchanged at this revelation, but he was more concerned with what was going through Sam's mind. Did she think he'd told her family they were dating? By golly, she always seemed to come at the worst possible time.

"It's not his girlfriend," Griffin corrected. "He said he's not gonna marry her, remember?"

If it was possible, Sam turned two shades darker, and Jackson closed his eyes, mortified. His family just couldn't help it. The more they tried *not* to embarrass him, the worse they were.

David spoke quickly before Griffin could say more. "Sam, how nice to see you again! You always happen to catch us at a crazy time. We're having a Monopoly marathon with the entire extended family. Everyone, this is Sam, one of Jackson's friends from school. I'd make official introductions, Sam, but I'm sure you'd never remember all the names at once. But maybe you'd like to stay and play a while with us? We have two games set up. You could get to know the people around Jackson's board."

"Oh, that's okay, Mr. Neunaber," she said, clearly flustered. "I should have texted before I stopped by. I just wanted to drop off your gloves, Jackson. You... ah... left them in the car the other day."

Jackson felt heat rise to his cheeks yet again at the admission. Obviously that meant the two had been together socially over the break, and the adults in the room all had knowing smiles on their faces. This was getting worse and worse.

"Come on," coaxed Faith. "I have to feed Hope anyhow. At least fill in my spot until I get back, will you?"

"Well..." Sam waffled. "I guess for a few minutes, sure."

Faith's face lit up in a smile as she acquainted Sam with the players at the kitchen table whom Sam hadn't met already. The proper introductions made, she concluded, "Help yourself to some snacks and make yourself comfy. I'll be back in a jiffy."

But it was much longer than a jiffy before Faith returned. She was gone an hour and a half, and when she finally came back, Sam was laughing and interacting with the others at the table, obviously enjoying herself and quite at ease.

"Sorry, guys," Faith said, plopping herself down on her husband's lap. "Couldn't help myself. I fell asleep up there with Hope. Guess I was more tired than I thought!"

Jackson glanced quickly at his sister, who was trying unsuccessfully to hide a smile. Who did she think she was fooling? She had orchestrated it that way on purpose, playing matchmaker, plain and simple. And from the smug look on her face, apparently she believed her plan had worked. He and Sam were teasing each other and sharing a bowl of Chex mix.

"So, Katie, why don't you tell everyone about your plans for your birthday?" he asked, deflecting attention away from his older sister's thinly veiled lie. Katie's eleventh birthday was coming up in less than two weeks.

Katie's eyes sparkled with excitement. "Mom and Dad said I could have a slumber party this year! I can invite all the girls in my class. I want to do a spa day with facials and manicures and pedicures."

"Oh, fun!" exclaimed Sam. "Who's gonna do the

manicures?" She asked this with a sly grin at Jackson, and he kicked her under the table and gave her a dark look. She burst out laughing, leaving those not in the know to exchange questioning glances.

"I don't know," confessed Katie, looking slightly disheartened. "I guess just Mom. Aunt Livy has something else that night."

"I can help," Sam offered. All eyes at the table turned to her, and she flushed. "You know, if you need someone…"

"Would you for real?" Katie asked hopefully. "It would be so much funner to have you! You look like you really work at a salon with your nose ring and your hair dyed. My friends would all be impressed."

"Katie!" admonished Jackson, embarrassed of her blunt assessment of Sam's appearance.

"It's true!" Katie insisted. "Besides, it's way cooler to have a senior helping than to have Mom help."

Everyone at their table laughed at the observation, and Sam said, "Then count me in. I'll bring along some nail polish I have at home. I have blue and green and even…" she lowered her voice dramatically, *"black."*

She grinned and winked at Katie, whose eyes widened at the revelation. "Awesome," she whispered, clearly impressed.

Jackson was impressed too. Maybe his family hadn't managed to scare her away completely. When Sam left an hour later, Jackson couldn't for the life of him concentrate on the game one bit. His mind was a million miles away. Or at least, five miles down the road with a certain young lady named Sam.

CHAPTER

10

"I've been thinking..." Grace began.

"Mmm?" replied her husband automatically, his mind clearly on whatever was on his computer screen.

"About next year," she continued.

"Okay." He still wasn't listening.

"I think maybe I'd like to go back to school. Get my degree after all."

David's head snapped up. That got his attention, alright. "Are you serious?"

"Yes, I'm serious. The girls will be in all-day kindergarten next fall, and I don't have any kind of job waiting for me. It seems like the perfect time to go back."

"What degree are we talking about?"

"Just an associate's."

David frowned slightly. "There's really not a lot you can do with an AA."

"I know, but I have to start somewhere. It would give me time to fit in the core classes and take a couple electives without the pressure of declaring a major."

Her husband did not look convinced, so she hastened on, her words tumbling over one another as she tried to get them all out before David could object. "I would only take two or three classes a semester. I picked up a course guide at Forest Springs Community College last week. There are still a couple of weeks before the application deadline for the fall semester. I could fit in a few classes during the day while everyone's at school, and the quiet house would give me time to study and do homework without sacrificing family time. I think I'd be able to do it."

David cleared his throat, obviously stalling for time. "Why?" he finally asked.

"Why, *what?*"

"Why do you suddenly want to get a degree? You've never mentioned this before."

"There's never been a good time before. It's not something a single mom can do easily, and then the twins were born barely a year after we got married, and... I just thought maybe... maybe now would be a good time. I'm not too old to do this."

"And would you hope to use your degree somehow?" She could hear the skepticism in his voice.

"Maybe eventually. But it at least gives me the groundwork so I could continue on or go back for a BA later if I so choose."

David rubbed his hand over his short salt-and-pepper hair, a nervous habit of his. Grace's heart plummeted. "You don't like the idea," she stated flatly.

"I didn't say that," he protested. "I just don't know that it's necessarily worth the cost without a clear goal in mind."

Grace blinked back tears and felt heat rise to her face. "So you're saying I'm not worth it," she accused. "Always the issue of money."

"No, that's *not* what I'm saying, Grace," he returned testily.

"I mean that we have a lot of other expenses to consider as well. Next year we'll be paying college tuition for Jackson, and with his broken leg, his football scholarship is off the table, meaning more money out of pocket for us. I don't know that we want to tack on even more college expenses, especially if you're only taking classes for the fun of it."

His words stung. "Maybe you don't get this, but I *want* to get a degree, David! Faith is working toward her degree, and Jackson will have one soon enough too. My children are earning degrees and I don't have one!"

"You don't need to compete with them or prove yourself to anyone, Grace." His voice was more gentle now. "Whether or not you have a college degree doesn't affect your worth in the least."

"David, I really want to do this. Please? Just consider it. Yes, it would be an expense, but there's financial aid available too. And besides, I… I need this." She looked at him pleadingly and dropped her voice to a near whisper. "Remember why I quit in the first place? I don't want *that* to be the way I remember college." She still carried emotional baggage from the abortion she'd gotten in college, which eventually caused her to drop out.

David nodded somberly, and she pressed her advantage. "All I ask is for you to consider it. I'll leave the catalog out for you to look through. I highlighted the classes I'm interested in, and the tuition information is in the front. See if we can fit this into our budget. Please, David, just do this for me?"

"Fair enough," he answered, holding out his hand for the catalog. "I'll take a look at the figures and give you my honest opinion. Okay?"

"Thanks, hon. I appreciate it. I love you." She gave him an excited little squeeze around his neck and scooted out of the room before he could say anything else. She'd done her part in pleading her case. Now all she could do was wait.

David sat in the living room with the course catalog in his hands, an inner debate raging. He'd checked the tuition costs and was disheartened to find that they were only slightly cheaper than fees at Jackson's school of choice, The University of Michigan—Ann Arbor. At least U of M was a well-known school. Forest Springs Community College, on the other hand, was a complete no-namer.

Sighing deeply, he removed his glasses and closed his eyes to think. They would be worrying about college costs for the next decade and a half as it was, and David's principal salary was nothing to get excited about. With the size of their family and the amount he made every year, they fell under federal poverty guidelines. And since the twins would be in kindergarten next year, David had been secretly hoping Grace would get a part-time job herself.

She didn't see what he saw. Each month, their checking account decreased by a few hundred dollars. He'd had a sizable amount in savings when they'd gotten married five years ago, and their savings account was still sufficient to cover unforeseen expenses. Yet despite the yearly raise he received, their growing family ate up the extra money. They didn't spend frivolously, by any means. They didn't even have cable. But with a mortgage, car payments, insurance for a teenage driver, and payments to cover the deductible from Jackson's surgery, money was tight. Not to mention Jackson's follow-up surgery to get his metal plate removed later this year. There was another full deductible. They'd just finished paying off Jackson's braces in time to start paying for Freddie's. David had needed to transfer money from savings to checking more than once over the past few months. It was not a situation that could continue indefinitely.

But at the same time, how could he deny his wife this one request? She didn't ask for much. He couldn't even remember the last time she'd bought new clothes for herself. So who was he to shoot down her dream of getting a degree? The one thing she finally asked for was to better her intellect and perhaps someday open up a new world of possibilities for her in terms of career. He knew if he stood against her on this, it would be a crushing blow to her.

David knew what he had to do. He walked upstairs to the room he shared with Grace. She was already in bed, leafing through a magazine. When he entered, she shut her eyes.

"You came up too fast," she said in a tiny voice. "You don't think I should do it."

His heart broke a little at her response, and he walked to her side of the bed to sit down next to her. Pulling her against his chest, he said, "Actually, quite the opposite. I say go for it."

"*Really?*" she squealed incredulously, pushing away from him to search his face. "Are you serious?"

"Absolutely. I think it's a great idea, and we'll make it work." They could always refinance their mortgage. They'd opted for a twenty-year payoff, but they could switch to thirty to save money in the immediate future.

"But can we afford that on top of everything else?" Her face scrunched as she waited for his response.

"We'll make it work," he repeated. "God's always taken care of us in the past. He won't let us down now. Do it, Grace. I'm proud of you for wanting to get your degree."

"Oh, David!" Tears swam in her eyes, and she leaped out from under the covers to tackle him in a bear hug.

Laughing, he fell backward and pulled her down on top of

him. "Matter of fact, I'll call tomorrow to make reservations for Le Poisson to celebrate," he said, throwing caution to the wind. Never mind the fact that dinner there cost a small fortune.

"Even better!" she exclaimed. "You surprise me, David. I didn't think you'd agree."

"Hey, it's not every day my wife decides to get her degree. Who am I to hold you back? Knock 'em dead, kiddo."

Her eyes shone with the look she reserved only for him, and as she drew close to kiss him, David knew there were certain things far more valuable than money.

CHAPTER

11

"So I was wondering if maybe… if, like, you would go out with me. Be my girlfriend." Jackson couldn't believe how hard his heart was pounding as he asked the question.

For a long moment, Sam was silent, gazing past him into the distance with a pensive look on her face. Jackson's stomach tightened. It didn't look like she was exactly jumping at the opportunity.

At length, Sam sighed. "Jackson, there's a lot about me you don't know. Stuff I'm not ready to tell you."

"That's fine. You don't know everything about me either."

"But I have a feeling you don't have the kind of heavy stuff I do."

She was probably referring to her brother, but Jackson thought that was irrelevant to the topic at hand. What difference did it make to him if her brother had schizophrenia? He'd never even met the guy. "So I don't know your whole history. I just know I like you and want to go out with you."

"Do you like me as a friend, or are you only in this because you want me to be your girlfriend?"

He was taken aback by the question and didn't know how to answer. Leave it to Sam to make this super awkward. "I... um... No, I'm not just looking for a romantic relationship. I consider you a good friend. It's just that the more I get to know you... as a *friend*... the more I realize that I'd like to go out with you too."

There was another long pause before she spoke again. "Jackson, I *do* want to go out with you. But right now, I need you more as a friend than a boyfriend. You're the best friend I have. Really, you're the *only* friend. I've told you stuff I haven't told anyone else, and you haven't laughed at me or judged me. You're a great guy. And I don't want to mess up our friendship by venturing into the realm of dating. Does that make sense?"

She looked at him worriedly, as though she feared she'd offended him. Swallowing his disappointment, Jackson spoke. "I suppose I can see where you're coming from," he lied. He had no idea what she was talking about.

"Besides," she continued, "come fall we're off our separate ways. Rival schools, at that." She had been accepted at Michigan State University, a long-time rival school to U of M. "Neither of us needs the pressure of keeping up a long-distance romance right off the bat."

"I guess so."

"But in the meantime, I still want to hang out together like we have been—you know, like, as friends. Can we do that?"

"Of course," he assured.

She smiled, obviously relieved. "Then how about we go to the movies this weekend? My treat. There's one I've been wanting to see, and it'll be out of theaters soon if I'm not careful. You game for that?"

"Sounds great," Jackson affirmed, giving her as genuine a smile as he could. She grinned back and got out of the car, thanking him for the ride home from school.

As he drove back home, Jackson wondered at the exchange. He probably could have asked half the girls in his class to date him, and every one of them would have said yes in a heartbeat. Why did he have to ask the one who said no? She admitted to having feelings for him, but chose friendship over romance. He shook his head. His stepfather was right. Women were completely impossible to understand.

CHAPTER

12

Faith snuggled closer to Spencer and nuzzled her face against his neck. "Just a few more minutes," she murmured sleepily in response to his alarm. "You have a late class this morning. The kids aren't awake. Stay in bed with me."

"How can I refuse such an offer?" he grinned, pulling her onto his chest. It was far too comfortable next to his wife to do something so drastic as to get out of bed. The two lay there contentedly until his phone rang.

Groaning, Faith glanced at the clock. It was barely seven. "Don't get it," she advised. "Let it go to voicemail."

Spencer checked the screen. "It's my mom," he announced with a slight frown. His mother rarely called, and never at this time of the morning.

"Probably a pocket dial," said Faith. Vivian Young had been known to do such things. "Don't answer, please?" She tightened her arms around him and pressed herself even closer in an effort to entice him away from the phone.

"Don't worry. I'll just be a few minutes," he said, hitting the "accept" button on his screen, even as Faith punched him on the arm and pouted.

"Mom?"

Vivian's voice was strained on the other end. "Darling, I'm so sorry... It's your father... He had a heart attack."

Spencer sat straight up in bed, pushing Faith aside. "Where did they take him?" His voice sounded harsh, which he hadn't intended.

"No, darling, you don't understand. He... He didn't make it. He's gone."

Without even replying, he hung up, completely in shock. "What is it?" Faith asked fearfully, scrambling up to sit next to him. "Spencer, what's wrong?"

His eyes were unfocused as he looked at his wife. He couldn't even say the words out loud yet. Instead, he announced, "I'm not going to class today."

Faith drove the entire three-hour trip to Mapleport, Spencer still reeling from shock. Griffin chattered away in the back seat and pestered them with questions they weren't ready to answer, so neither of them responded. When they got to the Youngs' house, Faith was relieved to see her mom's car in the driveway. Vivian needed someone there.

When they entered the house, Spencer went straight to his mom and pulled her into a fierce hug. Vivian wept quietly on his shoulder. It was the first time Faith had seen her cry. Spencer wasn't crying, but he clenched his jaw tightly.

"He was right next to me in bed," Vivian fretted. "I should have sensed something was wrong. If only I'd woken up sooner..."

"At least he was home, though," Spencer said. "He was in his own bed next to you, not in another country all alone. That's the way he would have wanted it."

"But, darling, he was so young! He was only fifty-six. He had so much life left to live."

"I know, Mom. It's not fair. But he went quickly, right? He wasn't in pain and didn't have to go through a prolonged illness. It could have been a lot worse."

Something about the scene bothered Faith very much, and she realized there was a key component missing. Spencer was doing his best to put his mother's mind at ease, but his assurances could only go so far. Mr. Young hadn't been a believer. The family couldn't console themselves with the knowledge that they'd see him again. He *wasn't* in a better place. The thought made Faith's blood run cold. What a terrible way to meet one's Maker, as Judge rather than Redeemer.

Poor Spencer. She couldn't even imagine how he was feeling now. Her tears began to fall for the man who had been so gruff to her. Although they hadn't had a close relationship by any stretch, she didn't wish to see him die in unbelief.

Spencer reached out an arm to her, and she welcomed his embrace, putting her own arms around Vivian. The three of them stood together, grieving. Faith heard her mother quietly round up Griffin and Hope, and she knew Grace was taking them to the Neunabers' house. That was a relief. The last thing Vivian needed right now was for Griffin to ask if Grandpa was in heaven, as that was *not* a discussion she wished to have then and there.

Once the kids were out of the house, Spencer led the two women into the living room, where they all sat together on the couch, Spencer in the middle with one arm around each of them.

"Dearest, I don't even know where to begin," his mother said sadly.

"Do Parker and Callan know?"

"I called them after I called you."

Faith found it interesting that she'd called her youngest son first. Spencer was clearly the one to whom his mother felt closest.

"Are they coming?"

She found it even more intriguing that Spencer had to ask. Would his brothers seriously consider *not* coming to their own father's funeral?

"Yes, they're both checking on flights. They should be able to get in late tonight or tomorrow sometime."

"That's good. Did you contact the funeral home?"

Vivian dabbed at her eyes. "No, darling, I haven't done anything yet. I'm so overwhelmed."

"I'll do it," promised Spencer. "Leave the arrangements to me. Just let me know if he had any specific requests."

"What about a minister?" Vivian asked worriedly.

"I'll see if my pastor will lead the memorial," he said.

Faith wondered what that service would look like. What comfort could a pastor give to mourners if not the certainty of the resurrection?

"Thank you, darling," Vivian sighed. "I just don't have the strength to deal with this."

"I know, Mom. We're here to help. Don't worry."

The three settled into a contemplative silence until Faith dared to ask a question. "How did you and your husband meet?" she asked. She hoped that would be a happy memory for her mother-in-law.

A small smile played upon Vivian's lips. "We met at a company dinner years ago. He was to receive the Junior Associate of the Year award. I was working with the catering company. While I was serving drinks, I stubbed my toe on his chair, causing me to spill the entire tray of champagne all over his expensive suit. I was certain he would get me fired for it, but he laughed and said, 'I don't like champagne anyway. How about I buy you a drink at the bar instead?' Of course I was working, so I couldn't take him up on his offer, but he stayed around until my shift was over and took me out for drinks afterward. We stayed out until three in the morning. That was a good day." A private smile graced her face as she relived the memory.

Faith was shocked by the account. She couldn't reconcile the stern Mr. Young she knew with the picture Vivian painted of him, laughing off a clumsy waitress spilling champagne all over him. Apparently at one time he'd been far more easygoing. Charming, even.

"How come I never heard that story?" Spencer raised an eyebrow at his mother.

"Well, dear, you never asked."

That didn't surprise Faith. The Youngs were generally a private family. Reminiscing wasn't something they did often, if at all.

Vivian sighed wearily next to Spencer, and he urged, "Mom, why don't you take a little nap? Faith and I will start making arrangements. Take a sedative, and we promise we won't bother you while you're resting."

"I think I will, darling. Thank you. You wouldn't believe the headache I have right now."

Spencer helped his mother to a standing position, then accompanied her upstairs to her room. When he came back down, he looked considerably more haggard than he had when his mother was with them. Clearly he'd been trying to hold himself together for her sake.

Faith rose and met him with a hug, and the two stood that

way for a long time without speaking. She wished there was something she could say to make him feel better, but there wasn't. Words were completely inadequate at a time like this.

CHAPTER

13

Faith felt like she walked through the next few days in a trance. Vivian, likewise, had a vacant look in her eyes that hadn't been there before, and Faith worried for her mother-in-law. Spencer took care of the practical arrangements that needed to be made. Even his older brothers looked to him for guidance when it came to decisions.

While Faith had met Callan a handful of times, Parker she'd only met at their wedding. The Young brothers were not close to one another geographically or emotionally, nor did they have a particularly close bond with their mother. Callan stayed at the Youngs' house, but Parker opted to stay in a hotel, which Faith found very odd. The family dynamic between the Youngs was nothing like the relationship between Faith's own family.

The visitation passed tediously on Thursday. Since Mr. Young was well-known in his company and traveled so widely, there were a number of coworkers and visitors from other countries who had come to pay their respects. Faith barely knew anyone at the visitation, and she wore a mask to protect

herself from the germs of so many strangers. She knew Parker
and Callan both thought she was ridiculous to do so, but she
couldn't take chances.

Friday morning came too soon, and Faith woke up wishing
she could skip the funeral. She didn't envy Pastor Chris having
to give the message to a family when he couldn't tell them their
loved one was in heaven.

The funeral home's chapel was packed, with standing room
only. The service began with a hymn, which had been added at
Spencer's insistence. Although "Amazing Grace" was a familiar
enough song, those in attendance mumbled their way through it.

That being done, one of Mr. Young's coworkers got up to
read a poem, followed by a handful of others who had been
asked to give eulogies. Faith was surprised when they spoke.
Each of his coworkers talked about him with such fond
memories that she felt like they were talking about another
person entirely. They spoke of a man who was patient in
answering their questions, who was kind and affable to
potential clients, and who was a natural leader. Each of the
speakers clearly admired Leonard Young a great deal.

Once the eulogies were over, Pastor Chris stood. "Lord
God, we come before You today with heavy hearts," he prayed.
"We pray for Your comfort as we mourn the loss of Leonard
Young. Be with his family and friends and coworkers as they
move on without him, and we pray for peace for every heart
here, Lord—the peace that only You can give. Amen."

Pastor Chris looked out at the assembly. "It was a critical
situation," he began. "Lazarus was very ill, beyond the help of
doctors. The time was drawing near for him to die. But his
family had one last hope: a man named Jesus. Jesus was a
family friend of Lazarus and his two sisters. He had already
healed others, and Lazarus' sisters had no doubt Jesus could

and would heal their brother also. They sent word to Jesus urging Him to come, but Jesus didn't hurry off to heal His friend. Instead, He stayed two extra days where He was, almost like He was wasting time. So by the time He reached Bethany, the town where Lazarus and his two sisters lived, Lazarus had been dead four days."

As he spoke, Pastor Chris paced the front of the room, his voice well suited to retelling the narrative. Faith was captivated by his manner of storytelling, and even though she already knew the account well, she found herself drawn in.

"Mary and Martha, Lazarus' sisters, lamented that if only Jesus had been there, Lazarus would not have died. So final was death in their minds that Jesus could do nothing more for their brother. Sure, He could heal a sick person, but raise the dead? No way. After Martha voiced her complaint that Jesus could have healed her brother, Jesus told her, 'Your brother will live again.' Martha said, in effect, 'Yeah, I know, I know. He'll rise at the resurrection of the dead. But that doesn't help me *now*.' And Jesus' answer is the verse I want you to remember."

Pastor Chris returned to the podium and opened his Bible to read, "'I am the resurrection and the life. Whoever believes in me, though he die, yet shall he live, and everyone who lives and believes in me shall never die. Do you believe this?'"

He turned his eyes back to the crowd before him. "I find it interesting that Jesus leaves her with a question. He makes a statement, but then He turns it over to her. 'Do *you* believe this?' He makes it personal. And Martha's answer is one of the most beautiful professions of faith in Scripture. She says, 'Yes, Lord; I believe that you are the Christ, the Son of God, who is coming into the world.' She knew who Jesus was and why He had come. He was the Son of God, come to the earth to save the world."

Tears sprang to Faith's eyes. She was so grateful she knew Jesus the way Martha knew Him—as Savior.

"But maybe sometimes you wish Jesus would save you a little more immediately," Pastor Chris went on. "Like Martha, perhaps you wish that the promise of heaven isn't so far off; that Jesus would ease you of the burden you're carrying *now*. Jesus knows your pain. Yes, He was the Son of God, but He was also a man. Like us, He knows the pain of losing a loved one. When they showed Him Lazarus' grave, He cried, seeing how death affected His dear friends. He felt their pain. But He didn't stop there.

"Jesus went on to raise Lazarus from the dead with just three simple words: 'Lazarus, come out.' He only had to speak, and death was defeated. Death didn't have the final say after all. Nor did death have the final say later when Jesus Himself was crucified, bearing our sins upon the cross. Three days after He died, He rose again. Even death could not hold Him. Death is not the end for us either, because whoever lives and believes in Christ will have eternal life.

"So now I ask you the same question Jesus asked Martha: Do you believe this? Do you believe that Jesus has taken your sin away? that He has taken your punishment upon Himself? Do you believe in Him as your Savior?"

Faith's heart pounded as Pastor Chris stepped away from the podium. He was getting personal, and she wondered how Spencer's brothers and mother would respond. Deliberately, she stared straight at Pastor Chris, not daring to glance at anyone in Spencer's family.

"I'm sure that some of you *do* know Christ as your Savior," Pastor Chris said earnestly. He glanced briefly at Spencer before continuing. "You're living your life for Him. You keep in touch with Jesus on a regular basis, reading and studying His

Word, gathering with others to praise Him in worship, talking with Him daily in your prayers, and depending on Him to see you through tough and challenging times. You can say with Martha, 'Yes, Lord; I believe that You are the Christ, the Son of God, who is coming into the world.'"

He took a step closer to the crowd. "Then again, perhaps there is someone sitting out there who is living life without Christ. Maybe you've never been introduced to Jesus. Or perhaps you've been too busy with your own life to bother with religion. Maybe some things have happened in your life which made you question God's love and care for you. Or it could be that you've gradually drifted away from God, like a stray sheep that nibbles and nibbles itself away from the flock till it's lost and out of touch with the Shepherd.

"I don't know where all of you are in your relationship to Jesus, but I know where He would want you to be: living your life with Him, believing in Him as the resurrection and the life, knowing that you will live forever with Him one day in heaven. Amen."

Faith glanced covertly at Spencer's brothers as Pastor Chris walked back to his seat and a soloist got up to sing. Parker was looking down at the floor, a slight scowl on his face, and Callan fiddled with his tie. She wondered if either of them had listened and taken the message to heart. It might be too late for Mr. Young, but it wasn't too late for his sons.

After a catered lunch at the country club, the Young family returned home and filed into the kitchen silently. Vivian offered to make iced tea, but no one was thirsty. Instead, they sat around the kitchen table, each lost in thought. Faith certainly wasn't going to be the one to break the silence.

Finally, Vivian asked, "Have you made arrangements to fly

back yet, Parker?"

"I have a seven fifteen flight in the morning."

"Tomorrow morning already?"

"Yes. I need to get back and catch up on work I missed this week."

"But, darling, it's the weekend!" she protested. "Surely you can catch up next week? I barely got to see you at all while you were here!"

"Work doesn't wait for anyone, Mom. Without advance planning, there's no way I can take off more time than I absolutely have to. I'm sorry."

Poor Vivian looked like she was fighting tears, and Faith felt a surge of resentment toward Spencer's oldest brother. Didn't he care that his mother was grieving? Was is too much to ask that he stay more than the obligatory three days?

"Callan, what about you?" Vivian asked.

"I'm here until Monday. I've been able to get work done on my computer."

She seemed grateful for his reply. "And Spencer, darling, I imagine you and Faith will need to get back for class. You've both missed nearly the entire week as it is."

Spencer answered for both of them. "We should probably leave on Sunday afternoon. Our profs know why we're out, but we do have assignments and reading to catch up on before class on Monday morning."

"I understand. I'm glad you could get away for so long. I don't know what I would have done without you." She was silent for a moment before venturing to ask, "Lovely service today, wasn't it?"

"It was," Faith agreed, glancing at Parker across the table, who snorted at his mother's comment. "It was neat to hear Leonard's coworkers talk about him and share their memories.

I never got a chance to see that side of him. It was nice to hear from people who knew him professionally."

"Yes, that was a nice addition, wasn't it?" Vivian responded. "Leonard would have enjoyed hearing the eulogies."

"Those were fine, but honest to goodness, whose idea was it to get that quack preacher up there?" Parker asked.

Next to her, Spencer stiffened. Faith could practically feel the tension radiating from him. "I asked him to preach," said Spencer. "Faith and I go to his church sometimes when we're visiting. I appreciated his message."

"Oh, little bro," Parker said in a condescending voice, shaking his head. "Since when did you get religion? Who filled your mind with that kind of nonsense? I don't think Dad would have appreciated all that God talk at his own funeral."

"What better place to talk about God than at a funeral?" Faith challenged. Goodness, Parker reminded her so much of his father. "People there are hurting and sad, looking for comfort. What better hope is there than to hear that Jesus defeated death for us?"

Parker scoffed. "Okay, that answers my question. Your pretty little bride here has managed to brainwash you, Spence. I had more confidence in you than that."

"Parker!" Vivian commanded sharply. "This is neither the time nor the place!"

"Why not? When else can we have this conversation?" asked Parker, raising his palms. "We're so rarely together as it is. Why not discuss it now? All I'm saying is that if you two want to believe all that junk, fine. It's none of my business. But how dare you force it down our throats at the funeral? Have some respect for what other people believe. Remember, there are plenty of other religions out there. You make it seem like the Bible is the only path to heaven."

"That's because it *is* the only path to heaven," said Spencer.

Parker's eyes narrowed and he leaned forward menacingly. "See, *that's* what I'm talking about, man!" His finger punctuated his words as he jabbed it toward Spencer. "Throwing around these outlandish statements like you're some big know-it-all. You don't know *anything*, kid. You have no idea what you're talking about."

"Boys!" pleaded Vivian. "Please stop!"

"I'm not making this up, Parker," answered Spencer, ignoring his mother's request. "Read the Bible for yourself. See what it says about Jesus."

He leaned back in his chair with a little smirk. "Oh, yeah, that guy who lived two thousand years ago and managed to gain a cult following that continues to this day?" Parker scoffed. "Classic founder of a religion. Just like Mohammed or Joseph Smith or anyone else who claims to be sent from God. He's just any other guy, Spence. He lived and died and that's it. No big deal."

"But He didn't stay dead," said Faith. "*That's* the big deal! Didn't you listen to the message today? Jesus died, yes. He died for our sins." Parker was shaking his head and chuckling to himself, but she continued. "He lived a perfect life for us—for *you*, Parker—and then died on the cross for you! But three days later, He rose from the dead. He proved that He really is true God by coming back to life. And because I believe that, I know I'll be in heaven with Him when I die."

Parker laughed out loud and clapped his hands together slowly a few times. "Lovely story. Well told. Straight from your days of Sunday School, I imagine. You learned well. But not all of us grew up with that. And not everyone needs your Jesus. Dad got to where he was by his own hard work. He climbed the proverbial career ladder and earned money by working for it, plain and simple. He was a self-made man, and he didn't need your God to help him out."

"But everyone needs God," Faith said. "It's just that a lot of people don't realize that until it's too late."

Parker leaned forward again and fixed her with a cold stare. "So was it too late for my dad?" Callan looked at Faith as his brother made the challenge, though Faith couldn't read the expression in Callan's eyes.

The question hung heavily in the air, and Faith wished she hadn't gotten herself involved in this discussion. How was she to answer diplomatically? Before she could formulate an answer, Spencer spoke up. "That's between him and God," he said quietly. "We can't judge what's in someone else's heart."

"But you think that if he didn't believe in Jesus, he didn't go to heaven, right?" pressed Parker. "Am I understanding your narrow views correctly?"

Spencer stared intently at his hands clasped together on the table. "Jesus told His disciples that He was the Way, the truth, and the life. He didn't say He was *a* way or *one* way, but *the* way." He raised his eyes to meet his oldest brother's gaze. "So yes, only by believing in Jesus can anyone get to heaven."

A long moment of silence followed his statement as he and Parker continued to look one another in the eye. Finally, Parker stood and said in a low, threatening voice, "If you *ever* so much as mention religion to me, I swear, I will never speak to you again."

With that, he wheeled around on one heel, stomped to the door, and slammed it shut behind him. Moments later, Faith heard his rental car start outside, and Parker revved the engine loudly before driving off, his tires squealing.

They didn't see Parker at all the rest of his visit.

CHAPTER

14

The remainder of the weekend was strained after the fiasco with Parker, and Faith saw firsthand that what Spencer had once told her was true. Their family didn't apologize to one another or bring up unpleasant encounters. They simply ignored the incident and pretended it hadn't happened. Sunday afternoon was a welcome relief as she and Spencer loaded the kids into the car to make the trip back to Ann Arbor.

On Tuesday evening after the kids were asleep, Faith walked into their bedroom to find Spencer lying on the bed staring blankly at the ceiling, his face void of expression. Her heart ached for her husband who had tried so hard to be strong for his mother, but who was also grieving himself. She walked over to sit next to him, pulling his head into her lap. He squeezed his eyes shut, but a tear escaped down each cheek nonetheless.

"I didn't know him at all, Faith," he said, his voice cracking. "He was my dad, but he was practically a stranger. At his funeral, I... I tried to cry, but I couldn't. What kind of terrible person does that make me?"

She stroked his hair and assured him, "You're not a terrible person, Spencer. Everyone processes grief differently. No way is better or worse than another."

"Listening to his coworkers talk about him—I mean, they knew him better than *I* did! They all respected him as this great leader who was always ready to answer their questions, who could charm potential clients... I didn't know him that way at all! It's like he had two lives, one at work and the other at home. At home he was cold and indifferent toward me most of the time. I can't recall a single time he told me he loved me. I don't know if he did. I think I was a mistake. They only wanted two kids."

Anger flared inside Faith. Had his parents actually told him such a callous thing? "Even if that's true, Spencer, you are *not* a mistake. Would you say the same thing about Griffin? We didn't plan him either. We shouldn't have been sleeping together, and I had no business having a baby in high school. But even so, would you ever call him a mistake?"

"No, but that's not how my parents think."

"Your mom adores you. I can't speak for your dad, but *she* loves you."

He sighed wearily and sat up. "My family is so broken. Parker barely tolerates me, and if I ever mention religion to him again, apparently he'll disown me." He barked out a bitter laugh. "What difference does it make anyhow? I see him once a year, if that. And Callan is off in California in his own world. Basically, it's just me and my mom. We're all alone now."

Faith's heart wrenched. "But you're *not* alone. You have us."

"It's not the same," he retorted, almost harshly. "Your family can't understand. You guys have everyone all in the same area—your grandparents, your aunt and uncle, all your siblings. I have no one!"

"Spencer, my family *is* your family," she insisted, trying not to be offended by his words. "For your mom too. They'll look out for her. They consider both of you family. And besides, you have a wife and two children who need you here. You aren't alone."

He shook his head sadly. "My dad was," he said. Tears welled in his eyes again. "Alone, I mean. Despite all the praise his coworkers heaped on him and no matter how much money he made, in the end he faced death completely alone. I can't imagine anything worse." Now he did start to cry, and he wiped impatiently at his eyes. Faith put her arms around him and pulled his head to her chest in a protective embrace.

"Faith, none of my family believes," he whispered. "Not one of them. And despite how strained our relationship was, I didn't want my dad to die without saving faith!" He pulled away from her. "But what did I do to change that? Nothing! I never once tried to witness to him or mention Jesus or anything! I'll feel guilty about that the rest of my life."

"But even if you had tried to witness to him, there's no guarantee he would have listened," argued Faith. "Look what happened with Parker. Sometimes family members don't want to listen to other family members about something so personal as religion. They'll listen to a friend or coworker, maybe, but not family."

"But I should have at least tried."

"I should have tried too. Neither of us thought to do it before."

"But why not?" Spencer threw up his hands in a hopeless gesture. "I mean, why aren't we witnessing to more people? If my roommate hadn't kept after me to go to church, I wouldn't be a Christian right now. But he cared enough to invite me, to witness to me."

"That's true. And if Mom hadn't met David, none of my family would be Christian either."

"So think of all the people we *could* be witnessing to but aren't. We both know all sorts of people who aren't Christian. I know it's not politically correct to talk about Jesus in public, but think back to the apostles in the Bible. They talked about Jesus everywhere they went! They wouldn't have considered *not* talking about Him! It's part of who they were. My own witnessing is pretty lame in comparison."

"It's a different time, though too," she reminded him, "with different means of witnessing. Back then people traveled from town to town preaching and teaching. That was their culture. Nowadays people just don't do that. We have more effective ways to communicate than traveling by foot from one town to another. We can text or email people on the other side of the world without even leaving our own homes. Besides, don't sell yourself short. You *did* witness to your family last week."

"Not very well," he said dejectedly. "I completely messed it up. Probably scared them all away from Christianity forever. Especially Parker."

"It has nothing to do with you," Faith said gently.

"What's that supposed to mean?" He gave her a suspicious glance out of the corner of his eye.

She took a deep breath. "Let's say Parker miraculously believed the Good News on Friday and professed belief in Jesus. Who would be responsible for his change of heart?"

Spencer ran a hand through his already-disheveled hair. "God."

"Not you, even a little? I mean, you're the one who witnessed to him."

"I'd be the instrument, but it's still God's work."

"So if you wouldn't pat yourself on the back for 'saving' a

person, why are you beating yourself up for *not* saving him? Unbelief always falls back on the unbeliever. Always."

"But if I'd said it differently or—"

"It's *not* your fault, Spencer," she interrupted. "Parker is set in his ways and doesn't want his little brother coming in to tell him he's wrong. I'd have been very surprised if he'd reacted any other way. That's just what unbelief does best—fighting against and rejecting God. I'm proud of you for speaking to him about your faith."

Spencer swallowed hard, and she continued. "The fact is that none of us witness as well as we ought to. My own dad isn't a Christian. Why haven't I talked to him about God before? And why am I not praying for him to come to faith? We can't change what happened with your dad, but maybe this is God's wake-up call for both of us, to open our eyes to people we could tell about Him, and to pray for Him to soften the hearts of our friends and family who aren't Christian yet."

"Maybe." Spencer shrugged. "That's a good way of looking at things."

Spencer let a few moments of silence pass before abruptly announcing, "I've decided I'm not going into cardiology."

Faith gasped. "But, Spencer, you've wanted to do cardiology as long as I've known you!"

"Yes, and my dad just *died* from a heart attack."

"And that's why I thought you wanted to do it—it's personal for you."

"*Too* personal. Every time I see a patient, I'll think of my dad. I'll wonder if his cardiologist missed something; wonder if *I'm* missing anything. I don't want that kind of pressure hanging over me at every single visit."

She cocked her head to the side as she pondered this. "Okay. That's fair. So I assume you have something else in mind?"

"Yeah…" Spencer rubbed the back of his neck, something he did when he was self-conscious.

"Oh, no. Please tell me you aren't thinking of being a pastor with all this talk about witnessing. I'm sorry, but I totally can't see you doing that. You've already put in way too much time toward getting your MD, and you're at the top of your class. Don't throw that away because you feel guilty."

"No, I'm not thinking of becoming a pastor," Spencer said with a wave of his hand. "I can't see myself doing that either. I still want to be a doctor, but in a different field. I… I'm thinking pediatrics."

"You want to be a *pediatrician*?" That didn't fit the mental picture Faith had of her husband in his career either.

"Not a pediatrician. Like, pediatric surgery."

"Oh." She took a moment to digest this bit of news. "When did you start thinking about this?"

"It's been rattling around in the back of my mind since your accident, when Katie was in the children's hospital."

"Really? That long? So this isn't just a knee-jerk reaction to your dad?"

"Yes and no. I was still leaning toward cardiology until recently. I guess my dad's death was the defining moment for me. But at the same time, I've been considering it for a while. In a way, it's almost like a special type of… I don't know… ministry, I guess. Like—oh, never mind. It's stupid."

"No, it's not. Tell me." She was genuinely curious to see what was on Spencer's mind.

He didn't answer right away, and Faith was afraid he wasn't going to elaborate. Eventually, he released a long breath and spoke. "When I took you to the children's hospital to see Katie and your family, I stayed out in the hallway, remember?" She wasn't likely to forget *that* visit. It hadn't exactly been pleasant.

Spencer went on. "While I was there, I saw doctors going into the rooms, talking to families, giving them comfort and assurance. I mean, parents are desperate when their kids are sick enough to be in the hospital, you know? Imagine if Hope or Griffin had a life-threatening illness. We'd be a mess. So I thought, if I can be there for them to answer questions and calm their fears, maybe even pray with them… Who knows whose lives I can touch?"

He'd been staring intently at the comforter, not daring to meet her eyes, but Faith put her hand on his cheek and gently turned his head so she could see his face. "I think it's a *great* idea, Spencer. If that's what you want to do, go for it."

She leaned over to kiss him, amazed at the changes she'd witnessed in his life over the past number of years. The Spencer she'd dated in high school would never have viewed a medical career as a type of ministry. Then again, she'd changed quite a bit herself. Such was the power of God to transform lives.

She prayed that in time, Spencer's family would experience that power themselves.

CHAPTER

15

Jackson slunk into the living room, looking around furtively.

"What's up, Macgyver?" David asked with a small grin.

"Huh?" Jackson was clearly confused.

David's smile broadened. The TV show *Macgyver* was well before Jackson's time, but it had been one of David's favorite shows years ago, watching Macgyver find ingenious ways to get out òf impossible situations.

"Never mind," he chuckled. "Just an old TV show reference. Why are you sneaking around?"

"Is Mom in bed?" He was evading the question.

"Yes. She's still fighting that sinus infection."

"Yeah, I know." Jackson stuffed his hands into his pockets.

"Can I help you with anything?" prompted David after a moment of silence.

Jackson flushed. "I… uh, I need your advice."

"Alright." David tried to mask his surprise. Jackson didn't ask him for anything, except for the handful of times he'd grudgingly sought help with math.

"But I don't want you to tell Mom about it," added Jackson.

"Okay." Now he was really curious.

"For real?"

"I won't tell your mom. I promise."

Walking over to plop down on the loveseat, Jackson said, "Sam's birthday is coming up and I don't know what to get her." He blushed even more at the admission.

"Ah." David bit back a smile. "Are you guys dating?" He had to ask. It was March, and the two had spent a lot of time together over the past few months, but Jackson was surprisingly tight-lipped about the status of their relationship.

"Uh, no… no, we aren't," Jackson admitted. David's eyebrows raised in surprise, and his stepson hastened on. "I asked her if she would be my girlfriend, and she told me she just wanted to be friends, so…"

"So you're just friends."

"Something like that." Jackson looked at him and shrugged. "You were right. Women are impossible to understand."

David chuckled and nodded. "That they are. I really thought she liked you, just from the interactions I've seen between you. Add that to the fact that you go out together regularly, I kind of just assumed…"

"Yeah, well, she *does* like me," clarified Jackson, as if he needed to defend his honor. "But she told me she needs me as a friend more than a boyfriend right now."

"And you're okay with that?"

"I don't really have a choice, do I?" They both laughed, and Jackson continued. "I mean, do I want her to change her mind? Sure. But at the same time, it's kind of nice to have a friend who's a girl. Sam and I actually *talk*. I can tell her stuff I wouldn't tell Tyler or Landon. I know she won't make fun of me or spread it around. She's probably the best friend I've ever had. Sam doesn't want to mess that up. Like she says, dating 'complicates' things." He did air quotes and rolled his eyes.

David shook his head in an attempt to commiserate with Jackson. "So you need a 'friend' gift that won't make it look like you're trying to woo her?"

"I guess."

"Hmm. That *is* tricky. You don't want to offend her by something either too serious or too impersonal. It's a fine line you're walking. I'm thinking jewelry would be out, huh?"

"I'd say so."

"Flowers too."

"Definitely."

"Chocolate? That's always a winner with your mom."

Jackson smiled. Everyone knew Grace was a hopeless chocoholic. "That's a good idea, but not necessarily as the main thing. I want to be a little more creative."

Creativity was not David's strong suit. He thought for a moment before deflecting the question back to Jackson. "Then think of stuff she likes. Any hobbies or interests you could work with? Music? Art? Or maybe something you guys could do together? A gift certificate to Krazy Katz or the movies? Just something fun, not like dinner at a fancy restaurant."

"Maybe." Jackson stared thoughtfully into the distance. "I could work with that."

Both men sat in silence, contemplating other ideas until Jackson asked, "Hey, does Katie still have that jewelry making thingy she got for her birthday?"

"I would imagine so, yes. May I ask why?"

"I think I just got an idea," Jackson responded mysteriously. He rubbed his hands together as a slow smile spread across his face. Without elaborating, he stood and walked out of the living room, lost in thought.

"Glad I could help," David called after him, well aware of

the fact that he hadn't done a thing. But a goofy smile spread across his face nonetheless. That was the first time Jackson had sought his advice on anything. He hoped it wouldn't be the last.

"Happy Birthday!" Jackson proudly handed Sam an envelope and a small wrapped box.

"Why, thank you!" she exclaimed, her eyes lighting up.

"Open the card first," he instructed.

Smiling, she ripped open the envelope and pulled out the card. She read the message and found a gift card inside for the Java House, a local coffee shop. "You can get a couple of those tea latte things you like," Jackson explained. "But you have to promise me you'll take me there at least once."

"Deal. I'll make you a tea latte lover yet." She arched an eyebrow smugly at him, and he snorted.

"Not likely. I'll stick with iced capps, thank you very much."

She grinned and opened the wrapped box to find two identical green friendship bracelets inside. At her quizzical look, Jackson explained. "I had Katie help me make those. One is for you and one is for me. It can be our own version of the green ribbon."

Sam stared at the matching bracelets, tears in her eyes. Jackson smiled proudly, glad he had thought of such a meaningful gift. At last she looked at him, her eyes pained. "I can't ask you to wear this," she whispered hoarsely.

What's that *supposed to mean?* Jackson wondered, blinking in confusion.

"But… you *aren't* asking me to wear it. I'm offering. I *want* to wear it. To show support for you and your brother. Your family."

"You really don't know what you're offering to support."

His frown deepened. Why did she have to make things so awkward? "I'm supporting *you*, Sam."

"And my brother by association."

"Yeah, and?"

She looked away and bit her lip. "Chris is in jail, Jackson," she said in a low voice.

"Okay," he replied stupidly, not knowing what else to say.

"For murder." She looked him in the eye as she said this.

"I see." Another lame response.

"The voices in his head told him to do it. He was off his meds, and…" Her voice caught and she looked away again. "Not all people who have schizophrenia are violent. Most aren't. And with the right medication, a lot of them can lead normal lives. Chris just… Well, he happened to not be one of them."

"Mm-hmm." Jackson's mind was racing to process this sudden revelation.

"People who are mentally sick need *help*, Jackson. They need mental hospitals. But those cost money and have too much of a stigma. You know, like padded walls and straitjackets and experiments and being strapped to a cold metal table! So we shut down these hospitals and institutions and turn our heads and let the patients and their families deal with the fallout. And then they commit crimes and end up in jail. Locked up in a different way. Only now their families are in their own type of prison with them."

Tears slid down her cheeks, and Jackson started to put his arms around her, but she shoved him away, almost angrily.

"Don't you *get* it, Jackson?" she yelled. "My brother *killed* someone! Why do you think we moved here? We had to get away from the stigma that followed us everywhere we went back home. The whispers, the looks, the speculation… You have no idea what this has done to our family. What it's *still* doing to us. My parents have completely changed. They never laugh anymore. They won't even talk about Chris. It's like they're trying to pretend none of this ever happened; like he doesn't even exist anymore. My family is falling apart, and there's absolutely nothing I can do about it!"

She looked at him with a wild look in her eyes and continued. "And who knows? Maybe it runs in the family! My mom had an aunt with schizophrenia. You don't want to get close to me, Jackson. For all you know, *I* might develop it too!"

The statement hung between them, and Jackson saw in Sam's eyes the raw terror at having finally expressed out loud her secret fear.

Rather than respond, he reached out and pulled her into a tight hug. This time she didn't resist. Instead, she clung to his shirt and sobbed. Jackson didn't offer trite assurances or try to calm her down. He didn't know what to say anyhow. Instead, he slid his bracelet on his own arm and tightened it. She needed his support now more than ever. There was no way he would let her go through this alone.

"Is there any sin God can't forgive?"

As he gave Evelyn a push on the swing, David looked up in surprise at Jackson's question. Without really thinking, he rattled off the stock Sunday School answer. "The only unforgivable sin is the sin against the Holy Spirit—unbelief. Other than that, no. There's nothing too big or too awful for God to forgive."

"Murder?" Jackson avoided looking his way as he gave Charlotte a push.

"King David arranged to have Uriah killed. He repented and was forgiven."

"Yeah."

David waited him out, pushing Evelyn and wondering where Jackson was going with this line of questioning.

"But what if you don't know what you did was wrong?" posed Jackson. "Like, say you had mental problems and a voice in your head told you to do it. Are you still guilty then?"

"Why do you ask?"

Jackson squirmed ever so slightly and gave his younger sister two pushes before he answered. "We… uh, we were talking about mental illness in psych last week, and we got into this discussion about being accountable if you're out of your mind. Like the 'not guilty by reason of insanity' defense. It made me think about it from a religious standpoint. Does God hold people accountable if they're not thinking straight?"

David pondered this. "Well, yes, we're all accountable before God for our actions. Even those sins we don't know we've committed. In fact, it even talks about that in the Office of the Keys part of the catechism, doesn't it? 'Before God we should plead guilty of all sins, even those of which we are unaware…' So I guess that would include sins committed while 'out of your mind,' so to speak. But to get back to your original question, God can and does forgive even those sins."

"Okay, so let's just pose a scenario here. Let's say you're in a nursing home someday." David couldn't help but smile at his stepson's example. "And you're rooming with this guy who killed someone years ago because voices in his head told him to. He's scared to die because he thinks God can't forgive him. What would you tell him?"

"If he was truly repentant, I would assure him that God has already forgiven him."

"So you would look him in the eye and tell him Jesus died for him and that he'll go to heaven?"

"Yep."

"A murderer."

"Mm-hmm."

"Cool. I thought so. But you're smarter than me when it comes to theological stuff."

The two lapsed back into silence, pushing the twins on the swings, but David kept the conversation in mind, thinking he had grossly underestimated his stepson.

CHAPTER

16

Sam knew Jackson was mad about the game. More specifically, he was upset about his performance in the game. He had long been Mapleport's go-to pitcher and hitter, but his leg wasn't making it easy on him this year. Although he'd been completely cleared by Dr. Kahn for every type of physical activity, his limp persisted, a fact Sam knew irritated Jackson to no end.

At today's game, it was obvious his windup wasn't what it used to be. He couldn't bring his left knee up as much as he should. And it was downright painful to watch him land on that same leg after the pitch. Then there was his running. He was a strong hitter, but he'd been thrown out twice today because his limp slowed him down. Sam even heard Miranda giggling behind her in the stands after one such throw out, and it had taken all of Sam's self-restraint not to turn around and slap her.

"Who am I kidding, Sam?" asked Jackson as the two sipped Oreo milkshakes at Applebee's afterward. "I'm slowing down the team. The coach only let me on because of my history with them. But I guarantee I wouldn't have made it otherwise. My pitching is terrible, and I can't even make it to first anymore. It's embarrassing."

"Since when is Jackson Williams embarrassed about anything related to sports?" she teased gently. "I thought you didn't care what other people thought."

"That was before I broke my leg. Now I look like a fool out there."

"You don't look like a fool," she assured him. "And it's not your fault. Everyone knows you broke your leg five months ago. A femur takes a lot of time to heal. Be patient with yourself."

"Yeah." He was obviously not convinced. He took a sip of his milkshake and said, "I'm not going to do sports in college."

Sam gasped. "At all?"

"At all."

"Jackson, hold on. I get that you're frustrated right now, but don't let this one game color your outlook on next year. You have plenty of time between now and then."

"Not enough," he insisted. "Football's already a thing of the past. I'm damaged goods. There's no way I can compete with the other guys who will be trying out. And to be honest, I don't know that I even want to play anymore."

At her skeptical look, he explained himself. "I don't know, Sam. I'm more... tentative now. When that line drive came at me today, I cowered away, thinking it might hit my leg and hurt it all over again."

"It scares me to death when you're pitching," she confessed. "I'm always worried a line drive will hit you. It happened to my sixth-grade teacher during recess. One of the kids in our class hit a ball right into his face and broke his nose. It freaks me out when you're on the mound."

Jackson allowed a half smile. "My mom gets freaked out too. But it never used to bother me before. I thought I was more or less invincible. Injuries only happened to other people. But after my leg, I'm not sure I even *want* to try football again. I'm scared I'll reinjure myself. The thought of getting tackled makes me break into a sweat. Mentally and physically, I know I wouldn't be at my top game."

Sam sat quietly, digesting this information. He had a point. "Then don't," she finally said.

He looked at her in surprise. Obviously, he'd been expecting her to try to persuade him otherwise. "Don't?"

"You know yourself, Jackson. If you're skittish about it, don't force yourself to do it. You don't have to prove anything to anyone. Football is a major contact sport, and you're right—you don't want to hurt your leg again. Nor do you want to play like you're scared. So don't do football. At least for now. It doesn't have to be a final decision for the rest of your life. Maybe you could do an intervarsity league or something. Still playing, but not at the fierce level of competition and pressure. It would probably be more fun that way, anyhow."

He nodded slowly. "That's a good idea. I might do that." He seemed lost in thought for a few moments until he mumbled, "I want to coach."

"Huh?" She wasn't sure she'd even heard him correctly.

"In answer to your question about what I want to do with my life. I want to be a high school coach. I don't have the patience for anyone younger, and I don't want the insane pressure of coaching at the college level. But high school would be perfect."

"I kind of figured you'd end up doing that," she said with a smile. "You love the game too much to walk away from it entirely. You'll be great at it."

"Thanks. I hope so." He fell silent and seemed to be struggling with whether or not to say more. At last he said, "I was thinking I might... like, I could maybe... um, you know, teach too. Maybe science."

His face was crimson at the confession, and he stared into his milkshake, poking his straw around aimlessly. When she didn't speak right away, he filled the void. "I know, pretty stupid idea, isn't it?"

"Actually, I think it's a fabulous idea," she said. He glanced at her face as she continued. "I think you'd make an awesome teacher, Jackson. When we were paired up for that awful pig dissection lab, I had no clue what I was doing, but you showed me what I was looking for and how to identity the different organs. It made complete sense when you explained it, and I actually got a decent grade on that test. Plus you have the sort of personality that demands respect. Your students would look up to you. I think you'd be great at it."

His face still red, Jackson muttered, "Thanks." He cleared his throat and spoke more clearly. "I'm not entirely sure yet, but I've been thinking about it a lot, and it just seems like a good fit. But I haven't even told my family. It's kind of embarrassing. I mean, my stepdad is a teacher, or at least he was before he became principal. It seems weird for me to want to teach too, like I'm following in his footsteps. And I'm pretty sure my family would laugh at me for even considering it. I don't exactly have the demeanor of a teacher."

"Look at you, throwing around fancy words like 'demeanor,'" she teased. "And besides, who defines what a teacher's demeanor is supposed to be?"

"I'm not patient at all."

"So? You're talking about high school, Jackson, not preschool. It's not that you aren't patient, but that you won't tolerate goofing off. You could handle a team of football jocks, and you could handle a classroom full of silly high schoolers, and you'd be awesome at both."

"I doubt my family will see it that way."

"Well, families can be weird," she replied. "Totally supportive on some things and completely closed-minded on others."

"What's yours?"

"What's mine, *what*?" She squinted at him, confused.

"Is your family supportive of what you want to do or closed-minded?"

Now it was her turn to avoid eye contact as she stirred her milkshake. "I, um… I haven't told them what I want to do yet," she confessed.

Jackson stared at her incredulously. "Are you kidding?"

"You're the only person I've told."

"*What?*"

"My parents have their own problems to worry about, and besides, I don't think they'll be thrilled about the plan. They don't always take me seriously. I'm the baby of the family. They seem to think I should go off to beauty school or something. You know, since I dye my own hair, why not dye hair for other people?" A sarcastic edge crept into her voice. "Perfectly logical, right? Plus I'm not the best student in the world, and psychiatry is a lot of hard work. Like, twelve years of hard work. Four years of pre-med, four years of medical school, and then four years of residency on top of that. It's expensive and challenging, and I'm pretty sure my parents don't think I can handle it."

She stared into her glass, feeling very sorry for herself. Jackson reached across the table and put his hand on top of hers, causing her to look at him. "I think you can do it, Sam. In fact, I think you *need* to do it. For your own sake, and also for your brother. You can relate to patients and their families in a unique way. I don't know anyone with mental illness, so I wouldn't know how to empathize. It'll be a challenge, yes. But you have the desire and the drive, and that counts for a lot. You can do this."

Sam brushed impatiently at the tears welling in her eyes at his sincere vote of confidence and whispered, "Thanks, Jackson." She took a deep breath and continued. "Another reason I haven't told them yet is that I know my dad is totally jaded about the psychiatry profession in general. Like, somehow it was the psychiatrist's fault that Chris ended up in jail. He has to blame someone, and since he won't blame God, then of course it must be that the psychiatrist wasn't doing his job right. My dad doesn't think it's a worthwhile career."

"Do *you* think it is?"

"Yes. Absolutely."

"Then go for it."

She grinned at him and straightened her shoulders. "Then I will."

"And while we're at it, let's make another deal. I'll tell my family that I'm considering teaching if you tell your parents that you want to be a psychiatrist."

He looked her in the eye, and she held his gaze for a long moment, wavering. At last, she shrugged and said, "Why not? They'll eventually find out anyhow. May as well break the news to them and let it have time to sink in."

"This weekend?" His eyes dared her to accept his challenge.

"Sheesh, Jackson, are you sure you don't want to go into politics or business or something? You'd be a great salesman."

He chuckled, but refused to back down, so she rolled her eyes and replied, "Fine. This weekend."

He held out his hand for her to shake on it, then broke into a huge grin and took a long slurp of his milkshake. Sam only hoped neither of them would regret the deal they'd just made.

CHAPTER

17

Jackson wasn't too worried about telling his family his plans. Although they'd probably be surprised that he was thinking about teaching, he knew his mom and David would be supportive of him. After all, it was logical to pair teaching with coaching. He'd made the deal with Sam more for her sake than his. She seemed to have a slightly more complicated relationship with her parents.

By Sunday evening, Jackson had long since made the announcement to his family, but he still hadn't heard anything from Sam. If she thought he'd let this one slip quietly into the night, she had another thought coming to her. She'd made a deal, and he would see that she kept it.

How'd it go? he texted her.

A few minutes later her reply came back. *I can't do it.*

Jackson considered this. Obviously the girl needed some help. He'd go over and give her a boost of confidence.

I'll be right there, he typed quickly.

No, don't come. Pls.

He pretended he hadn't seen her text. He was already on his

way out.

Ten minutes later, he knocked on Sam's front door. He realized with surprise that he'd never met her parents before. He'd picked her up a few times, but she usually ran out to the car before he could get out. And when he dropped her off, she never invited him in. He was curious to meet Mr. and Mrs. Lewis at last.

When Sam opened the door, it was only a crack. "What are you doing here?" she hissed. "I told you not to come."

"I'm here to help you hold up your end of the bargain," he answered. "Besides, I haven't met your parents yet. I'll introduce myself and we can steer the conversation toward college plans. It's perfect."

"Jackson, I can handle this on my own," she insisted. "Just go away."

"Samantha, who's at the door?" a voice called from inside. Sam shut her eyes.

"A… friend from school, Dad," she called back. "I'll be right there." Her eyes looked slightly panicked as she turned to Jackson and whispered, "Go!"

It was too late for either of them to do anything, because Mr. Lewis appeared in the entryway and opened the door fully. When he saw Jackson there, he frowned. "Can I help you?" he asked sternly.

"Oh! Hi, Mr. Lewis. I'm Jackson Williams. I just stopped by to talk to Sam."

"Samantha is not allowed to date."

Whatever he'd been expecting, it wasn't this. Was this guy living in the 1950's? Sam was eighteen years old, for crying out loud.

"Oh, no, sir. We aren't dating. We're just friends." For once, Jackson was grateful for that fact. He could be completely truthful with Sam's father.

"Then you can talk to each other at school tomorrow. There's no reason you need to be here at this time of the evening. Good night."

Without allowing him a chance to respond, Sam's dad shut the door in his face. Anger surged through Jackson's body, and he had an almost overwhelming urge to pound on the door and give her dad a piece of his mind, but he knew that would only make things worse for him. And for Sam.

Instead, he clenched his jaw and turned to walk back to his car, stopping to fiercely kick a rock on the sidewalk. Naturally, it flew into the passenger door of his car, leaving a nice scratch mark. Jackson gritted his teeth. Just his luck.

Inside the house, James Lewis turned to his daughter and crossed his arms. "Is *that* the friend you've been going out with?"

Sam was crestfallen. "Yes," she whispered.

"Samantha Marie, you are not allowed to date anyone in high school!"

"We aren't dating!"

"You go out together after games. You go to the mall together. You go out to eat together. That sounds like dating to me."

"Dad, Jackson is my best friend!" she protested. "Friends go out together. It's not a big deal!"

"Not to you, maybe. You have broken my trust, young lady."

"Father! I am eighteen years old! I think I'm old enough to be friends with a guy. And for the record, I'm plenty old enough to date too. Your rule is ridiculous! I'm not going to do anything dumb."

"Let me see your phone."

"What? Why?" She didn't like the sound of this.

"Let me see it," he insisted more forcefully, holding out his hand.

"Dad!" Sam was starting to panic.

"Now!"

Defiantly, she slapped the phone into his hand, and her father scanned through her texts to and from Jackson. Then he deftly blocked Jackson's number, and with a swipe of his finger, deleted the entire thread of texts between the two.

"Dad! No!" she yelled, feeling sick. He handed the phone back to her, but she shoved it away. "I don't even need it now! He's the only one I contact! Just *keep* the stupid thing!"

With that, she fled to her room and slammed the door. She threw herself onto her bed and allowed hot tears to fall. Why, oh why, had Jackson come after she'd told him not to? And what in the world was he going to think of her now? Her dad was a stickler when it came to boys, but he'd been downright rude to Jackson. And then to delete all their texts...

She tried halfheartedly not to harbor bitterness against her father, but quickly gave up that pretense and allowed herself to think spiteful thoughts. When had he become so uptight, so calloused? Did he even care about her feelings, or was he too wrapped up in his own pain? She briefly considered running away. *Maybe* that *would get his attention,* she thought resentfully.

Her ears perked up when she heard the garage door, and knew her mother had arrived home from the grocery store. After a few minutes of rustling as her mother brought in bags and put the groceries away, Sam heard her mom enter the living room where her dad was sitting. Undoubtedly he was on his computer, as always. The man seemed to spend all his time on that blasted thing, as if he could block everyone else out and stay in his own little world.

"Thanks for helping," Sam's mom said sarcastically. That was another thing. Her parents were always snarky toward each other nowadays. It was almost like they *wanted* to keep hurting one another.

"You could have asked if you needed help," James returned testily.

Sam decided the time had come for her to plead her cause. Her mom was already upset with her dad. She'd take her side when she found out what had happened. Throwing open her door, Sam flounced out to the living room, knowing full well how awful she still looked after her crying.

"Samantha!" exclaimed Brenda as she approached. "What in the world is wrong?"

Sam glared at her father and said, "Ask *him*."

James had gone decidedly pale at Sam's appearance, and his wife now turned to eye him with suspicion. "Well?" she demanded.

"Ah… You see…"

"I had a friend stop by," Sam interrupted coldly, "and Dad sent him away and shut the door in his face! And *then* he deleted all my texts from him!" She blinked furiously, trying not to succumb to tears again.

Brenda looked at her husband in astonishment. "You did *what*? James!"

"Samantha knows the rules—she is not allowed to have a boyfriend in high school."

"He's not my boyfriend!"

"Young lady, we've already had this talk. Go back to your room while your mother and I *discuss* this." He said this in a mocking tone, indicating that he knew it would be more of a fight than a discussion.

Sam glared at him a moment longer for good measure, then stomped back to her room and slammed the door again. But immediately she opened it to eavesdrop. Not that she needed the door open. Her parents' voices weren't exactly hushed.

"What happened?" Brenda's voice was hard.

"I didn't hear a knock or anything. Suddenly I just heard voices in the entryway and walked in to find Samantha whispering to this boy who was standing at our front door. It was like they were sneaking around. I may have overreacted, but I was surprised and upset to think she was hiding something from me. She knows she's not allowed to date."

"So you shut the door in this poor boy's face? That's rude no matter what!"

"Not if they're sneaking around together behind our backs!"

"James! Samantha is a senior in high school! If you can't trust her now…"

"I don't want her to get hurt. Most relationships at that age are purely superficial anyhow. It's best if she avoids them altogether."

"Oh, for heaven's sake. Listen to yourself! James, your rules are stifling! *I* don't even agree with that one. And if you insist on ruling with an iron fist, all you'll end up doing is making her resent you, just like you're making *me* resent you! I can't live like this anymore, James! I can't!"

There was a moment of silence in the living room, and Sam's heart pounded. It wasn't the first time her mother had made such an accusation of her father, but the desperation she heard in her mother's voice was a first.

"What exactly are you saying, Brenda?" Her father's voice was quiet.

"This isn't working, James. I need to get away."

"Oh, that's rich," he snorted. "*You* need to get away? That's why we moved here in the first place! You didn't want to face everyone back home. You felt like they were all looking at you, gossiping about our family, judging you behind your back. You quit your job, you quit going to church with us, and you shelled yourself up at home just to avoid everyone! We moved here for *you*! I quit my job and found a part-time job here just so *you* could get away from other people's speculation!" His voice was no longer quiet.

"I know! You remind me of that all the time! It's *my* fault we moved, right? *I'm* the one who made you quit your dream job and uproot the family to come here. Everything is always my fault. No, James. It's not my fault that our son is a murderer!"

"He's *sick*, Brenda. There's a difference."

"And maybe if you would have admitted that sooner, we could have gotten him help before it was too late! You thought a psychiatrist was a waste of money!"

"So then it's *my* fault? Mental illness runs on *your* side, my dear."

Brenda's gasp was audible. "James! How *dare* you! I don't even know you anymore. You are not the man I married. I can't keep on pretending like this. My feelings for you have been dead for so long I can't even remember being in love with you. Maybe I never was to begin with." Sam sincerely hoped her mom was speaking out of anger and didn't truly mean what she was saying.

Brenda spat out her words as if they were arrows intended to pierce her husband's heart. "I was afraid I'd be alone in life if I didn't take the first guy who showed an interest in me. And now I have a husband who's a stubborn jerk and a son in jail and a daughter whose father is suffocating her with ridiculous rules! I'm done, James."

"Oh, and where do you think you'll go?"

"I'll live with my sister."

James scoffed. "Susie? When Samantha stayed with her last summer, she came back with green hair and a nose ring! Our daughter looks like a punk now. Who knows what crazy thing Susie will talk *you* into?"

Tears of frustration and shame welled in Sam's eyes at her father's words. *Don't bring me into this,* she begged silently. She didn't want them fighting over her.

"Oh, please, James. Susie is a free spirit, that's all. It'll be refreshing to live with someone like that rather than someone authoritarian like *you.*"

"You'd better make sure she doesn't already have another live-in," said James, his voice biting. "She may not have room for you."

"I'll take my chances," she shot back coldly.

There was a pause, and Sam imagined her father taking a deep breath like he often did when things got heated. "Come on, Brenda," he said, more quietly. "We're both mad at each other, but let's not overreact. Neither of us is in any frame of mind to make rash decisions now. Things will look better in the morning. They always do."

"No, James. Not this time. I'm done," her mother answered, her voice chilling and low. Sam shivered at the tone as much as the words. She'd never heard her mother talk like this.

Sam scrambled away from the door as she realized her mom had left the living room and was walking past her room. Then again, she doubted very much her mother would even notice her door. She listened as her mom walked the wrong way down the hall to the guest room. Apparently she didn't even want to sleep in the same room as her husband.

Feeling nauseous, Sam stumbled over to her bed. Would

her mom really leave? Or was she just making threats in the heat of the moment? Her parents had been fighting a lot lately, but Sam always assumed they'd work through it. They were all dealing with Chris' situation in their own way. But her mom wouldn't just leave them. Would she?

She'd thought her tears were spent earlier, but now she found there were plenty more inside. Sam cried herself to sleep, fearing very much that she had just contributed to the further breakdown of her family.

CHAPTER

18

Jackson entered the cafeteria and scanned the noisy room until he found Sam. She was sitting alone at a table in the corner. At least she was here. He'd waited at her locker that morning but she hadn't come. Either she was tardy or she'd gone straight to homeroom. But he was relieved to see her there now and made a beeline for her.

"Sam!" he called as he approached.

She glanced at him dully as he pulled out the chair opposite her. "This isn't your lunch period," she said flatly.

"I took a bathroom break from trig. I can't follow that stuff anyhow, whether I'm in class or not."

The corner of her mouth pulled up ever so slightly, and he went on. "What even *happened* last night? You didn't answer my texts or calls or anything. Is everything okay?"

Her eyes filled with tears and she bit her lip. "Nothing is okay. I don't know that it ever will be again."

"Because of me?"

"Because of everything. You, me, Chris, my parents—it's a mess."

"How come you didn't text me back? I sent, like, ten messages."

She tucked a lock of hair behind her ear. "My dad blocked your number and deleted our texts."

Jackson felt rage well up inside him at this man whom he barely knew. Didn't he care about his daughter at all? He had to know that would crush her. Taking a deep breath, Jackson willed his blood to stop boiling. "I'm sorry, Sam. I shouldn't have come when you told me not to. I should have listened. It's my fault."

"No, it isn't. That's just how my dad is. He's way overprotective of me. He thinks boys at this age are distracting. Plus, I'm his baby. He still treats me like I'm twelve. It might be his way of dealing with Chris somehow. I don't know." She lifted one shoulder despondently. "But that's not even the worst of it."

"What does that mean?" Jackson asked, wondering if he wanted to know.

"My parents got into a huge fight last night. It was partly my fault. Mom was gone when you came over, and when she got back I told her what Dad did. Then she got all mad at him and they got into a shouting match, and she threatened to leave."

Sam stopped abruptly and bit her lip again, blinking furiously as if trying not to cry right there in the school cafeteria. Now that he looked more closely at her, Jackson could tell her eyes were already puffy. Poor Sam. His heart ached for her. He was glad he'd been young when his parents had divorced. At least he didn't remember their fights.

"Do you think she's serious about leaving?"

"She might be." Sam blew out a frustrated breath. "I don't know, Jackson. They've fought before. That's nothing new.

Once everything happened with Chris it was like they suddenly started playing the blame game, pointing fingers at each other. But last night… Last night was different. I could hear it in my mom's voice. She sounded desperate. Hopeless. Hateful, even. Like she doesn't want to try to work out their relationship anymore. She didn't even sleep in their room with him last night. That's the first time she's ever done that."

Having no idea how to respond, Jackson simply remained quiet, taking the advice Sam had given him at the food court. He didn't want to give her some pat answer and make her more upset. Besides, he didn't *have* a reassuring response. He didn't know her parents at all, other than the ten-second exchange with her dad the night before. If he was like that all the time, he didn't blame Sam's mom for getting fed up.

Sam put her face in her hands. "I just wish I could go back and redo last night. I shouldn't have gone out there to tattle on my dad to my mom. I knew it would make her mad at him, and I still did it deliberately. I'm such an idiot!"

"No, you aren't," Jackson said. "If anyone's an idiot here, it's me. I didn't listen when you told me not to come. I'm the reason the whole fight happened in the first place."

Massaging her temples, Sam shook her head. "Even if both of us acted stupidly last night, ultimately it's my parents' fault. They've been like this for a long time now, arguing and growing bitter toward each other. Yes, I wish I could erase my actions last night, but that one incident isn't going to make or break their marriage. It's been building up for awhile. An ultimatum was bound to happen eventually."

"I guess." He was not entirely convinced. "Is there anything I can do?" He didn't know if that was the right thing to say, but felt he had to make the offer.

"Not much you *can* do, especially now that my dad expressly forbids me to see you outside of school.

"Can you still come to my baseball games?"

"I don't know yet."

"Can I—"

"Williams!" a voice barked. Jackson turned to see Mr. Vance approaching. "This is not your lunch period. Quit flirting and get back to class."

Jackson flushed and hastily stood to obey the principal's orders. "Save me a seat in bio," he whispered to Sam as he left. It was an exceedingly small consolation, but if she wasn't allowed to see him socially, at least they still had biology class.

The knock on her bedroom door made Sam close her eyes. She had a sinking feeling she knew what was coming.

"Samantha? Can I come in, honey?"

"Yes, Mom. Come in."

Her mother entered, looking as though she hadn't slept much the previous night either. Her eyes were red-rimmed, and Sam could tell she'd been crying a lot. Brenda perched on the edge of Sam's bed, smoothing an imaginary wrinkle on the comforter as she collected her thoughts. She opened her mouth to speak, then shut her mouth, pinched her lips together, and took a deep breath before trying again.

"I've rehearsed what I wanted to say about two hundred times in my mind," Brenda confessed, her voice quavering, "but I'm drawing a blank now that I have to say it." At last she looked at Sam and said gently, "Your father and I have decided to give each other some space."

Although she'd expected as much, the finality of hearing her mother say the words out loud took Sam's breath away. She felt like she'd been punched in the gut. "You're getting a divorce?" she whispered.

"No, sweetie, not a divorce. We're just taking a step back for awhile."

"Is this because of last night?" She had to know.

"Oh, honey, it's because of everything. The last few *years*. Both he and I have changed a lot since Chris was diagnosed, and we don't see eye to eye on anything anymore. We hoped this move would be good for us to have a fresh start in a town where no one knows us, but it... it's just not working. We both have too much baggage we're carrying around. Your father stayed home from work today and we talked about it. I'm going to live with Aunt Susie for the summer. We need our own space. I'll leave today so this doesn't become a long, drawn-out process."

"So you're just going to leave us like *that*?" Sam's voice was both accusatory and pleading. "Today? Are you kidding me? I'm a month away from graduating, Mom! Can't you tolerate us at least that much longer? Stay in the guest room, for all I care!" Now her voice had turned harsh.

Her mother winced. "Samantha, you know I love you more than anything. But I know you heard us last night. And three days ago. And last week. Honey, all we ever do is fight anymore. I don't want you to keep witnessing that. And *I* can't keep doing this either. We need some time to cool off. But of course I'll be back for your graduation. And if you want to come down to spend the summer with me before college, I'd love to have you."

Sam looked away, angry tears splashing down her cheeks. "So now I have to choose between you and Dad? Which one of you will I pick for the summer? Who do I love more? Is that how we're gonna play this game?"

"Oh, sweetie, no," her mother insisted. She scooted closer to hug her, but Sam stood and evaded her. She was broken-hearted, yes, but she was also mad. How dare her mother put her in a position where she had to choose between her parents?

"Samantha, sweetheart, please listen to me," pleaded Brenda. "I don't want you to think you have to pick sides. I just mean that I'll miss you terribly, and if you want to spend part of the summer with me, I'd be thrilled."

"Mom, you're running off to Indianapolis! I don't know anyone there! I've barely had time to get to know anyone *here!* And the one person I do consider my friend, Dad won't let me see! Now you're leaving me too! You think *your* life is hard? Try mine for awhile!" She turned away and clenched her jaw, willing herself to stop crying, but it was no use. Now that her tears were falling, she couldn't stop them. She put her head in her hands, her shoulders shaking from the sobs.

The bed rustled behind her, and her mother came over to hug her. This time Sam didn't push her away. She buried her face in her mom's shoulder as both women cried. Brenda smoothed her hair the way she used to when she was a child, and Sam yearned for those days back, when she'd believed life was rosy and her family was normal and happy, the days when all it took was a kiss from her mother to take her mind off her troubles.

Eventually their tears lessened to sniffles, but her mother continued to stroke her hair. "This is the hardest thing I've ever had to do," she whispered. "It breaks my heart to leave you like this. But if I don't leave now, I'll lose my willpower to do so and nothing will ever change. Your dad and I have to do this. We need to go our separate ways for a while." She pulled back and looked Sam in the face. "But I need you to know that I am very proud of you. You are a beautiful, capable young woman, and I love you more than I can express. Always remember that, Samantha."

"I will," she whispered, tears threatening to spill over once more.

Her mother gave her another tight hug, and for a few minutes they stood, clinging to each other, not knowing how long it would be before they would hug each other again. At last, Sam's mom broke the spell and stepped away.

"I'd better get going," she said softly. "The longer I stay, the harder it will be on both of us. I love you, honey."

"I love you too, Mom," she managed, her voice breaking.

Brenda squeezed her hands in response, attempted an encouraging smile, and walked out of the room. Sam felt rooted in place as she watched her go. This wasn't really happening, was it? The whole thing was surreal. How was it possible to feel broken-hearted on the one hand and yet detached on the other, as if observing the scene as an outsider?

She heard low voices in the living room and assumed her parents were saying their goodbyes. Even when the front door opened, she couldn't move. Her legs felt like cement. But when her mother's car started, she bolted to the window and watched as her mother drove away. She wanted to chase her and beg her not to go. It wasn't supposed to happen like this. Surely her parents could get counseling and work through this, right? They didn't need something this drastic.

A soft knock on her bedroom door startled her, and she turned to find her dad there, looking rather defeated himself. "Want to talk about it?" he asked quietly.

"No, Dad, I don't," she answered shortly. She didn't have the strength to deal with another emotional conversation. She was still trying to process what had just happened.

He looked disappointed at her response but simply nodded and walked away. Sam shut the door behind him and flung herself onto her bed. She felt more alone than she ever had before. Her mother had just left, she was mad at her father, and she wasn't allowed to contact her best friend.

You can pray.

The thought came to her, but she angrily pushed it out of her mind. *Yeah, right,* she thought. *Like God even cares anyhow. Look at this mess our family is in.*

She didn't care that it was only four fifteen in the afternoon or that she hadn't touched her homework. All she knew was that she couldn't feel pain if she was sleeping. A good long nap sounded like an excellent idea right about now.

CHAPTER

19

"Would you like to have a graduation party? That's coming up, you know. We need to make plans."

Sam scoffed at the question her father posed at the dinner table. It had been a week since her mother had left, and in that time she'd done little else at home than sleep and stay in her room. She was even letting her homework slip, and knew if she wasn't careful, she was in danger of not passing at least two of her classes. But she was so empty inside she almost didn't care. She'd done her best to avoid her father all week, but tonight he'd insisted she come to the dinner table with him or get nothing at all.

"Who would I invite?" she shot back scornfully.

"Friends from school."

"I don't *have* any friends, Dad! Don't you get it? Jackson's my only friend! And you chased him away! Do you have any idea how humiliating that was?" Now that she had started talking, she couldn't stop as she vented her pent-up frustration and anger toward her father. "I'll be leaving for college in three months. If you can't trust me to make good decisions now, what do you expect will happen in college? Will I have to check with you on everyone I meet, just to be sure it's okay for me to hang out with them? You treat me like a child! It's no wonder Mom left! You try to control us all!"

Sam pushed away from the table and stomped to her room, deciding she didn't care if she wasn't allowed to eat. She could always sneak out to the kitchen later for a snack, but she couldn't stay out there and make pointless small talk.

A few minutes later, there was a soft knock on her door as her father entered. Coming to sit on the bed next to her, he put his arm around her shoulders and pulled her against his chest. She stiffened but didn't resist. As much as she hated to admit it, she liked the feel of his touch. It was reassuring to know he still loved her.

"Do you think I don't miss her too?" he asked quietly.

She hadn't been expecting that. "I don't know. Do you?"

"Very much," he said, his voice catching.

"But—I mean, you guys argued all the time. I figured you'd be glad to be done with that."

Her father sighed deeply. "I don't miss the arguing. I miss the relationship we used to have, the one we let slip away. We dealt with our grief differently and got resentful of each other in the process. She always told me I was too uptight, too strict. Especially with you. And she's right."

Sam pulled away so she could see his face as he asked, "Do you like this boy?"

"Jackson? Yes, I do."

"As in, boyfriend like?"

"Yeah."

"Does he like you?"

"Mm-hmm."

"But you aren't dating?"

"You wouldn't let me anyhow, so what difference does it make?" She tried without much success to hide the scorn in her voice.

"I highly doubt you'd tell him your father doesn't want you to have a boyfriend. Would you go out with him if he asked?"

"It's complicated," she moaned. "He did ask me to go out with him, but… I don't know, Dad. He's the best friend I have. I even told him about Chris, and he was totally supportive and didn't judge our family or tell anyone at school or anything. I don't want to mess up our friendship by dating him. Like, what happens if we break up, you know? Then we wasted a friendship. I don't want to risk it."

Her dad nodded thoughtfully, and Sam decided now was as good a time as any to have the conversation she was supposed to have a week and a half ago. She and her dad were actually having a decent discussion. No telling when that would happen again. "Jackson is also the only one who knows what I want to do with my life," she ventured.

"Oh?" her father prompted. "And what is that?"

"I want to be a psychiatrist. I want to help families like us deal with mental illness because I know what it's like."

James swallowed hard as he looked at his daughter. "Sweetie, I'm sorry," he whispered, pulling her into another hug. "I've been so caught up in my own pain I've been ignoring yours. I think that's a wonderful idea. I'm glad you have a friend like Jackson you can talk to about stuff like that. Someone who was there for you when I wasn't. I'm sorry, honey. You deserve better."

Sam burrowed her face against his chest, smelling the familiar scent of his aftershave. "It's okay, Daddy," she said. "I know this has been hard for you. Everything. Chris, Mom, your job… It's too much."

"But that's no excuse. You're right—I've been treating you like a child. Maybe that's my way of trying to protect you. But you've turned into a fine young lady, and I'm proud of you."

"Thanks, Dad."

He rested his chin on top of her head and asked gently, "Is Jackson really your only friend?"

"More or less. There are a few girls I hang out with, but I don't talk to them like I talk to Jackson. They barely know anything about me. Certainly not about Chris. We're superficial friends, that's it. When we graduate, we won't keep in touch."

"What about Katie? You went to her birthday party with a couple of other girls, right?"

Sam's face warmed. "Katie is Jackson's younger sister," she admitted.

"Ah. And Faith? You had a good time playing games with her family during Christmas break."

"Faith is Jackson's older sister," she divulged, more blood rushing to her face.

"I see." His voice made it clear he was not pleased at the information.

"I didn't mean to lie to you, Dad," she insisted, pulling out of his embrace to look him in the eye. "But I didn't want you to tell me I couldn't go. He has a great family, and they're a lot of fun to be around. He has four sisters and a brother, and his aunt and uncle are the McNeals from church. His own family goes to St. John. His stepdad is the principal there. They all really like me." She stopped abruptly, realizing she'd just confessed to spending enough time with them to allow them to get to know and like her.

Her father mulled this over in his mind. "It would appear I'm the one who is mistaken," he finally admitted. "I'm sorry I put you in a position where you felt like you had to lie to me. Jackson seems like exactly the type of friend you need. I *do* trust you to make wise choices. I guess I was just trying to hold onto you as long as I could," he finished with a sad smile.

"So what does that mean?" Sam asked, slightly hopeful.

He pulled her phone out of his pocket and tapped the screen a few times before handing it over to her. "Here. I'm not saying you can date him, but why don't you invite Jackson for dinner tomorrow? If he's your best friend, I'd like to get to know him. Give him a better impression of me than the one I gave him a week ago."

"Oh, Daddy!" Sam squealed, throwing her arms around his neck. "Thank you! You'll really like him, I promise. And I know he'll like you too." She planted a kiss on his cheek as he grinned back at her.

"And while we're at it, allow me to propose an alternative to a graduation party," he said. "How about if we invite Jackson's family out for a nice dinner somewhere after the ceremony? My treat."

"What family do you mean, exactly? He has five siblings, and his older sister is married with two kids of her own."

"That's fine."

She was probably pushing her luck, but she continued anyhow. "His extended family is all in town too. The McNeals and his grandparents—probably both sets of grandparents will be at graduation, the ones from Detroit too."

"Why not? They can come. It's still less than throwing a huge party for the entire class."

She giggled. "That's true. I'll ask them. Thanks, Daddy. But…" She paused.

"But what?"

"Um, will… will Mom be there?" She studied her

fingernails as she waited for his answer.

"Your mother promised she'd come back for your graduation, yes. Probably Aunt Susie too."

"But I mean, would you invite them to the dinner?" She peeked at his face, trying to read his expression.

He smiled sadly. "Everything is so much more complicated now, isn't it? Yes, sweetheart, I'll invite your mom and Aunt Susie too. This is *your* celebration. Your mother and I will be polite to one another. I promise. I want that day to be a happy one for you."

"Thanks, Daddy. It will be a good day. I'm excited about it." Having something like that to look forward to was enough motivation to do her homework and ensure she'd pass all her classes.

"So am I." He smiled at her and prompted, "Don't you have a phone call to make?"

Sam flashed him a dazzling smile and turned to her phone as her father let himself out of the room. She was talking to Jackson even before the door was shut.

CHAPTER

20

"Want to meet my mom?" Sam asked.

"Sure," Jackson said, giving up his attempt to locate his family in the crowd. "I don't know where my parents are anyhow."

The two of them, along with the rest of their newly-graduated class, were milling around the football stadium after the ceremony, people flashing pictures and hugging, laughing, and talking loudly.

"Dad said they'd be on the fifty-yard line by the bleachers." She scanned the area, then pointed. "There! Come on, let's go!" She grabbed him by the hand and dragged him to the appointed spot, where Mr. Lewis was standing with two women. Had Jackson not known the two were sisters, he might not have made the connection. He figured Sam's mom was the older one, dressed sensibly in an outfit Jackson's own mother might have worn.

Sam's aunt, on the other hand, wore a long sweater over jeggings, plus high heel boots that came up to her knees. Her hair was short and spiky, dyed bright pink, and she wore heavy eyeliner and hot pink lipstick to match her hair. Her feather earrings dangled all the way down to her shoulders. Jackson would never have guessed this woman had grown up with Sam's mom.

"There you are, honey!" Mrs. Lewis said as Sam and Jackson reached them. She gave Sam a hug. "What a big day! I'm so proud of you!"

"Thanks, Mom. I—"

"Oh, sugar, congrats!" squealed her aunt, cutting her off. She practically lunged at Sam, giving her an excited hug. While Sam was still fighting to maintain her balance, her aunt released her and turned to Jackson. "So this is your 'friend'"— she made air quotes with her fingers—"you were telling me about?" She gave Sam a knowing smile and a dramatic wink as she lowered her voice to a stage whisper. "You're right. He's hot!"

Sam turned dark red and Jackson felt heat rise to his own cheeks, although he fought back a smile, secretly pleased.

"Susie!" Sam's mom chastised. "Allow Samantha to make the proper introductions without giving us your own commentary!" She turned to Jackson. "I'm so sorry. I'm Brenda Lewis, Samantha's mother."

Jackson shook her outstretched hand. "Very nice to meet you, Mrs. Lewis."

"Ooh, and good manners too!" exclaimed Susie. "I like him already, Sammie." She held out her own hand to Jackson. "And I'm her aunt. Don't bother with formalities. Just call me Susie."

"Nice to meet you," he replied, shaking her hand.

"Susie?" she prompted mischievously.

"Susie," he repeated, feeling very much like a little kid following a parent's instructions.

"Hey, hey, hey! Look who I found!"

Jackson froze at the sound of the voice behind him. Dang it, what was *he* doing here? He hadn't invited his father. Heat crept up his neck as he realized his mother must have invited Bob. She hadn't even given him the courtesy of asking if he wanted his dad there. He didn't. Now he was mad at both his mom and his dad.

Bob slapped him hard on the back. "Congrats, son. I'm proud of you."

Jackson had to physically bite his tongue not to make a sharp retort. His dad *knew* he didn't want him calling him "son," and what right had he to be proud of him, anyhow? Bob hadn't done a single thing to support or encourage him in his education or upbringing since he left years ago. He couldn't be proud of a son he didn't know.

"Oh, and who is *this*?" Susie purred. "Given the striking resemblance and the way he addressed you, I'll go out on a limb here and say this is your father, hmm? I see where you get your good looks." She batted her fake eyelashes at Bob, who had a wide grin on his face, clearly quite pleased with himself. Jackson rolled his eyes. His dad's ego was even bigger than his own.

"Bob Coleman," offered his father, taking Susie's hand in his own and kissing it with a dramatic flair as he bowed slightly. She giggled again, and Jackson gave Sam a dark look, communicating his displeasure at the situation. She didn't look so happy herself.

Sam's dad took over the conversation. "Mr. Coleman, glad to make your acquaintance," he said. "This is Jackson's friend, Samantha. I'm her dad, James Lewis, and this is her mother, Brenda."

"A pleasure," Bob replied affably, nodding at everyone in turn.

"So you'll be joining us for dinner?" Susie asked hopefully.

"He can't," answered Jackson shortly.

"Well, I wasn't planning on it, but I can rearrange my schedule if need be," replied Bob, ignoring Jackson's comment entirely.

"Please do," Suzie begged, slipping her arm into his. "It would be lovely to get to know you better."

It was all Jackson could do not to gag. Could this woman be any more obvious? "My father will not be joining us today," he informed them, more loudly this time. He saw Sam's parents exchange looks with one another. "Now if you'll excuse me, I need to find my own family. We'll see you at the restaurant. *Without* my dad."

He whirled around and stomped off grouchily, furious that his dad had turned up unannounced yet again. This was supposed to be a happy day for him, and instead his dad had to come and ruin the moment. He knew that Sam was following him, but he didn't speak to her as he scanned the crowd looking for his family, getting more and more upset by the second. When he heard his aunt's loud laughter, he followed the sound to find his entire family crowded together, talking and laughing.

"Jackson! Sam! Congratulations!" exclaimed Grace when she saw them. Her smile quickly faded when she saw Jackson's expression. "What is it?" she asked.

Jackson took her elbow and steered her away a few paces. "Why did you invite *him*?" he demanded in a loud whisper.

Grace's expression clouded. "Who?"

"Dad!" he practically exploded, causing people around them to look over in surprise. He fought to lower his voice and maintain control as he continued. "You didn't tell me you'd invited Dad. You didn't even *ask* me if I wanted him here. And now he's over there flirting with Sam's aunt, and they've invited him to dinner with us and I don't want him there and—"

"Honey, calm down," Grace interrupted, her soothing tone further grating on Jackson's nerves. "I didn't mean to offend you, and I didn't actually invite him. I just told him when your graduation was."

"That's the same thing," he groused.

"Jackson, you have to let it go," his mother pleaded. "Let go of your resentment. Whether you like it or not, he *is* your father, and although he hurt us in the past, he's also been there for us when it counted most. Need I remind you that he gave Faith part of his liver? Nearly cost him his own life." Bob had gotten a bile duct infection after his operation, and being as stubborn as he was he refused to go to the doctor until he nearly died.

"I know!" His voice was getting loud again. He took a deep breath and continued softly. "Why is it that everyone seems to think he's the big hero now? Like that one thing makes up for everything else he did to us? Yes, I'm grateful he donated his liver! But good grief, it's the *least* he could do. Any of the rest of you would have done it in a heartbeat, but he just so happened to have the right blood type. It's dumb luck, nothing else."

"Or maybe that was God's way of putting him back into our lives," Grace said gently.

Jackson grunted. "Yeah, right."

"Honey, if you really don't want him to come to dinner with us, I'll talk to him privately and tell him not to come."

He sighed heavily. "So that would make me the spoiled kid insisting on his own way. No, Mom, he's here now, and Susie is already hanging on his arm. I'll just sit at the opposite end of the table and let them flirt with each other while we eat." His words dripped with scorn.

"Jackson?" Sam's voice was tentative as she appeared next to him. "Are you okay?"

He looked down into her concerned eyes and blew out a slow breath. He knew this was her way of reminding him that his family was waiting for him, wondering what was going on. "Yes, I'm fine," he answered, putting his arm around her shoulders. "Sorry. Let's talk to my family."

They turned to rejoin the noisy bunch, and his younger siblings clamored around him, begging to see his diploma and tasseled mortar board. He caught David's questioning look at Grace, and knew he had deduced the problem. At least David would take his side. He knew his stepfather was as uneasy around Bob as he. David was such a good fit for their family. He'd become an instant dad when he'd married Grace, and Jackson had never fully appreciated that until now. To accept responsibility for four children who weren't his own must have been intimidating, and Jackson sure hadn't always been accepting or respectful of him. He saw his stepfather with new eyes now. He'd stepped in to fill the void Bob had left.

Bob. Thinking of his father made Jackson's stomach turn sour again, anticipating the dinner to follow.

"Hey, man, it's okay."

Jackson startled at the sound of Spencer's voice next to him. He'd hardly been paying attention to everyone talking at once.

"Huh?"

"I know you and your dad don't get along, and I totally get that. My own dad didn't even come to my graduation. His out-of-town business was more important."

Jackson could only stare at his brother-in-law. Spencer never confided in him, and after his father's death neither of them had mentioned Mr. Young to the other. Jackson steeled himself for a moral lesson about how Spencer never appreciated his dad until he was gone, or about how he should forgive and forget before it was too late, but Spencer didn't go there. Instead, he told Jackson, "Faith and I will sit by him if he comes to the dinner. We'll act as a buffer between you guys so you can enjoy the time with Sam's family."

"I—uh, thanks," he stammered stupidly as Spencer walked away.

Sam appeared beside him again. "Ready for some pictures?" she asked.

"Yeah, let's do it," he grinned, willing himself to put his dad out of his mind. He couldn't do anything about his father's presence, but he wasn't going to let Bob ruin the day for him or for Sam. She was excited to have both her parents there. He'd just pretend his father had never shown up at all.

CHAPTER

21

When July rolled around, Jackson had another surgery to remove the metal plate from his leg. The recovery time was much shorter than it had been when he first broke his leg, but he was still on restricted duty for a while, much to his irritation. When he returned home from the hospital, Sam stopped by with a care package for him.

His mom ushered Sam into the living room, where he was recuperating on the couch with his leg elevated. "Hmm, now why does this scene look familiar?" she teased as she entered. "What's this? No salon duty this time?"

Jackson chuckled good-naturedly. "No, but you just missed an epic Barbie playtime," he joked back.

They laughed together, and Sam held up the paper bag she'd brought. With a devious grin, she said, "That's why I brought this." She handed the bag to him and he peeked inside to discover a variety of nail polish jars. He threw his head back and laughed out loud.

"Shall I call the girls?" she asked, arching an eyebrow smartly.

"Go for it," he replied.

Evelyn and Charlotte were only too happy to get their nails painted "fancy." Charlotte chose a sensible pastel pink, while Evelyn opted for a rainbow, each nail a different color. To complete the look, she requested sparkles on top. Even Katie took advantage of the service, although she insisted Sam be the one to do her manicure.

While the girls were waving their hands in the air to make them dry, Evelyn asked, "Are you gonna paint Sam's nails now, Jackson?"

"You know, I think that's a fabulous idea, Evy," he agreed, smiling at Sam. "And I know just the color for her."

Ten minutes later, Sam's nails were freshly painted emerald green, even if they were a bit sloppy. Jackson was, after all, a guy. Painting nails wasn't his forte. But Sam didn't seem to mind one bit. She declared it the best manicure she'd ever received. Jackson grinned proudly. Sam was the only one in the world who could get him to do something so drastic as paint nails.

The summer passed far too quickly for Grace's liking. Even with the chaos of five kids home from school, she knew the fall would bring a huge change—Jackson leaving for college. He'd always been her most challenging child by far. He was the one to push the envelope, the one she likened to taming a wild mustang. Yet somehow, over the past number of years, he really *had* grown up. The wild mustang had been broken. Sure, he still had his moments, but overall, Jackson had finally matured.

He and Sam spent a lot of time together, and Grace knew the two of them often spoke about Sam's parents' separation. Sam was still reeling from the shock of everything, struggling with how to feel and how to act toward both of her parents, and Jackson had become an excellent listener and sounding board for her. He had, in fact, stepped into the role of "psychiatrist" for her now. It was a side of Jackson that Grace hadn't even known was there, and it warmed her heart to see a gentle side of him emerge.

As August progressed and the time approached for Jackson to leave for college, Grace became more and more emotional. It got to the point where she cried just looking at her son. This was different from Faith's leaving for college four years ago. She'd still been close enough to see on a regular basis. And by the time Faith and Spencer got married, Grace was used to not seeing her every day. But this was completely different. Jackson would just be gone. It was a cold turkey separation, and she didn't like it one bit.

When she and David drove Jackson to Ann Arbor to move him in, Grace was overwhelmed by the chaos of all the freshmen checking in, finding their dorms, and moving their stuff into the tiny rooms. Fresh, eager faces were optimistic as they looked forward to starting classes and experiencing campus life. Grace busied herself with the task of getting Jackson settled in, then took him to Faith and Spencer's apartment for a family dinner, but when that was over, there was no choice but to drive him back to campus.

"Want us to drop you off in front, or should we walk you in?" Grace asked as they pulled up.

"Nah. Just in front is fine," replied Jackson.

Grace knew it would be better that way so his roommate didn't have to witness their goodbyes, but still her heart ached at his answer. He was ready to start a new chapter in his life completely apart from them.

David pulled the car off to the side, and the three got out

and looked at one another uncertainly. None of them wanted to be the first to say goodbye. Grace turned to look at her son, realizing that he had grown into a man sometime over the past number of months. Yet despite the fact that she now had to look up to see his face, she saw in his eyes a flicker of vulnerability, reminding her of the boy he used to be.

That did it. Grace burst into tears. She'd been holding it in all day. Blindly reaching out, she put her arms around Jackson and held on tight, burrowing her face in his chest. He hugged her in return, resting his cheek on the top of her head.

"Oh, Jackson," she sobbed, "I'm going to miss you so much. It won't be the same without you at home."

She pulled back just enough to look into his eyes. She needed to be sure he heard her next words. "But I am so proud of you. I always have been. And I love you very much. Remember that."

Jackson cleared his throat. "I know, Mom. I love you too."

"Your determination is one of your strongest assets," she continued. "Use that to help you reach your goals. I have no doubt you can accomplish anything you want to with that determination."

Jackson nodded, and Grace reverted to "mom" mode for final instructions. "Have fun at college, but not *too* much fun. If you go to parties, be careful. Don't drink; don't mess with drugs. Be wise about the people you hang out with. Remember to eat well, and be sure to go to church. If you ever need anything at all, Faith and Spencer are here. Make time to see them as often as possible. Please don't forget your poor lonely mother. Call me when you can, and text as often as you want. And remember, college is harder than high school. Allow enough time for homework and studying."

David put a gentle restraining hand on her back, signaling

her to stop. Jackson didn't need a sermon. He reached out to shake Jackson's hand.

"I second everything your mom said. We're very proud of you. And even though you and I don't share the same last name, I've long considered you my son, and I love you."

Jackson actually teared up slightly at the comment, and hid that fact by hugging his stepfather, surprising Grace. He had never initiated a hug with David before.

"Thanks for stepping into the role of 'dad' when I needed one," he said. "You're the best thing to happen to our family in a long time."

Jackson gave him a parting slap on the back to signal the end of the discussion. Sentimentality was not something with which he was comfortable.

"Well," he said, drawing in a deep breath, "I guess this is it, huh?"

"Guess so," Grace responded. "Better go finish settling in. Meet your dorm mates, get to know your way around… Give me one more hug and then be on your way."

Jackson hugged her again, giving her a little squeeze. Then he turned to walk away with one quick wave as he left. David put his arm around Grace, and together they watched as Jackson disappeared into his new life. Then David led her back to their car, got in, and drove away slowly. But Grace felt very much like a little piece of herself had been left behind with Jackson.

CHAPTER

22

"I want to go by 'Fred.'"

"What?" Grace looked up as Freddie made the announcement to her and David after his siblings were in bed.

"In high school. 'Freddie' is too babyish."

Grace felt another piece of her shatter inside. She'd been dreading this conversation, but she'd had a feeling it was coming. Her children were all growing up, and she wasn't ready for it. Faith was married with two children, and Jackson was off to college. She wasn't at all sure she could handle one more of her children making a change, even one as mundane as dropping a nickname. Though it had been chaos, she missed the days when the kids were younger and still living at home together. It was all Grace could do not to cry right then and there.

Thankfully, David seemed much less shaken by Freddie's statement and responded matter-of-factly, "All right, son. That's a fair request. But bear with us here at home. We've been calling you 'Freddie' for so long, it'll take awhile to get used to 'Fred.' But this is as good a time as any to make the change. Only a handful of students at high school will know you from St. John. The rest can start out calling you 'Fred' and it will hardly be an issue."

Freddie—*Fred*, rather—smiled and nodded, obviously pleased that his family would try to honor his wishes. He walked over and sat by his mother on the couch. Grace sensed there was more he wanted to say.

After a minute of silence, she prompted, "Something else on your mind, honey?"

Fred sighed and said in a very small voice, "I'm scared."

Grace turned to look at him fully. "Of…?"

"High school," he admitted. "It's a big change. There were only eight kids in my class at St. John, and now there will be a few hundred. And most of them already know each other. I'll be the new old kid. They won't even remember me from first grade all those years ago."

He had a point. Before she'd met David, all her kids had gone to the public school. Grace doubted many of the kids from his first-grade class would remember him.

"And, Mom, I'm not like Faith or Jackson or even Katie," he went on. "Faith was popular because she's pretty and nice. Even after she got pregnant and wasn't in with the cool kids anymore, I think people still respected her. Jackson is awesome at sports, so everyone knew him and liked him. Even if they didn't, Jackson wouldn't have cared. It didn't matter to him if people liked him or not. And Katie is so outgoing people can't help but like her. Me?" He shrugged despondently. "I'm not like that. I'm not outgoing, I'm not athletic, and I *do* care what other people think of me. I want them to like me. But I'm afraid no one will. I'm just too… *average.*"

Grace paused for a moment before answering. "Want to know a secret?" she asked. "I'm scared too."

He looked at her in surprise. "Of what?"

"Going back to college."

"Really?"

"Mm-hmm. It's very daunting to go into something new, something you haven't experienced before. I'm not outgoing or popular either, Freddie… ah, *Fred*. I'm pretty average myself. I was always a little jealous of Olivia because she was so pretty and outgoing. So I think I know a little bit how you feel. And even now, I'm scared to go back to school with kids that are twenty years younger than I am. I'll probably be older than some of the professors! What will the other students in the class think of me—a middle-aged woman just now trying to get her degree? New ventures are pretty daunting."

"I still get nervous at the beginning of each school year," confessed David. "It's natural to be jittery about new stuff."

"And I'll bet even Jackson is nervous starting out at U of M," said Grace. "He's not a big shot football star there, and there are a lot more students than here at Mapleport. He may seem confident and brave on the outside, but he's probably scared on the inside."

"Maybe," conceded Fred. "But I'm still not like him at all."

"And that's okay!" she said. "I wouldn't want two Jacksons in the same house. Could you imagine? You are your own person, unique and gifted in the way God made you. And we love you exactly the way you are."

"Yeah, I know." He didn't sound entirely convinced, but he wasn't dismissive of her answer either. Grace took that as a small victory.

There was a thoughtful pause until Fred spoke again. "I never thought I'd say this, but I miss Jackson."

Grace's eyes misted over. "So do I," she whispered.

"It's so… empty without him here. Even with the girls. It's

funny. When we were younger, I couldn't wait until I'd have my own room and be rid of Jackson. Now that he's really gone, I miss having him here. Life is weird like that. But Jackson really grew up a lot the last year or two. He isn't the same as he was when we shared a room. He was mean to me and made fun of me a lot back then, but he's not like that anymore. Or at least, not as much," he amended.

"You're right," Grace said, her throat tight. "He *has* grown up a lot. And I miss having his exuberance here too."

"Do you really think he's going to be a teacher?" Fred asked.

"I don't know," she said. "Lots of people change their minds about their majors in college. Spencer did, after a fashion. But you know how Jackson is. Once he makes up his mind about something, he's pretty determined to see it through."

Fred heaved a sigh. "I don't have any idea what I want to do when I grow up."

"Freddie—ach, *Fred*, you're only going into high school this year. I bet the vast majority of freshmen haven't even given it a second thought," Grace protested. "You know what I wanted to do when I was in junior high? I wanted to be a stewardess and fly all over the world."

"And I wanted to be a spy," said David with a grin. "Or a Secret Service agent."

"See?" Grace said. "Neither of us had anything planned back then. You don't need to make any decisions so soon."

"I know. But I've kind of been thinking about it lately because of Jackson. For a while I was thinking about being a teacher too. But not if Jackson's going to be one."

"Why not?"

"I don't want it to seem like I copy everything he does."

Grace bit back a smile and was pretty sure her husband did so as well. Fred was nothing like his older brother. One could hardly say he copied *anything* Jackson did.

"I was thinking about going into music," continued Fred. "I really like band. But a lot of people who go into music end up teaching."

David spoke up. "But directing a band or choir is much different from classroom teaching like Jackson's going to do. He'll be dissecting pigs and teaching the periodic table, while you're working on intonation and balance. I wouldn't consider that copying him."

"I suppose."

"You know," Grace said, "I don't even have a specific goal in mind for going back to college. Yes, I want to get my associate's degree, but then what? I'm hoping that being exposed to different classes will help me discover new interests. So don't feel bad. I *still* don't know what I want to do when I grow up!"

Fred laughed. "I guess if you're brave enough to try something new at your age, I can be brave about starting high school."

"Atta boy!" she encouraged, choosing to ignore the barb. She knew Fred wasn't trying to be mean or disrespectful. "And I tell you what—let's make a deal. At ten thirty each morning, let's say a little prayer for each other. That way you know I'm thinking about you, and we can kind of be 'together' in a sense. What do you say?"

"I like it." Fred grinned. "Thanks, Mom. For everything. I love you." He gave her a little hug and then stood.

"I love you too, sweetie."

Her son made his way upstairs to go to bed, and Grace sat quietly, pondering the conversation in her mind. In all honesty, she was a little nervous for Fred herself. He *was* pretty shy and skittish of new endeavors. The switch from the public school to

St. John had been good for him. He'd blossomed with the smaller class size and more individualized attention from the teachers. But now she wondered what the transition back would be like for him. Try as she could to shake the uneasy feeling, she suspected it wouldn't be nearly as seamless.

CHAPTER

23

"Can I be homeschooled?"

Fred's question stopped dinner conversation as all eyes turned to him.

"What are you even talking about?" Katie frowned. "Who would *ever* want to be homeschooled? Mom wouldn't have the first clue what to do!"

"Thanks, sweetheart," protested Grace, although she knew full well Katie was right. She hadn't the slightest inclination to homeschool any of her children. Ever.

"Then Dad can!" Fred shot back. "He's a teacher. Besides, I'm way ahead of most of those kids anyhow. The stuff we're doing in math is stuff I did in, like, seventh grade. I could practically take a year off and still be at the same level."

"I take it you didn't have a great day, huh?" asked David sympathetically.

"Oh, it was *fabulous*," Fred returned sarcastically. "I just wanted to try homeschooling to see how fun that could be too!"

"Fred!" reprimanded Grace, shocked by his rudeness. Fred rarely resorted to sarcasm, especially to his parents. "Do *not* speak that way to us! We're trying to have a discussion with you. Sarcasm is not needed."

"*Sorry*," he retorted, though his tone indicated he was anything but. "You want to have a *discussion*? Fine. Yes, I had a crappy day. Gym was mortifying. Some of the guys figured out who I was, so now I'm little 'Freddie Williamth' with a lisp who can't throw a ball to save his life!" He was practically fighting tears. "So much for being my own person! When they found out I'm nothing like Jackson, they all made fun of me. I *hate* having an older brother who's perfect, because there's no way I can ever measure up to that!"

Grace was indignant. How could kids be so cruel to one another?

"And guess what else?" Fred continued. "You know what time gym starts, Mother? Ten thirty! So your dumb little idea of thinking of each other right then totally backfired! If you said a prayer for me this morning, it didn't work at all. In fact, that was the *worst* part of my day! So just forget the whole thing!"

With that, he shoved away from the table and stormed upstairs to his room, slamming the door behind him. The other family members looked at one another in astonishment. Fred rarely got worked up over anything. If he'd ever slammed a door before, Grace couldn't recall it.

"He kind of sounded like Jackson," Evelyn said.

"I don't think we ought to compare him to Jackson at all," remarked David somberly. "It sounds like that's partly why he's so mad right now. So how about we all agree not to do that, okay?"

Grace looked at David. "Should I…?"

"I think he needs some time to cool off first," he replied. "Why don't you finish eating and talk to him afterward while

Katie and I clean up down here?"

The family continued their meal in silence, even Katie unusually reserved. Grace's heart was breaking for her son. She'd been afraid something like this would happen. High school could be brutal, and unfortunately, Fred was finding that out the hard way.

When she brought a plate of reheated food up to Fred later that evening, Grace knocked twice before letting herself in. "I thought you might be hungry," she commented. "You didn't eat much at dinner."

Fred shrugged from his desk chair and said nothing.

"What are you working on?" she asked, peeking over his shoulder.

"Just drawing," he replied shortly.

"Can I see?"

Reluctantly, he moved the sketch pad over enough for her to see his work. It was a drawing of his dog, Pluto.

"Fred, that's terrific! It looks just like her! Is this for an assignment or just for fun?"

"For art class. We're supposed to make a pencil drawing of something living. It can be a plant, person, animal, whatever."

"It's already due tomorrow?" she asked in surprise. It seemed an ambitious assignment for the very first day of school.

"Next week. But I figured I'd start working on it right away. I'm not sure I like her legs yet. I might redo it."

"So at least art class went okay, huh?" she asked cautiously.

Fred sighed and put his pencil down. "I don't mind the real classes. It's gym I hate. They all made fun of me today."

Grace pulled her son into a hug. "Sweetie, remember way back when you were in first grade with those guys, and you threw rocks at that car one day? Do you remember what I said?

You didn't want them to tease you about your lisp, and I told you there will always be people who will make fun of you for one reason or another. They make fun of other people to make themselves feel better."

She released him from the hug to look into his face. "As hard as it is, you can't allow mean-spirited people determine how you feel about yourself. If they have nothing better to do than make fun of you for a lisp you had years ago, they aren't worth your time. You'll make other friends who will appreciate you for who you are."

His only response was a snort.

"Is Paul in any of your classes?" Paul was Fred's closest friend from St. John.

"A few. At least we have the same lunch hour so we can sit together. But we don't have the same gym period. The only one I know in gym is Matt, and he's the reason they started making fun of me in the first place. He told them I throw like a girl and close my eyes when I swing the bat."

"I'm sorry, honey. I wish I could make it better for you." She really did. This was one of the most difficult things about being a parent—seeing her child hurting, but realizing she was powerless to fix the situation.

There was a pause before she ventured, "Do you want to know why I picked ten thirty? That's the time my first class starts. So right before class today, I said a prayer for you. Truthfully, I didn't have a great first day myself. The professor handed out the syllabus, and it's pretty overwhelming. There's a lot of work involved, and I could hardly follow her lecture today. After class I was pretty dejected. I don't know if I can do this after all. It's been an awfully long time since I've been in school."

"I guess that prayer thing didn't work for either of us, then, huh?"

"I don't know about that. Maybe God knew both of us would *need* an extra prayer at that time of the day."

Fred looked at her dubiously, clearly not convinced.

"Look, this is only the first day. Even though I'm overwhelmed and think I may not be able to do this after all, I'm not about to give up already. And even though you had one bad class today, I'd hardly be pushing for homeschool yet. Give it time. Probably by next week those guys will have other stuff to talk about or other people to tease. At least you have a few classes you enjoy—art and band went okay, right?" He nodded, and she continued. "Then instead of dwelling on the one period that was crummy, think instead about the ones that went well. Can you do that?"

Fred didn't answer, so Grace kissed him on the top of the head. "Whether you want me to or not, I'll still say a prayer for you at ten thirty. Now I can be more specific in my prayers."

"Sure."

"And no matter what happens at school or who's mean to you, we all love you here at home. Even as un-Jackson-like as you are."

Fred allowed a small smile at her last comment, and Grace gave him one last kiss before letting herself out of the room. She knew that her little pep talk hadn't accomplished much. He still felt lousy. Nothing had been solved. Grace desperately wished she could make everything better for him, like she used to be able to magically heal an owie with a kiss when he was little. But unfortunately, growing up was painful.

This was one boo-boo she couldn't kiss away.

CHAPTER

24

Fred walked into the locker room, dreading what was sure to be the worst hour of the day. Scott saw him coming, as if he'd been watching for him. "Hey, Thlugger!" he cackled when he caught sight of Fred. Apparently this was to be his unofficial nickname. Fred hated it.

"Hey, you know this is Star Wars period, don't you?" Scott joked, wiggling his eyebrows. "May the 'fourth' be with you, right, Thlugger?" The other boys guffawed at the lame joke, and Fred gritted his teeth as he yanked on his shorts.

The general ribbing went on until the gym teacher hustled into the locker room with a shrill blast on his whistle. "Let's *move*, gentlemen!" Coach Navarro barked. "You're worse than the ladies! What are you doing in here—powdering your faces? Get out there and start running laps! Go, go, go!"

Obediently, everyone shuffled out of the locker room and started jogging around the gym. As Fred ran, a student with shaggy hair came up next to him, keeping stride so they were together. Fred glanced in his direction and had to look down. Even though Fred was under the average height for his age, this kid was a good six inches shorter still. He looked familiar, and Fred tried to place him.

"Don't worry about them," the other student panted as they jogged. "They're a bunch of bullies, and everyone knows it. They still make fun of me for scoring for the other team last year in basketball. Only shot I made the entire year. They call me 'Hoops.'"

Despite himself, Fred smiled. At least he wasn't the only unathletic one. He liked this kid already.

"But my real name is Zep," his running partner continued. "And I'll make you a deal. I'll call you 'Fred' if you call me 'Zep.' Forget these stupid nicknames."

"Sounds good to me," Fred agreed.

"My mom says guys like that make fun of me 'cause they're trying to make themselves feel better."

Fred looked at him in surprise. "My mom says the same thing!"

"Do you believe her?"

"No. Do you?"

"Nope." They both laughed, and Zep continued. "You're in band, right? Trumpet?"

"Mm-hmm."

"I play saxophone."

Ah, *that's* why he looked familiar. "Yeah, I've seen you across the room."

Zep flashed a lopsided grin and wiggled his eyebrows. "See, these guys may be jocks, but can they read music? Hmm?"

Fred chuckled. He highly doubted that any of them would consider that a loss.

"Okay! Flag football today!" Coach Navarro barked after a blast on his ubiquitous whistle. "Bring it in, boys! Scott, Clayton, you're team captains. Start picking teams. Now!"

Zep and Fred looked at each other in dread. They knew what was coming. Soon enough, it was just the two of them left standing there, the rest of the kids already selected. Scott sighed deeply. "I'll take Hoops, I guess. You get Thlugger."

"Good luck," Zep mumbled to Fred. "This is my least favorite game of all. But at least we've got band to look forward to."

As Fred jogged over to grab a red pinney, he allowed a ghost of a smile. He *did* enjoy band, and now, thanks to Zep, gym class might be slightly more tolerable after all. Slightly.

"David? Do you have a minute?" Grace's voice was tentative. David looked at his wife standing in the living room doorway, biting her lip.

"Of course, sweetie. What's wrong?"

"I was wondering if you could do me a favor." She fiddled unnecessarily with the corner of a paper she was holding.

"For you, anything."

She advanced into the room. "I know this might sound dumb, but could you read through a paper I'm working on? It's been a long time since I've had to write a paper, and I'm not very good at it. You're smarter than me anyhow, so I need you to see if it makes sense or if there are mistakes. Can you do that?"

"Of course," he assured, resisting the urge to correct her grammar: *"You're smarter than I am," Grace, not "You're smarter than me."* He doubted she'd take kindly to that, especially given the statement in question. "I'd be happy to help. But for the record, I'm not smarter than you."

"Yes, you are. And we both know it. At least in terms of book smarts."

"Do you want me to read it right now?" He wasn't about to

start a debate about who was smarter.

"May as well." She handed him the paper she was holding and perched next to him on the couch, sitting practically on the edge of the cushion like she was going to bolt at any moment.

David accepted the paper from her and started reading. A few sentences in, he realized he'd never read anything she'd written before. And there was a reason for that. Her writing wasn't very good. She didn't stay on topic in each paragraph, and he spotted a number of misspellings and grammatical errors as well. This was going to be challenging. He'd seen papers written by eighth graders that were better than this.

He read slowly, stalling for time as he tried to figure out the most tactful way to make suggestions. But eventually he knew he had to give her his opinion, so he turned back to the opening page and set the paper on his lap, signaling he'd finished reading it.

"Well?" Grace asked worriedly.

"You have a good start," he began. "It just needs some work."

Grace moaned and sank back against the couch. "That's what you tell the kids when their homework is terrible. It's your way of trying to put the best construction on things."

"That's not what I meant," he protested. "I have some suggestions, that's all. Some technical ones like grammar that are easy enough to fix, and some that may call for reworking a few parts."

It surprised him to see a tear running down his wife's cheek. "David, who am I kidding? I know it's awful. I don't even know *how* to write a paper anymore. It was stupid of me to want to go back to school. I'm the oldest one there by far, and I'm making a fool of myself. Besides, I'm only there for an AA. What can I do with that? I'll stop wasting my time and our money and just drop out."

"Whoa, whoa, whoa! Where did this come from? You will do no such thing! I get that you're frustrated right now, but what would you tell Jackson if he came home from college and told you what you just told me? Would you accept defeat from him already, barely a month in?"

"No, but this is different. He's there so he can get a teaching degree and go out and make a living. I'm just there for the fun of it, with no actual goal in mind. It's pointless."

"It is not pointless. And you are not quitting. Period."

"What difference does it make to you? We'd save money if I dropped out." He didn't miss the slightly scornful edge to her voice.

"Because you are not a quitter, Grace. You can do this. It's challenging, yes. But that'll make it all the more meaningful when you get your degree in another couple of years. Besides, it's good for the kids to see their mom going back to college. You're showing them that you're not afraid to try new things and learn more as an adult. You're teaching them a valuable life lesson. They need to see you do your best. And dropping out is not your best."

She groaned. "It's so much harder than I thought it would be."

"Anything worth doing takes effort."

She merely shook her head.

"When is this paper due?"

"Friday."

"Okay. That gives us four days. Let's work on the topical stuff tonight. See if we can figure out a way to rearrange some of the paragraphs to flow together better. Then tomorrow we can go over it for spelling and grammar. Then you can make the changes on the computer on Thursday and be done a day early! How's that?"

"Do you really think I can get a decent grade on this thing?"

"Absolutely." He hoped his voice conveyed none of the secret doubts he harbored.

She slowly pushed herself away from the back of the couch. "Then let's get this over with."

"That's the spirit!" he grinned. "One thing I learned from my composition class in college was to read your writing out loud. I know that sounds like a weird trick, but it works. Your ears catch what your eyes don't. So start reading this out loud and stop when you think something sounds funny or doesn't make sense."

"You know this is going to take forever, right?"

"Then I guess we'd better get started," he teased.

Grace smiled half-heartedly and turned her attention to her paper, and David took a deep breath. He hoped he'd have the patience and diplomacy to deal with the task ahead without offending his wife. He was proud of her for going back to school, yes, but he'd never considered how much work it would be, both for her and for him.

CHAPTER

25

Want a ride home this weekend for Homecoming?

Jackson sent the text to Sam and waited for an answer. He couldn't believe October was half over. The first month and a half of college had flown by. He was enjoying the pace of college life and the 24/7 activity of a town like Ann Arbor. By now he knew his way around campus, had a routine for classes, homework, and working out, and had been to a handful of parties. He was debating between two fraternities to join come spring, and was getting to know a few guys from each. He and his roommate weren't best friends, but they got along well enough. All in all, it had been a decent adjustment.

A few minutes passed before his phone beeped. Sam texted back, *Sure! When?*

Friday btwn 2–4. Gotta be back before the game at 7.

Make it 3:30. I'll text directions to my dorm later. In class now. Lol

Jackson grinned. It would be good to see Sam again. The two texted frequently, but he missed seeing her in person. He'd even take her out after the game, just like old times. They needed to catch up and have a real conversation.

The next day after a freshman class, someone stopped Jackson on his way out the door.

"Hey, Forty-Three," greeted Miranda with a flirtatious wink.

It was good to see a familiar face from home. "No one here knows I used to be a football star," he chuckled. "You need to find a new nickname for me."

"I like it," she insisted. "It suits you. Besides, this weekend is Homecoming. Everyone back home knows your old number. You're going, I assume? We have to crown the new King and Queen."

"Yeah, I'll be there. Are you going?"

"That depends on you."

"On me?"

"I don't have a car," she explained. "I know you saved up money over the last few summers with all the big bucks you made mowing lawns, but I am among the underprivileged few who don't have a car. Can you give me a lift?"

"Sure. I can do that."

Her face lit up excitedly. "Great! Thanks!"

She started to walk away, but Jackson stopped her. "FYI, I'm stopping by Michigan State to get Sam on the way."

That made Miranda pause, but she quickly regained her composure. "That's fine," she assured, even if her tone didn't quite match the words. "It'll be good to see her again. So I'll meet you at your dorm Friday afternoon?"

"I'll pick you up at yours. Text me which one. I'll get you around two fifteen."

"Deal. Thanks, Forty-Three." She kissed him on the cheek and traipsed off down the hall, hurrying to catch up to a male student and slip her arm coyly in his. Jackson shook his head and grinned. Miranda certainly hadn't lost any of her feminine charm.

"I miss it, Sam. I do," Jackson confessed.

The two were sitting together over Oreo shakes again at Applebee's. The game was over, Jackson and Miranda had turned over their titles to the excited new King and Queen, and now Sam and Jackson finally had a chance to talk, just the two of them. The ride home with Miranda had been pleasant enough, but they'd stayed on neutral topics like classes and professors. Now, in the relative privacy of a public restaurant, they could really talk.

"I knew you'd miss football," she responded. Sam always seemed to understand what he meant.

"Watching the team out there tonight—it brought back all the memories, you know? Yes, I broke my leg playing football, and I suppose that really should scare me off, but I still miss it. Being part of a team, working together, everything."

"I would imagine so." Sam nodded and took a sip of her milkshake.

"You know, I love that about you," he said a few moments later.

She laughed in astonishment. "What on earth are you talking about?"

"You don't try to give pep talks when you respond. You empathize and leave it at that. None of this, 'But at least...' stuff. You don't try to cheer me up or talk me out of the way I'm feeling. I think that's a good trait for a psychiatrist to have. You just let me talk while you listen. You aren't trying to solve my problems."

Sam seemed pleased by his insight. "Thanks, Jackson. It's not something I do consciously."

"And it's even better that way. You're completely genuine about it."

"Now you're going to make me self-conscious about it, though," she said with a small smile, twirling the straw in her shake.

"Then forget I said anything. Getting back to sports, I'm going to try out for football next year after all."

"Seriously?" Sam squealed. Her eyes positively lit up at his comment.

"I can't help myself," he said. "I have to at least try. This past year was too soon after my broken leg. I wasn't at the top of my game physically or mentally. But I'm ready now. I've been working out and lifting weights to keep in shape, and I don't limp anymore. They have open tryouts in January or February, and they have my highlight reel from high school. I think I'd have a halfway decent chance of making it if I try out."

"Oh, Jackson, that's great!" she encouraged, reaching over to give his hand a quick little squeeze. "I had a feeling you'd pull something like this."

"Ah, it's purely selfish motives," he said with a grin. "It looks better on my resumé if I play college football. Makes me more marketable as a coach someday."

She laughed. "Selfish motives or not, I think it's awesome! I'll even come to some of your home games." She lowered her voice to a theatrical whisper, leaning closer to him over the table. "Just don't spread it around East Lansing that I'm rooting for maize and blue!"

It was Jackson's turn to chuckle. "I haven't made the team yet," he reminded her.

"You will. When Jackson Williams makes up his mind to do something, you can bet that he'll see it through."

Her compliment sent a rush of warmth through him, and he smiled his thanks before changing the subject. "So are you going to join a sorority?"

Sam laughed out loud. "Not on your life! Can you imagine me doing that?"

"Depends on the sorority. You should try it! Miranda already has hers picked out."

"Why doesn't that surprise me?" She rolled her eyes good-naturedly. "No, I'm not a sorority girl. But I'm sure you're going to be a frat boy, huh?"

"Of course!" Jackson was surprised she'd even asked.

"Please tell me you don't have to do something crazy or illegal as part of your hazing," she pleaded.

"Hazing isn't even allowed anymore, don't you know that?" Jackson asked with an indignant sniff. "Fraternities are much more sophisticated than people give them credit for."

Sam raised an eyebrow. "Mm-hmm. You're joining a fraternity so you can be sophisticated?"

"Of course not. I'm joining for the parties."

She burst out laughing. "Aha! That's the Jackson I know." She smiled at him as they both sipped their milkshakes.

"So…" Sam trailed off, her face turning serious. The lightness of the previous conversation was gone. "Mom and Dad are getting a divorce. It's official."

"Oh, Sam…" Jackson felt a heaviness settle upon him. "I don't even know what to say."

She blinked back tears. "Me neither," she said. "Yeah, Mom was living with her sister, but I thought that was temporary while they both went through counseling and gave each other space. And I hoped…" Her voice cracked and she cleared her throat before speaking again. "I don't know, maybe with me out of the house, I hoped they'd work things out on their own."

She shook her head with a sad smile. "I guess I'm completely naïve."

Sam looked into Jackson's face. "So now what am I supposed to do? I mean, for holidays and stuff? Spend one with Mom and one with Dad? Where is 'home,' anyhow? We were only in Mapleport for a year before I went off to college. Only Dad is here. Chris is off to jail, and Mom's off to Indianapolis. My family is falling apart and there's nothing I can do!"

Jackson remained silent, his heart aching for her. His own family was exactly opposite. In his humble opinion, there were too many of them. At this rate, they could be their own reality show. Holidays were pure chaos in their household, but it made him sad to think of Sam celebrating Christmas just with one parent.

She sighed deeply and continued. "I wish none of this had ever happened at all."

"I know."

"You do it too, you know." She peeked at him over the top of her glasses with a tiny smile.

"I do what too?" Jackson was confused.

"You don't try to give me pep talks or say, 'Yeah, but…' You empathize well."

He guffawed. "If my family could hear you now… I'm the *least* empathetic person there is."

"Not with me," she insisted. "I can talk to you about stuff I'd never talk about with anyone else. You're my best friend."

While Jackson was touched by her words, he couldn't help but feel a sense of longing that she'd see him as more than a friend. Trying to push the thought aside, he answered, "And you're mine."

After a pause, Sam ventured, "So… have you heard from your dad lately?"

Jackson stiffened. Neither he nor Sam had mentioned his father since he'd shown up out of the blue at graduation.

"No. Why?"

She twirled her straw between her fingers. "He… um…" She sighed and shook her head. "He's dating my aunt."

Jackson clenched his jaw so tightly it hurt. Was his dad just determined to get under his skin? To keep showing up unwanted as often as he could? Of *course* he would end up dating Sam's aunt. The two were flirting so shamelessly at graduation it was embarrassing to watch them.

"Oh, that's just great," he muttered angrily.

"Jackson, why do you have such a grudge against him?"

He felt heat rush to his face at the question. "Sam! I've told you all about this! He ran off and left our family when I was six!"

"My mom just ran off and left too!" she protested, stubbornly jutting her jaw out. "You think I'm not struggling with that? But I still talk to her! It's awkward, and I go through periods of resentment, yes, but I at least make the effort."

"Sam, my dad ran off with some other woman when my mom was pregnant," he said in a hard voice. "And since Mom was an emotional mess and Faith was a girl, everyone looked to me to be the 'man of the house' and step up to be there for my mom. At the age of *six*! That's an awful lot of pressure to put on a kid, don't you think?"

She was silent a moment, squinting as she looked off into the distance. "Yes, it is," she said quietly. "You're right."

Somehow her answer made him more defensive. "But you still think I should let it go?"

Sighing heavily, she answered, "Life is a mess, Jackson. For everyone. I have no right to tell you to forgive your dad when I'm struggling to forgive my own family. I don't want to even *talk* to Chris, much less forgive him. He quit taking his meds because he didn't like how they made him feel, but then the voices in his head came back and he killed someone and messed up the rest of his life, leaving us all in his wake."

"That's sort of how I feel about my dad. His selfish actions messed up the rest of us for a long time."

"But he and Faith get along now?" She looked at him hopefully, as if she needed an affirmative answer. Jackson wondered if it was for his sake or her own.

"Mostly because he donated part of his liver to her. It's kind of hard to keep being mad at someone who saved your life."

"Probably true." She gave him a half smile and dabbed at spot on the table absentmindedly. "What about your mom? Has she forgiven him?"

"I think so. Mostly, yes."

"Forgiveness is so hard, isn't it? I still don't know who I'm mad at. My parents, my brother, God... Kind of everyone, in a way. And my dad would say we have to forgive others, but what if they aren't sorry? Chris has never apologized to me. Can I forgive someone who isn't remorseful?" Sam gestured toward Jackson. "Or what about your dad? Has he ever asked for your forgiveness? Are we supposed to forgive if the other person doesn't ask? And how about God? Is it even possible for a person to 'forgive' God?"

"I... don't know," he admitted. He was way over his head in this discussion. He'd never had much of a grasp on deep theology. "Since God is perfect, He doesn't sin," he said slowly, trying to put into words the jumbled thoughts in his brain. "So in that sense, we can't forgive Him. But... I think... like, there are times when He allows things to happen to us that maybe we think He could have prevented, like my dad leaving or Chris' illness. So then we might get mad at Him and have to come to terms with our… uh, with the burdens He allows, in which case, it's sort of like we're forgiving Him. But it's more like accepting His wisdom than forgiving Him. I think. Maybe."

She smiled faintly. "My dad keeps reminding me of that verse that talks about God working all things out for the good of those who love Him. Even when I can't see His plan, I have to trust it'll be for my good. Or so my dad believes."

"You don't?"

"I'm not sure yet."

"Fair enough." Jackson was silent a moment before continuing. "My mom has made the comment before that if Dad hadn't left, she never would have fallen in love with David, which means he wouldn't have invited her to church. None of us would be Christian now. So even though she had to go through years of being a single mom, struggling to make ends meet and deal with the demands of four young kids by herself, God did work it for her good—for the good of all of us—after Dad left. It took years to see how, but He did."

"What if I don't *want* to wait years to see any possible good to come of my family falling apart?"

"That's not really our choice to make."

She fixed him with a piercing gaze. "So even though you can see the good that came of your dad leaving, you're still holding a grudge against him?"

He bristled. "God brought good out of the situation, but my dad is still clearly in the wrong."

"Like Joseph's brothers, selling him into slavery? Remember what he told them? 'You intended evil against me, but God used it for good.'"

Jackson felt like she was challenging him to do something she couldn't bring herself to do, and that made him mad.

"Whose side are you on, anyhow?" he demanded. "On the one hand, you're telling me I should forgive and forget, but at the same time, you're telling me you won't forgive your brother, or even God!" He threw up his hands, exasperated. "You're mad at God, but you still use the Bible to make me feel guilty when it suits you to do so. You can't have it both ways."

Sam scoffed. "I'm still trying to figure out how I feel about everything, and I'm asking you all the questions I ask myself."

"Oh, really?" He snorted in disbelief.

"Yes, really. I think about this a lot. And I'm probably more honest about my struggles than you are about yours." She tossed her head defiantly as she looked him in the eye with a challenge in her own.

"What's that supposed to mean?" This conversation was taking a turn he did not like in the least.

"At least I'm acknowledging my conflicting emotions! You, on the other hand, pretend to have absolute confidence in God, but you're totally ignoring His command to forgive those who sin against you. In your case, that's your dad. You'd be content to pretend he doesn't exist, and you get mad whenever he shows up or whenever someone talks about him. Maybe God is challenging you to forgive him and actually live out what you believe."

Jackson shook his head. "I don't want to talk about this anymore."

"Fine! Keep pretending the problem doesn't exist!" She glared at him. "Someday, Jackson, you're going to have to make a decision whether you'll forgive your dad or hold a grudge forever. But I wouldn't want to be in your shoes if you choose hatred."

Standing abruptly, Jackson tossed some money on the table. "I'm leaving," he announced. "If you want a ride home, you'd better come now. And quit talking about forgiveness and God and my dad. This discussion is over."

He stormed outside, his entire body rigid from tension. He heard Sam scurry to catch up, pulling on her jacket as she followed him. They reached the car, and he didn't bother to open the door for her, but got in and started the engine without a word.

They drove to her house in silence, but when he pulled into her driveway, she said, "I'm sorry, Jackson. That was uncalled for back there. I don't want to fight with you, and I don't want to ruin our friendship. Let's just forget that discussion ever happened, okay? I won't preach to you about your dad anymore. It's not my place. Goodness knows, I have enough struggles of my own to deal with."

He blew out a slow breath. "It's okay, Sam. Our conversation just touched a nerve, and I got defensive. Talking about my dad is always a sensitive subject."

"I know. I'm sorry."

"It's okay. No hard feelings."

"Am I still your best friend?" She peeked at him out of the corner of her eye.

"Of course. Friends can disagree sometimes, can't they? And what are friends for, if not to speak honestly?"

She smiled in relief. "Thanks, Jackson. Call me tomorrow?"

"Sure."

She squeezed his hand and opened the door to get out. He watched to be sure she got inside safely, then backed out and drove away, his mind still on their conversation. How was it his dad always seemed to turn up and ruin things? He and Sam had been having a great time together until they started talking about his father. Resentment coursed through Jackson, but it was quickly followed by a sense of guilt. Despite what he said or thought, Sam hadn't been wrong in her accusations. It wasn't his dad who had ruined the evening.

It was Jackson himself.

CHAPTER

26

"Rise and shine! Breakfast is served!" Grace called cheerfully as she flipped on the light.

"Mother!" Jackson chastised with a groan. "It's nine in the morning! What are you doing?"

"We are going to have a nice family breakfast," she insisted. "We haven't seen you for a month and a half. It's not too much to ask. Up and at 'em!" With that, she marched back up the stairs, whistling. It was good to have her older son home again.

Ten minutes later, everyone was at the table except Fred. "Frederick Walter!" David called up the stairs. "Last call! If you aren't down here, you don't eat until lunch. Come *on!*"

A very reluctant Fred came down sullenly, dropping into a chair and avoiding eye contact with everyone. Grace exchanged a frown with her husband. This was not like Fred at all.

Over fried eggs, bacon, and cinnamon rolls, she peppered Jackson with questions about college. Katie and Evelyn added questions of their own, making for a lively conversation as everyone competed to be heard. Fred still seemed uncharacteristically silent, so Grace tried to draw him into the conversation. "Did you and Zep have fun at the game last night, sweetie?"

Fred's face darkened, and he turned to glare at Jackson. "No, we didn't. Thanks to *him*," he accused.

A frown appeared on Jackson's face as well, and he opened his mouth to respond, but Grace beat him to it. "Why? What happened, Fred?"

"Scott and Matt were teasing me and Zep like they always do, and—lo and behold—in swoops Jackson to defend me like some big hero." He turned to Jackson, his face hard. "Do you have any idea how embarrassing it was to have my *brother* come in and stick up for me? Like I can't take care of myself?"

"It didn't *look* like you were taking care of yourself!" Jackson shot back. "You just sat there and let those jerks insult you! Stand up for yourself! I was trying to help you out!"

"Well, you didn't! Now they're gonna be worse than ever, teasing me that my older brother has to rescue me!"

"Boys!" admonished Grace. "That's enough! We do *not* need to argue at the table!"

"Besides," Fred continued as if she hadn't spoken, "you told them not to pick on 'smaller kids.' Is that all I am to you? A smaller kid? Thanks for that. Thanks a lot."

"But you are! Those guys are way bigger than you!"

"Don't you think I know that?" exploded Fred. "I'm one of the scrawniest kids in my class! Look at me! I don't even weigh a hundred pounds yet! And here I have my muscular, athletic brother coming in to point that out. Rub salt in a wound, why don't you? I'm sick of being compared to you!"

With that, he stomped back to his room, leaving the rest of the family at the table. Grace sighed and blinked back tears. So much for a nice family breakfast.

* * *

Jackson knocked on Fred's door and waited a very long minute before the door opened and his younger brother glared out at him.

"What?" he demanded.

"Can I come in?"

"Did Mom make you come up here?"

"No. Can I come in?"

Reluctantly, Fred opened the door and stalked back to his bed, throwing himself down.

"I like how you rearranged the room," Jackson commented. "You made your own little astronomy corner by the dormer window. That looks nice."

"Why are you here?"

Okay, so no small talk. "Why didn't you tell me you were having trouble at school?"

Fred scoffed. "So now I have to report to you all about my pathetic social life? What would you do about it anyhow? Other than embarrass me, that is."

"I didn't mean—"

"Maybe you don't get it," interrupted Fred. "Not everyone is popular and awesome like you. And the fact that you were such a legend makes me look like a total loser in comparison. I'm the most unathletic person there is."

"There's more to life than sports." Jackson could hardly believe the words had come out of his mouth.

"Not in high school, there isn't! All you did in high school was practice and work out. Sports was your *life!*"

"Not anymore!" Jackson was out of patience. "As much of a 'legend' as I was at high school, I'm a no-namer at college! No one there knows me at all! I've made some friends, sure, but I'm not a football star anymore. Don't you think *I'm* having a hard time with that?"

"Welcome to my life!" Fred gestured grandly, spreading his arms wide as though making an entrance onto the stage.

Jackson gritted his teeth. Apparently his brother was determined to wallow in self-pity. "That's not what I mean!" he said. "You don't like sports anyhow. But you still get to do the things you love—you still have band and art class. Me? I don't get to do what *I* love! All I ever wanted to do through high school was make it to college football, and now I don't have that! Do you have any idea how hard it is for me to sit in the student section at those football games when I've been dreaming my whole life about being on that field instead?"

Fred paused briefly before conceding, "Okay, fine, that's true. But do people make fun of you like they make fun of me? I doubt it."

"College is different," insisted Jackson, plopping down on the end of the bed, one leg folded beneath him so he could face his brother. "Most of the people there are at least a little more mature than in high school. Look, you want them to quit teasing you? Stand up for yourself! Tell them to knock it off, and if they don't, beat 'em up!"

"Oh, sure," Fred scoffed. "Can you see me beating up anyone? Ever?"

"Want me to teach you how to punch someone the right way? I've been in my share of fights." Jackson grinned proudly.

"I'll pass. I don't want to get in a fight."

"Then join 'em."

"What?"

"You know that expression—'If you can't beat 'em, join 'em?' Do that."

"Whatever. You're such a dork." Fred tossed a pillow in his general direction, which Jackson caught and threw back.

"No, I'm serious! Listen, they do it because they know you hate it. But if you encourage them, the fun will be gone and they'll get tired of the whole charade. It's, like, reverse psychology."

"Brilliant, Jackson." Fred rolled his eyes. "Did Sam tell you that?"

"I had to endure psych class in high school, you know. I used reverse psychology on Mom all the time. Worked like a charm."

Eyeing him suspiciously, Fred asked, "So what, in your mind, would that look like?"

"Tease yourself back! Beat them to the punch. Like, you know, they call you 'Thlugger' and you say, 'My name is Freddie Williamth.' Or walk in and say, 'I hope we're playing bathketball today. I like it better than batheball.' Let them see it doesn't bother you if they tease you about your lisp. Which, by the way, you grew out of, like, six years ago. They're morons for teasing you about something that happened that long ago."

"Yeah, they are. But Matt started it. He went to St. John with me and always teased me about how bad I was at sports. He helpfully pointed that out to the guys in the locker room. Then when they made the lisp connection, it was the icing on the cake."

"Then take off their icing! Gosh, Freddie, have fun with this!" He gave Fred's leg a little push. "They're giving you an awesome opportunity to completely blow off PE. If you get the ball, totally overdo it like you have no clue what you're doing. When you play basketball, do a granny shot. Or fake missing the ball when you're up for kickball. If they're going to laugh at you anyhow, may as well make it seem like you *want* them to!"

"Then I won't get an A in gym."

Jackson waved away the protest impatiently. "I seriously

doubt Mom will be upset about that. And colleges won't care. They look at 'real' subjects."

Fred was silent for a moment, considering the advice. "That could maybe work," he grudgingly admitted.

"In the meantime, are you sure you don't want me to teach you how to fight? You can practice on me."

"Very tempting," laughed Fred. "I've long waited for the opportunity to punch you."

"Well…" Jackson gave him a sly grin.

"Nah. I'm good. Fighting is stupid."

"Okay, but if you ever change your mind…"

"I'll ask you if I can punch you."

"Exactly." He hopped to his feet. "Now, are you going to come down and eat your bacon and cinnamon roll or not? 'Cause if not, I will."

"Like you need the extra calories," Fred snorted. "You're getting fat, Jackson."

"I am not!" he protested, looking down at his broad chest. "Muscle weighs more than fat. I've been lifting weights at the gym."

"Tell yourself what you want. You just don't want to admit you're getting the 'Freshman Fifteen' or whatever they call it." Fred's devious smile made Jackson happy. His brother must be feeling better if he was teasing him.

"Okay, featherweight," he teased back. "If you're so concerned about me putting on the pounds, come eat your own food and start gaining weight yourself! You can even have the extra cinnamon roll Mom saved for me. Don't say I never did anything for you."

"That's a pretty gracious offer," Fred replied as he stood as well. "The whole thing?"

"Maybe we can split it fifty-fifty," Jackson amended.

"Deal," Fred chuckled. "You know, I've kind of missed having you around. It's not at all the same without you here."

"I believe it. Now you're stuck with three giggly sisters." He shook his head and placed a hand sympathetically on Fred's shoulder. "I feel for you, bro. But hey, I can teach you how to give a manicure if you want. They love it. I'm just that awesome—I can fight *and* do manicures. All in the same day." He placed his fists on his hips, swelled his chest, and looked off to the side in a Superman pose.

Fred laughed and gave him a little shove, and the two went back downstairs to polish off the breakfast remains. Jackson consoled himself with the fact that even if he'd messed up the previous evening with Sam, at least he'd made things right with his younger brother.

CHAPTER

27

When Sunday afternoon rolled around again, Jackson's mother bade him another tearful farewell before he chauffeured Sam and Miranda back to school.

After dropping Sam off and giving her a parting hug, Jackson got back into the car with Miranda. He brooded a bit as he drove off, knowing he wouldn't see Sam again until Thanksgiving. They'd gotten together on Saturday, but the discussion about forgiveness was still hanging over both of them.

"So are you guys dating?" Miranda broke into his somber thoughts.

"Huh? Me and Sam?"

"Who else?" she teased, swatting his arm playfully. "Are you dating?"

"Uh, no, actually."

"Why not?"

"What is this? Twenty Questions?"

"I'm just curious, that's all. It's obvious you guys already have a great relationship, and you're sitting over there mooning now that she's gone. Have you not asked her?"

Jackson scratched his head absently, stalling for time. He wasn't about to tell Miranda that he *had* asked Sam and she'd said no. "We're just really good friends, that's all."

Miranda gave him a long look. "So you *don't* like her?"

"Do we have to discuss this?"

"Yes."

"Why?"

"Because if you aren't going out with her, how about you go out with me?"

He glanced sideways at her from the driver's seat, hardly believing what he'd just heard. "Are you asking me out?"

"More or less, yeah."

"Seriously?" He stared at her a full three seconds before turning his eyes back to the road.

"You're one of the nicest guys I've ever known, Jackson. One of the few in high school who didn't try to make a pass or get physical with me. Heck, even a couple of my mom's live-in boyfriends have tried to come on to me." Jackson's stomach turned at the thought as Miranda went on. "You actually respect females, and that's pretty uncommon, at least in my experience. Most guys don't bother to see past my looks, but there's more to me than my body. I have a personality too. And a brain I can use on occasion."

Jackson was astonished by her reply. He'd always thought Miranda was so self-absorbed that she *liked* the attention she garnered from males. And she certainly dressed in such a way as to accentuate her curves. He assumed she was shallow and flighty, and really hadn't bothered to find out if she had a personality beyond that. He frankly had no interest in going out with her, but he could hardly say that.

"Miranda, I'm glad you think I'm a decent guy and all, but

you don't really want to go out with me."

"Actually, I do. Come on, Jackson, I'm practically groveling here. This is embarrassing."

He squirmed in his seat. "I'm just… not interested in dating anyone right now, that's all. It's nothing personal."

"Then let's go out a few times and see where that leads us."

He mulled this over in his mind. She was hardly going to let this drop. "Okay, how's this? Why don't you come to church with me next week? I usually go to my sister's house afterward for brunch, but you and I can go out to eat instead."

"Wow, Jackson. You're sweeping me off my feet. You really need to work on your pick-up lines," she replied dryly.

Heat flooded his face. "I'm not even *trying* to deliver a pick-up line!"

"Clearly. Just forget it." She looked out the window stonily, nursing her wounded pride.

Jackson started to say something, but quickly checked himself. It wasn't worth prolonging the discussion. They drove the remainder of the way in silence.

CHAPTER

28

Squaring his shoulders, Fred walked into the locker room to start changing.

"Whazzup, Thlugger?" Scott asked in a hearty voice when he approached.

Fred opened his locker and started getting his shorts on. "You know, you really need to get a new nickname for me... *Thcott.*"

There was a moment of silence as Matt and Scott exchanged confused glances.

Pulling his gym shirt on, Fred continued, "I heard we're playing thoccer today, which is great, becauth that'th one thport I can actually play. Latht year I thcored two runs all by mythelf."

By now he had finished changing, and Fred stood after tying his shoes. "Better go thart my lapth. You coming, Hoopth?" He walked out of the locker room without looking back.

"That. Was. Awesome," Zep breathed as he caught up to him, a smile of wonder on his face as the two started jogging.

When Coach Navarro blew his whistle to signal the official start of laps, Scott ran up beside Fred and kept pace with him long enough to say, "Not bad, Slugger," before running ahead.

Fred grinned proudly. Coming from Scott, that was high praise. Maybe Jackson knew a thing or two after all.

David looked up in alarm as Grace flung the door open. He'd just arrived home from school with the girls, and Fred was already home after the bus dropped him off.

"What's wro—"

She cut him off mid-sentence as she threw herself into his arms and kissed him soundly on the lips, eliciting exclamations of disgust from all four kids.

"I take it you had a good day," he laughed.

Without answering, Grace handed him the paper she'd received back from her professor. Scrawled across the top in red pen was the grade. She'd gotten an A minus. His heart swelled with pride as he beamed at his wife.

"That's wonderful, Grace!" he encouraged with a hug. "I'm so proud of you!"

"I have you to thank for that," she said. "If it wasn't for you, I wouldn't have done nearly so well."

"Not true," he protested. "I gave a few suggestions, that's all. You're the one who put the hard work into it. And it paid off! See? I *knew* you could do this! Kids, look! Your mom got an A on her paper. The very first one she's had to write in twenty years. Aren't you proud of her?"

"That's great, Mom!" exclaimed Fred.

"Way to go!" Katie seconded.

The twins shrugged at each other, clearly not comprehending the situation.

"Tell you what," David continued, still grinning at his wife.

"To celebrate, I'll make supper tonight. I'll grill my famous ribs. How does that sound?"

"Wonderful!" Grace said. "I can never refuse such an offer! Just so long as I change out of my white shirt first…" They both laughed. She was notorious for dripping barbecue sauce on her shirt when he grilled.

"Are you going to make cookies while I grill?" he teased. "You look cute with flour in your hair and chocolate smeared on your forehead."

"Might as well. I haven't tested the smoke alarm lately." The two dissolved in fits of laughter.

Fred and Katie looked at each other and rolled their eyes. Their parents were completely ridiculous sometimes.

CHAPTER

29

"Can I get a phone?"

Grace looked at her sixth grader in dismay. "Katie! We just got Fred one last year, and you're three years younger than he is!"

Katie heaved a dramatic sigh. "*Mother!*" she exclaimed in exasperation. "Seriously! *Everyone* in my class has one. Most of them have the latest model too. Even third and fourth graders have them. I'm so pathetic in comparison."

"Who would you call?"

"You don't even use a phone for calling anymore," her daughter informed her haughtily.

"Of course not. What was I thinking? Then what *would* you use it for, exactly?"

"Texting. Games. Social stuff."

"Ah, yes. 'Social stuff' meaning what? Facebook? Twitter?"

"Oh, Mom, those things are so old school! No one uses those anymore! That's for adults." Katie flung herself on the couch, rolling her eyes.

This was news to Grace. She'd only hopped on the

Facebook wagon a few years ago and still hadn't ventured into the Twitter world. Apparently she was hopelessly behind the times.

"Then what are kids your age using?"

"Instagram. Snapchat. Some do Tumblr."

Grace had no idea what any of those were. She knew for the first time how *her* mother must have felt when she came home in high school raving about "NKOTB," or New Kids on the Block. It was like a foreign language, and one she wasn't sure she wanted to learn.

"Besides, I'd even use it for school stuff," Katie said, clearly believing she was upping the ante. "There are apps for vocab and videos for science and games for math. There's even an interactive thing for band where I record my playing assignment and send it to the teacher from home."

"What do you do for those things now?"

"Use Dad's," said Katie dejectedly. "But then I can only use it when he's not."

"You could use mine, you know. You've never even mentioned any of those things to me before."

"That's because Dad didn't want me to bother you about it. He said you have enough on your mind with your own classes. Besides, he already downloaded all that stuff. I have my own folder."

"On Dad's phone?"

"Yeah."

"I see." Grace was surprised at this bit of information. Technology had come a long way even in the decade since Faith entered high school. Faith hadn't gotten her own phone until the end of her freshman year, and had used it mainly for texting and calling. Nowadays, Grace knew kids in early grade school were getting phones of their own, and many had accounts for various forms of social media. She didn't like that fact, but it was true.

"So will you at least think about it?" Katie pressed, snapping her out of her reverie. "Please?"

"I'll discuss it with Dad and see what he thinks," Grace promised.

"Tonight?" Katie's eyebrows raised hopefully.

"Don't press your luck, young lady. He has a meeting tonight. I'll discuss it when it's convenient for us to do so. Now go work on your math."

"Okay," sighed Katie. "But if I had a phone, I could start with my science video and write the summary already. Just saying…"

Katie scooted away before she could respond, leaving Grace to shake her head in exasperation. She had a love/hate relationship with technology. Yes, it had many good uses, and she certainly took advantage of a number of those things. She followed a few blogs, listened to music, kept up with the news, texted Faith and Jackson on a daily basis, looked up recipes and other tidbits of information, and occasionally even wasted time on social media and games.

But technology could also be dangerous. The lure of the glowing screen was a hard one to resist; a modern-day equivalent to the Sirens of Homer's *Odyssey*. She'd seen families at restaurants each looking at his or her own phone throughout the entire meal, barely interacting with one another at all. Nor was her own family immune to the temptation. David and Jackson were often glued to their phones or tablets, and even though she hated to admit it, she spent more time on hers than she should. It was shocking how quickly one could become addicted. She wanted to hold off her kids as long as possible. Because once they started, there was no going back.

* * *

"Katie wants her own phone," Grace informed her husband.

"I know. She mentions it every day on the way home from school."

"What do you think about it?" asked Grace. The two were in the living room that evening, ironically enough, both using their phones.

David sighed and placed his phone on the end table. "I don't like it very much, but she could probably handle it."

"In sixth grade?"

"She's pretty much the only one in her class who doesn't have one."

"That's what she told me." Grace was dismayed that David was confirming what Katie said. Her daughter wasn't exaggerating to make a point. "She also said Facebook and Twitter are 'old school.'"

"Oh, yes. Kids don't use those."

"*I* just started using Facebook!"

David nodded. "Exactly why kids don't. Their parents are on there. They don't want to be."

"Katie said now it's instant gem and snapshot."

"Instagram and Snapchat," corrected David with a chuckle.

"How do *you* know about these things?" It irked her that her husband was correcting her on the latest social media sites.

"I work in a grade school, you know," he replied, still grinning. "I try to stay current with things the kids are doing."

"That makes one of us."

"Don't worry," he assured her. "Social media is constantly changing. Soon enough, Instagram and Snapchat will be 'old school' and there'll be some new thing that's all the rage."

That was precisely the sort of thing that worried Grace. She could never keep up with the latest fads. "I don't like it," she told David. "Everything is moving too fast and kids are growing up too soon. Faith didn't get a phone until she was almost a sophomore. Jackson got one going into high school. Fred got one in eighth grade. Now Katie wants one in *sixth* already? At this rate, the twins will want one for their birthday!"

"Lots of kids already have them by fourth or fifth grade," David admitted. "Sometimes even younger."

Grace shook her head. "There's no reason a child needs to get addicted to a phone that early. What happened to playing outside? Or board games? Talking with a friend about boys? That's what I did with *my* friends!"

"And our parents worried that we listened to too much music on our boomboxes and played on the Nintendo too much," David countered. "And *their* parents were concerned that they listened to rock 'n' roll, which was straight from the devil. Parents have always worried that their kids were being corrupted by new inventions or advances in technology."

She thought about that. He did have a point. "I suppose," she conceded. "But don't tell me you aren't worried even a little that our kids won't know how to socialize because they're always on their electronic devices. I want them to actually *talk* to the people they're with, rather than ignoring them while texting or insta-gemming or whatever. Technology is too addicting. Even *we* use it too much."

"I know," David said, removing his glasses to wipe the lenses on his shirt. "You're right. It *is* very tempting. The round-the-clock connectivity is dangerous."

"I just want our kids to stay away from all that as long as possible."

"Me too. But like it or not, this is the world in which we

live." He squinted through his lenses before putting his glasses back on. "We're raising the Internet generation. They've never known a time when iPhones and computers didn't exist. And more and more stuff is being done online. A number of offices have completely done away with paperwork and only do online forms. Some textbooks are only available on the internet. Katie even has apps on my phone for some subjects."

"Yeah, she told me she has her own folder on your phone."

"She does. And I'm totally okay with that sort of stuff. It's a good use of technology."

"Granted. But that's not the main reason she wants her own phone."

"True. But I don't think it's unreasonable to get her one for Christmas or her birthday. We have the filtering program already set up on the family plan. We'll just add her as another user and set stiff restrictions so she can't wander onto inappropriate sites. We can set a certain time of day when she can use it, like for half an hour or forty-five minutes at seven thirty, for example. And that's only if she finishes her homework before then. If she wants to do Instagram or Snapchat—which she *will*, being our little social butterfly—she has to have us approve her followers, and one of us has to follow her as well. How does that sound?"

Grace mulled his suggestions over in her mind. "I guess if you're okay with it, I am too," she finally said. "I didn't feel this nervous about Fred getting a phone, because he doesn't really care about social media stuff. He has his games that he plays with his friends, but he's always been our responsible one anyhow. I trust him more than I trusted Jackson at that age— maybe more than I trust Jackson now! But Katie is so innocent and naïve sometimes. I just fear she'll do something dumb without realizing it."

"Which is why we need to be vigilant about what she's doing online," said David. "In a way, it's better to start out now, when her circle of followers is pretty much the other six girls in her class, than when she's off to high school and we don't know anyone there. This is sort of her 'training period,' if you will."

"I can see that. Okay, let's add her on our plan at Christmas. But in the meantime, how about you and I set a curfew for being on our own phones? We can actually *talk* at night when the kids are in bed."

"We're talking now!"

"Isn't it wonderful?"

David laughed. "Come here, you," he said, pulling her into a hug and resting his chin on her head. "I like your idea. Sometimes it's all too easy to get caught up in whatever I'm doing on the computer or phone, but I'd much rather end the day by talking to my wife. How about nine thirty?"

"Perfect. We can have an adult conversation without the girls interrupting every thirty seconds like they do at dinner."

"Maybe we'll even live large and break out the boxed wine now and then to relax."

"Life on the edge…" she teased with a laugh.

"I like to live dangerously," he grinned. "For tonight, though, how about we splurge and have some ice cream? I'll get some for us."

"You don't have to convince me! You know I'm a sucker for ice cream."

He kissed the top of her head before getting up to dish out their dessert. Grace smiled as she watched him go. There was no one with whom she'd rather live dangerously than David.

CHAPTER

30

Jackson grinned as he entered the party. Although it was December in Michigan, his fraternity of choice was throwing a Hawaiian luau to celebrate the end of the semester, complete with a pile of sand dumped in the middle of the floor and plastic palm trees surrounding it.

Everyone there wore some sort of tropical attire. Jackson sported Bermuda shorts and a gaudy floral shirt he'd picked up for the occasion. Many of the girls had bikini tops and grass skirts. A few guys were floating around handing out plastic leis to everyone, and Jackson got a hot pink one to complement his outfit. Loud music blared, the food table was loaded down, and tropical beverages were being served.

"Hey, Williams! You made it, man!" Pete Jennings, one of the fraternity brothers he'd gotten to know, came up and clapped him on the back. "Good food, cold drinks, pretty girls… Who could ask for anything more?" He handed Jackson a piña colada and walked away.

Jackson glanced around before taking a sip. It was good, but he knew there was alcohol in it. His mother would be appalled if she knew he was drinking at a party. But she wasn't here, and what she didn't know wouldn't hurt her, right? He'd only have one. It was harmless enough. Pushing all thoughts of his mother out of his mind, he had another sip and sauntered over to the food table.

While he was balancing his plate and drink at the same time, he heard a familiar giggle and turned toward the sound. Sure enough, it was Miranda. She was wearing a Hawaiian shirt with the top two buttons undone and the bottom half of the shirt tied in a knot, exposing her midriff and making the shirt into a halter top. A pair of super-short shorts accentuated the outfit. Undeniably, she looked good, and that fact did not escape the males in her vicinity.

As Jackson watched, a guy replaced the nearly empty glass in her hand with a full one, then slid around to stand behind her, his hands on her hips as he whispered something into her ear. Miranda giggled again, quite obviously drunk out of her mind. Her male companion smiled lewdly and pulled her against him, his hands sliding onto her stomach. His pinkies slid underneath the waistline of her shorts as he swayed her back and forth in time to the music. Jackson had no doubt what his intentions were, and something exploded inside him as he watched the scene unfold. He couldn't protect Miranda from creeps like this all the time, but he wasn't going to let this guy take advantage of her tonight.

Marching over to the pair, Jackson took her hand and firmly pulled her out of the grasp of her unsavory companion. "Come on, Miranda," he insisted. "It's time to go."

"Hey! What do you think you're doing?" the male protested. "She's with me!"

"Not anymore," Jackson said in a low but threatening voice, his teeth clenched.

"What, you want a piece of her too?" There was that awful lecherous grin again. Rather than respond, Jackson let his fist do the talking, causing those around them to scream as blood gushed from the guy's nose.

Jackson grabbed Miranda's hand again and walked away without looking back. She was barely coherent as it was, so she followed blindly, stumbling to keep up with his quick pace. As they left the party, Jackson consoled himself with the fact that no girl would have to fall prey to Mr. Wandering Hands that night.

Twenty minutes later, Jackson was half dragging, half carrying Miranda into Faith and Spencer's living room. By now, she was starting to moan, fully feeling the effects of the alcohol. Jackson wondered if the jerk at the party had slipped something else into her drink as well. Miranda had a headache and was sick to her stomach, and although Jackson didn't have experience with drunk people, he had a feeling she'd be throwing up before too long.

"I'm really sorry about this, guys," he apologized, keeping his voice low so as not to disturb Griffin and Hope as they slept. "I don't know what else to do. I don't want to leave her in her dorm room. Her roommate is out of town for the weekend, and she needs someone to look out for her. But I can't take her back to *my* room either. Imagine how bad that would look. You guys are the only ones I trust to take care of her."

"It's not a problem," assured Faith, setting a bucket next to the couch as Jackson lowered Miranda onto her side. "When you called, we knew she needed a place to stay. We're happy to help. Just don't make a habit of this."

"I wouldn't dream of it. Want me to stay to help clean up or get her to the bathroom or whatever?"

"We've got it," she assured him. "Spencer's in medical school. He can handle it, right, babe?" She winked at her husband.

"Yeah, thanks. Because I don't deal with enough bodily fluids with our kids."

"It's good practice for you," she insisted sweetly.

Jackson laughed. "Seriously, I'll stay if you want me to."

"You'd better not. If people find out neither of you made it back to your rooms after leaving a party together, they may talk," Faith pointed out. "Don't put yourself in that position."

"You're probably right. Hey, do you have something she can wear? Like an old sweatshirt?" Good grief, Miranda was practically spilling out of her top. It was embarrassing even to look at her.

"I'll find something," said Faith. "She *is* rather scantily clad, isn't she? I'll take care of it. You get on back to your room and call in the morning to check in."

"Will do. Hey, thanks again. I really appreciate this."

"So will she when she's coherent enough to realize what you did for her. Sounds like that guy at the party was a real jerk. I'm glad you were there to intervene."

"Me too," Jackson agreed with a shudder. "I don't even want to think about what would have happened otherwise."

The three exchanged somber glances. He'd been in the right place at the right time tonight, but Jackson was very uneasy. What if it happened again when he *wasn't* around?

The following morning, Jackson drove back to Faith's apartment to pick up Miranda. His sister wouldn't go into detail about what happened during the night, nor, quite frankly, did he want to know. When he arrived, he was glad to see Miranda sitting at the table, eating tiny bites of scrambled eggs and nibbling at dry toast. She had one of Faith's T-shirts on, plus a pair of yoga pants. There were huge bags under her bloodshot eyes, and her hair was a disaster, but oddly enough, her vulnerability made her seem more real to Jackson. Seeing her like this, she was prettier than when she dolled herself up and wore tight clothes.

When she caught sight of him, Miranda turned dark red and averted her eyes.

Griffin didn't miss a beat. "Hi, Uncle Jackson! Mommy said you were here last night when I was in bed, but you didn't wake me up to see you!" He pouted momentarily before brightening again. "But your friend is feeling better. Mommy said you dropped her off 'cause she was sick, and Daddy's almost a doctor! Are you gonna stay and play with me?"

Jackson grinned and ruffled his nephew's hair. "Maybe tomorrow after church, huh, bud? I need to get Miranda back to her room. Thanks for helping take care of her. I appreciate it. Your mom says you're a good helper."

Griffin puffed importantly. "Yeah, I am," he agreed.

Jackson chuckled at his candid admission, and Spencer pulled out a chair opposite Miranda. "Might as well stay and eat first. Faith made a double batch."

"How can I resist?" he replied. "It's either this or dry cereal back at the dorm. I'll take a nice hot breakfast any day."

Spencer walked to the kitchen to dish out a plate, and Jackson addressed Miranda in a low voice. "How are you feeling?"

"Better than I would be if you hadn't been at that party last night," she admitted in an equally quiet voice. "My head is pounding and I feel like crap, but it'll pass." She still avoided eye contact, choosing instead to fiddle with her fork.

Before either of them could say more, Spencer brought in a

heaping plate of eggs for Jackson, who promptly inhaled them all.

"Uncle Jackson is the fastest eater I know," Griffin boasted to Miranda. "And he eats more than anyone else too. That's because he works out. He used to play football 'til he broke his leg."

"I know," Miranda replied. "I went to high school with him. I was a cheerleader so I went to all his games. Even the one where he broke his leg."

"Oh!" Griffin was clearly impressed by this revelation, but then his forehead creased in confusion. "But you're not the one with green hair."

Spencer answered, "No, Uncle Jackson has lots of friends from school, G. That's Sam."

"Yeah. I like her. But Jackson said he's not gonna marry her." His face brightened. "So is he gonna marry you, then?"

Jackson and Miranda both flushed deeply, and Faith intervened with a nervous laugh as she set more eggs on the table, along with a bowl of cut-up fruit. "Oh, Griffin, you certainly do speak what's on your mind! We haven't quite figured out how to teach him to filter his thoughts yet," she added quietly to the college students. "So! Lots of homework this weekend, Jackson?"

"Not too much. But I do have to finish a paper I've been putting off."

"Are you going to have Mommy proofread it for you again?" inquired Griffin.

"You *do* realize you're raising a male version of Katie, don't you?" Jackson sighed to Faith. Their younger sister had always been blunt.

"It's okay," continued Griffin. "Evelyn said Grandpa helps Grandma with her papers too because he's a teacher. Well, kind of. He used to be, I think. Now he just sits in an office at the school. But maybe when you become a teacher, Uncle Jackson, you'll be smart like him!" Griffin smiled triumphantly, clearly proud to have made such a profound connection for a kindergartner.

Miranda actually giggled at that, and Jackson snuck a glance at his sister, the two exchanging a small smile. Sometimes it was convenient to have Griffin around. He had a way of breaking the ice.

After Jackson had polished off the last of the eggs, he stood and thanked Faith for the food. Then, turning to Miranda, he asked, "Ready?"

She stood self-consciously and turned to Faith with downcast eyes. "I'm really sorry to be an inconvenience," she mumbled. "But thank you for everything. I'll wash your clothes and give them to Jackson to return to you."

"It's no problem. I'm glad we were here to help. Let Jackson know if you need anything else."

Miranda followed Jackson out of the apartment and into his car. Clearly, Miranda did not desire conversation, and kept her face turned to stare out the passenger window. When they got back to campus, Jackson noted that she glanced around furtively and wondered why. Did she simply want to avoid other students seeing her in this condition? Or was she watching for signs of her male companion from the night before? Jackson wondered how much of the incident she even remembered. She'd seemed pretty out of it last night.

They reached her dorm, and Jackson walked her in, determined to see her safely to her room. After she unlocked her door, she walked in and Jackson started to leave, but she grabbed his arm.

"Jackson, wait. I… I want to thank you for stepping in last

night with Kevin. I wasn't thinking clearly, and didn't realize what he was up to at first. He was going to… I mean, if you hadn't been there, he would have…" She broke off with a sob, unable to complete the thought.

Jackson entered the room and drew her into a tight hug. "But I *was* there," he whispered. Her tears fell then, and once she started, it seemed she couldn't stop. Jackson held her close and let her cry.

"What if he comes back?" she asked fearfully. "I mean, now he's mad. Or what if he comes after *you*?"

"Don't worry about me," Jackson assured her. He could easily handle that scrawny punk. "Just be careful yourself. If you're going out, be sure you're around other people—people you trust. Give me a call if you ever need a lift or someone to walk with so you aren't alone, especially at parties. Have, like, a partner there so you can keep an eye on each other. And don't drink anything at a party. You never know what kind of stuff they put in the drinks." His own conscience was pricked as he said this. *He'd* been more than willing to sample the alcoholic beverages.

"Yeah," she said flatly.

A chilling thought occurred to Jackson. "You didn't give him your number or anything, did you? Or tell him where you live?"

"No. We talked about classes, and he asked which sorority I wanted to join, but nothing else really personal."

"You just met him last night? At the party?"

"Mm-hmm. He isn't even a student here. He goes to a community college."

That relieved Jackson somewhat, knowing Kevin wouldn't bump into Miranda around the campus, but still he was uneasy. "Did you take any pictures with him? Did he take any of you?

Did he ever have your phone?"

"*No*, Jackson," she said, sounding exasperated.

"I'm just asking. I want to be sure you're safe." With time stamps and digital fingerprints and such, hackers could find a great deal of information from something as innocuous as a photo. Jackson didn't trust this Kevin guy one bit. Coming to a party from off campus with one goal in mind seemed downright criminal. He wondered if there was anything legal that could be done if Miranda filed a police report against him. Unfortunately, probably not. He hadn't technically done anything, other than intentionally getting her drunk, and that would be next to impossible to prove.

As for his intentions, although Jackson had no doubt what Kevin would have done, again that couldn't be proven. It seemed horribly unjust. This guy was out there at large, probably waiting for the next party—maybe even at Miranda's sorority—and the next girl. And in the meantime, Miranda felt vulnerable and scared. What if this guy did show up on campus? And what if he *did* want a chance to finish what he'd started with Miranda?

Realizing his silence was making Miranda nervous, he spoke softly. "Hey, look at me. I need to tell you something important. You told me a while ago that there's more to you than your body. So take your own advice and start believing that about yourself. You're one of the prettiest girls I've ever met, and yeah, guys notice that right away. But you don't need to attract their attention by how you dress. I think you're prettier right now than I've ever seen you. Just be yourself and respect yourself, and guys will respect you too. If they can't see past your outward beauty, they aren't worth your time anyhow."

Her cheeks had turned bright pink at his candid words. "You're a good man, Jackson Williams," she said. "The world would be a better place if more people were like you." She kissed him on the cheek and patted his chest before turning to walk over to her bed. She still needed to sleep off the lingering effects of her hangover.

When she caught sight of her reflection in the mirror, she gasped. "Jackson! I look *dreadful*! And you think *this* is pretty?"

"Beautiful."

"Sheesh, if I knew it took so little to impress you, I wouldn't have spent all those hours in high school fixing my hair and putting on makeup."

He laughed amicably and asked, "So do you want to come to church with me tomorrow?"

"Still haven't improved that pick-up line, have you? You seriously need to think that one through. I'll pass, thanks."

"Okay. But consider it a standing offer. I'd have you anytime." Heat flooded his cheeks at the way his statement had come out, and he added hurriedly, "In church, I mean. I'd be happy to have you join me for church anytime."

She giggled at his discomfort and flopped down on her bed. He walked over to cover her with a blanket, then brushed her hair out of her face. "Sleep it off," he advised. "I'll come by later with some food for you. But don't hesitate to call if you need anything in the meantime. I'm here for you."

"I know," she affirmed, giving his hand a little squeeze. "You're the best. Everyone should have a friend like you."

She closed her eyes and started to drift off, and Jackson let himself out of her room, making sure to lock the door and shut it firmly behind him. He glanced up and down the hall, looking for any signs of Kevin lurking in the shadows. He kept his eyes peeled the entire way out of the dorm and back to his own room.

This was ridiculous. If *he* was this jumpy, he could only

imagine how Miranda must feel. Jackson clenched his jaw angrily. This situation had to be resolved. The problem was, there was nothing he could do about it.

CHAPTER

31

Faith sat with Spencer and Mrs. Young in the darkened living room, lit only by the white lights on the Christmas tree and the flickering glow of the fireplace. Outside, the snow fell gently. The scene was idyllic, almost picture-worthy. Hope and Griffin were asleep for the night, and the house was quiet.

Breaking the silence, Vivian sighed deeply. "I especially miss your father at times like this," she confessed. "When you boys were little, darling, he and I would come out here and do this very same thing—turn off all the lights and just look at the tree. I miss that."

Faith couldn't picture Mr. Young doing such a thing, but she remembered Vivian's story about how they'd met. The man had at one time been less intimidating and far more personable. She wondered when that had changed and why.

"It was a difficult Christmas this year," she went on. "I didn't have the heart to plan a family getaway. If not for the housekeeper, I wouldn't even have bothered with the tree."

Spencer put his arm around her. "We had a nice time with Faith's family instead. It was probably good for you to have so many other people around."

"Yes, dearest, I suppose it was." After a slight pause, she announced, "I'm going to move."

Faith and Spencer both gasped. "Where?" asked Spencer.

"Maybe Forest Springs. They have some nice townhouses there. I don't need this big house just for me. I feel so lonely rattling around in here all by myself. Darling, I don't even sleep in our room anymore. I usually sleep in your old bed. I can't bring myself to sleep in my own bed, because that's where I found him next to me that morning..." She trailed off and fidgeted with the rings on her fingers, fighting tears.

Faith exchanged a look with her husband and nodded at him. "Then come live with us," he invited.

Vivian's head shot up. "Oh, Spencer darling, that's completely absurd. I wouldn't do that to you. It would be dreadful for all of us and you know it."

"I didn't think we were *that* bad," teased Faith. "Spencer and I have already talked about this possibility, but we were afraid to bring it up to you. We've been looking for houses in Ann Arbor so we have more room than in our little apartment. There's one that won't go on the market until the New Year, but our realtor has an inside connection with the owner. If we make an offer, they'd likely accept it. The house has three bedrooms, and there's a separate apartment over the garage. Originally we thought we might turn it into guest housing, but we'd love for you to live there. That way you're not actually *with* us in the same house all the time. Everyone has their own space. It's perfect timing. We'd love to have you close by."

"Mom, there's nothing holding you to Mapleport," added Spencer before his mother could protest. "None of your kids are here anymore, Dad is gone, and your family isn't close by either. You just said you were lonely, so come live by us. You can see the kids every day."

Faith continued. "In fact, if you're willing, you could help us solve a problem. We need help with the kids. Spencer's classes are getting more demanding, and with his clinical hours, he'll be home less often. I'm still trying to get my degree too, and it's really hard to get my homework done with the kids around. Griffin will be in first grade next year, but I'd rather leave Hope with you than keep her in the school's daycare program."

"Well…" Vivian was clearly torn. She had a soft spot in her heart for her only granddaughter, and Faith knew it. She'd never had girls of her own, so Vivian could at last shower someone with frilly clothes and eventually jewelry.

"Besides," Spencer went on with a conspiratorial smile, "we don't want to put a toddler *and* an infant in daycare."

Vivian gasped as she realized the full import of his words. "You mean…?"

Faith beamed. "You're going to be a grandma again come July!"

"Oh, darling! That's wonderful! Oh, I'm so happy!" She leaned over to give Faith a hug first, then Spencer. "This is the best Christmas gift you could have given me. How marvelous to be celebrating life after losing your father earlier this year."

Spencer hugged her in return. "I know, Mom. It makes it all the more special."

"So does that sweeten the pot at all?" Faith cajoled. "We *need* you to live with us. You can be the stay-at-home grandma. Please?"

"How can I refuse now, darling? If you're both really okay with this plan, then count me in."

"We are," Faith promised, while Spencer nodded and squeezed his mother's hand.

"Who would have ever thought after all these years in small

town Americana that I'd be off to a place like Ann Arbor?"

"We'll make you a city girl yet," Spencer said with a grin. "Mapleport will always be home, but Ann Arbor has really grown on me. It has tons of options for restaurants, events, stores, and places to take the kids. It's a great town."

"You know, dearest, I'm actually excited about this!" exclaimed his mother. "This gives me something to look forward to and plan for. It makes me feel useful again. You're the best son and daughter-in-law anyone could ask for."

Spencer put his arm around her and reached over to squeeze Faith's shoulder. She beamed back at him happily. She and her mother-in-law had come a long way. Not so long ago, Faith would never have considered inviting Vivian to live in their garage, but now she found she was as excited about the new plan as was Spencer's mother. The three fell into contented silence as they gazed once more at the brightly lit Christmas tree, falling snow still visible through the window.

In the span of ten minutes, seemingly nothing had changed. And yet, everything had.

CHAPTER

32

The knock at her door surprised Sam. She opened it to find Jackson, grinning as widely as she'd ever seen.

"I'm in."

"You made the team?!" She leaped at him and threw her arms around his neck. "I knew you would! That's awesome! I'm so happy for you!"

He laughed, clearly pleased by her response. "I'm pretty excited myself. I haven't stopped smiling since I got the email."

"I should think so! How did your parents react when you told them?"

"I haven't told them yet."

"Are you serious?" She raised her eyebrows in surprise.

"They didn't even know I was trying out."

"*What?*"

"I didn't want to get their hopes up. If I didn't make it, I didn't want them to be any the wiser for it. You're the only one who knew."

Sam felt warmth spread through her entire body at his admission. The fact that Jackson confided things to her he didn't even tell his own family made her inordinately happy.

"So are you going to drive back to Mapleport to tell them in person?" she teased, knowing Jackson would do no such thing.

"Nah. An hour drive to Lansing I can handle, but it's not worth two more hours back to Mapleport. I'll call them tomorrow."

"Why not tonight?"

"Because I'm going to take you out to celebrate, that's why!"

"No, you aren't," she said. "I'm taking *you* out, you big hotshot football star. Oh, Jackson, I can hardly believe this! This is incredible!" She gave him another tight hug and turned to grab her bag from her room before slipping her arm into his as they walked out to his car.

Soon they were seated in a casual restaurant that was popular among college students, munching on mozzarella sticks as they waited for their burgers.

"Tell me about the tryout," urged Sam. "What was it like?"

"I was terrified," Jackson admitted. "You know how much I've been training and how hard I worked with the high school coaches over Christmas break, but even though I shaved half a second off my timed drills, I still wasn't as fast as I was in high school. And my bench press is decent, but I know high schoolers who can bench more. I was afraid I was just too slow and too weak."

Glancing at his sizeable biceps, Sam scoffed. "'Weak' is not a word I'd use to describe you. Ever."

He smiled. "It's all relative."

She popped the last bite of a mozzarella stick into her mouth. "How many guys were there?"

"I'd say about fifty."

"Did any of them make it too?"

"I don't think so. I could tell I was better and stronger than most of the guys trying out, but this isn't high school tryouts anymore. Walk-ons are the exception rather than the norm. If one or two guys make it out of fifty, that's pretty remarkable. I knew it was still a long shot, even if I was the best one out there. College scouts get the best guys out of high school. They don't rely on open tryouts."

"But the scouts had their eye on you in high school," she reminded him.

"That's probably why I got in," he said with a small smile. "At the very least, it helped my cause."

"You don't give yourself enough credit. You've worked really hard this past year to keep in shape and get better. That hard work paid off." She reached over and gave his hand an excited squeeze. "Jackson, holy cow, you're going to play for a Big Ten football team, do you realize that? You'll be on TV! The commentators will talk about you. Hey, maybe they'll do a vignette about Mapleport! Put that little town on the map!"

Jackson leaned back in his chair and chuckled. "Don't get ahead of yourself, Sam. I'm on the team, sure, but I'll be a benchwarmer. I'll probably be third-string."

She waved away the comment. "So you might not be a starter right away, but you'll get there. By senior year, you'll be a household name across the country."

By the smile on his face, Sam could tell that her response meant a lot to him. "You've always been my biggest fan," he said with a look in his eye that made Sam's stomach flip-flop. "Other than my mom, who doesn't count." He leaned forward as if to say more, but their burgers arrived just then, cutting him off.

Sam busied herself squirting ketchup on her fries and taking the onions off her burger, avoiding further eye contact with Jackson at all costs. She didn't want to deal with the jumbled emotions that had welled up when he'd looked at her like that. The easy camaraderie they'd shared just moments ago had suddenly vanished. Instead of friendly banter between good friends, it was like they were awkward high schoolers on a first date, both trying to do everything right under the scrutiny of the other. Did Jackson feel the shift too?

Daring a glance in his direction, Sam saw Jackson hold out his hand, and she laughed, the tension of the last minute melting away. She handed him the onions she'd just removed from her burger, and he popped them into his mouth all at once.

"You'd better not have plans to kiss anyone tonight," she teased with a giggle, then felt the blood rush to her face as she realized what she'd just said. Instantly, the tension was back.

"Not unless you're volunteering for the position," he replied. His voice was light, but that look in his eyes was back.

"Jackson…" Her face was still flaming. How on earth had she gotten herself into this conversation?

"Sam, let's try it," he said softly, leaning toward her.

"What, kissing?" She tried unsuccessfully to pull off a flippant comment.

"Dating."

She dragged a fry slowly through her ketchup, trying to think up an appropriate response.

Jackson lowered his voice even more. "What are you afraid of, Sam?"

I've already lost a brother and my mom, and my dad's not the man I grew up with. I can't bear to lose anyone else, Jackson. Especially you.

Struggling to keep her voice even, she lied, "Nothing at all!" She laughed nervously and went on. "I just don't like the idea of long-distance relationships. They tend not to work out so well."

"*We've* been friends long distance since September," he pointed out. "It's working for us."

She lifted one shoulder. "I don't know, Jackson. It's just that… if we try dating and it doesn't work out, we will have ruined a great friendship. I don't want to take that risk. Your friendship means too much to me."

He opened his mouth to respond, but she didn't give him the chance. Desperately trying to recapture the light-heartedness from before, she said, "Besides, you're a football star now, remember? You'll be surrounded by cheerleaders and college fan girls vying for your attention just like in high school. You should be able to enjoy that without being tied down to one person, especially someone from MSU. Try explaining *that* one to your teammates."

Her voice was teasing, but it was all she could do not to cry right there. She was fiercely proud of Jackson for making the team, but that did change things considerably. He'd go from an anonymous—albeit handsome—face in a sea of students to an elite group of players almost instantly. People would know who he was. *Girls* would know who he was. And while she'd like to think Jackson wasn't the kind of guy whose head could be turned by a pretty face, neither could he be immune to girls fawning over him. Visions of pretty cheerleaders wearing halter tops that revealed their midriffs and short skirts that showcased their long tanned legs flashed through Sam's head. She could never compete with that.

Jackson frowned slightly. "So… you *want* me to date other girls?"

Her heart shattered a little at the question. No, of course she didn't want him to date anyone else. "Absolutely," she fibbed. "Enjoy your college experience. We don't need to rush

RUTH E. MEYER

into anything."

"*Rush?*" He snorted an ungraceful laugh. "I'm pretty sure no one would ever think we were rushing into anything, Sam. You've been putting me off for over a year now."

Her stomach knotted. This was not how she wanted their evening to go. "Jackson—"

"No, it's fine," he interrupted in a tight voice. "If you aren't ready, I'm not going to force the issue." Breathing out a mirthless laugh, he shook his head. "I don't think I'll ever understand you," he mumbled. He took a bite of his burger, but Sam noted that the excited light in his eyes had dulled considerably, and he looked very disappointed in her answer.

The rest of the meal was quieter than was comfortable for the two of them, and Sam found herself wishing to be back at her dorm. It was the first time she hadn't enjoyed her time with Jackson, and she scolded herself for ruining what should have been a celebratory evening for him.

Later, when he dropped her off at her dorm, she gave him a hug and said, "Hey, let's not be mad at each other, okay? I'm sorry I made things awkward at dinner. I'm really proud of you for making the team, and I'm just not ready to venture into dating."

"I know, Sam. I get it. I'm not mad, I promise." His voice wasn't completely convincing, but he gave her his usual bear hug before turning to go.

"Text me when you get back," she called after him.

He wheeled around and grinned at her while walking backward. "Spoken like a true girlfriend," he yelled back in a jaunty voice.

His voice was loud enough she was certain other people on the floor heard him, and her face flamed.

"Shut up!" she hissed, but Jackson only laughed as he gave a little farewell wave and turned around, heading out the door.

Sam closed the door behind her and tossed her bag next to her desk. They'd parted on good terms, back to their usual friendly banter, but she had an uneasy feeling about the exchange at dinner. Walking to her bed, she threw herself face-down and tried to muffle her sobs with her pillow.

Despite her desire to keep things as they were, she had a feeling she'd just ruined things with Jackson after all.

CHAPTER

33

"Jackson! *Jackson*! Open up!"

The pounding on his door and shrieking on the other side woke Jackson from a deep sleep. At the sound of panic in Miranda's voice, he shot out of bed, his legs getting tangled in the sheets and causing him to fall on the floor, landing painfully on his knees.

Groaning as he hobbled to the door, he flung it open, and Miranda darted inside and slammed the door shut behind them.

"What's wrong?" he demanded. "Are you okay?"

"He's here," she whispered.

"Kevin?" he asked, a knot forming in his stomach.

"Yes. I saw him—" Miranda cut herself off. "Did I wake you up?"

"Yeah. It's fine. Don't worry about it." He was pulling on a T-shirt to cover his bare chest.

"It's ten thirty," she pointed out.

"I always sleep in on Saturdays."

She shook her head. "You might want to comb your hair

too."

Jackson flushed as he ran a hand through the hair he knew was sticking straight up. "You know, two minutes ago I was sound asleep. Most people don't have picture-worthy hair when they wake up. Including you, for the record. Now, did you just come here to insult me, or do you have something more important to say?"

It was Miranda's turn to blush, and she hastened on apologetically. "Sorry. Yes, Kevin is here. I've seen him three times this past week."

"Three times? And you're just now telling me?"

"What could you do? The first time I saw him in the courtyard when I was walking to class. It's a public enough place. I don't know if he even saw me, and I thought maybe it was a fluke. Then on Thursday I saw him in the hall after class. He had on sunglasses and his face was turned the other way, so I couldn't tell if he saw me then either. But today he was at the cafeteria, and that's just too many coincidences too soon. Especially for someone who doesn't attend school here."

"Agreed." Jackson tried not to show how alarmed he was at this news. Either Kevin was playing games with Miranda or actually stalking her. And those were only the times she'd spotted him. Who knows if he'd been able to avoid detection other times?

"So what now? What should I do? Jackson, I am *freaking out.*"

"Okay, okay. Hold on. Let me think." Problem-solving was not his strong suit, especially so soon after waking up. "Did he follow you when you left the cafeteria?"

"I don't think so, but I went a circuitous way anyhow, just in case. And I came here instead of going back to my room. I don't want him following me there."

"That was good thinking."

"And I got a picture of him today."

"On your phone?"

She scoffed at the question. "What else?"

"Did he see you do it?"

"No. I pretended I was texting for awhile first, like giggling and smiling and stuff. Then I zoomed in on the camera and got a few pretty decent pictures of his face."

"That was really, really smart, Miranda. That could be very useful. I'm impressed you were level-headed enough to do that instead of just panicking and running off."

"After I got the picture I panicked and ran off."

Jackson smiled faintly at her admission. "How did he find you, I wonder? You're sure you didn't tell him any details about your schedule or anything?"

"Nothing." She shook her head, making her blond curls bounce. Her eyes were wide with innocence.

"Ohh. Maybe you didn't have to." A sudden insight dawned on Jackson. "Pull up Instagram."

"*Instagram?*" she asked incredulously. "You want me to check Instagram right now?"

"Just do it."

Shrugging, she pulled it up on her phone before handing it over to him. He scanned it quickly, becoming more and more concerned. "Miranda, this is an open book of your life! Don't you get it? You're practically inviting him to come find you! You by your dorm, selfies in classes, shots in the cafeteria, parties—and all with captions telling exactly where you are! You're advertising your schedule!"

She frowned and bit her lower lip. "Okay, but only my followers can see my stuff."

"Yeah, all seven hundred forty-eight of them! Are you

kidding me? You really know every one of those people personally?" He stared at her in disbelief.

Miranda absently twirled a lock of hair around her finger, avoiding his gaze. "Some of them I accepted because they were in class with me or whatever. There were a few requests from some really cute guys who go here that I couldn't resist. So maybe there's a few people I haven't actually met…"

"Miranda! Any one of those 'cute guys' could well be Kevin! Or worse! They don't have to use their real pictures. You have no idea who you're giving this information to!"

"Is all *your* social media safe?" she threw back, jutting out her chin. "Let's check yours next, shall we?"

"No, you're right," he admitted. "But right now we need to focus on *your* profile. First of all, I need you to weed through this massive list of followers and take off anyone you don't know personally. Then we'll work on the stuff that's visible to anyone. In theory, prospective followers should only be able to see your name and pic. That's it. No recent photos or videos or anything."

"Jackson, this is ridiculous. I'll try to be more careful about what I post, okay? But I don't think any of this is necessary."

"Why do you think we're having this discussion in the first place?"

"This is all pure speculation! We don't know for sure why Kevin's been on campus. For all I know, maybe he does take a class here, and that would explain it. And you have no proof that he's been getting my info off Instagram. We don't even know if he's one of my followers! Besides, plenty of people advertise their lives on social media with no drastic side effects. Your theory is a worst-case scenario." She flipped her hair over her shoulder and crossed her arms.

Jackson rubbed a hand across his forehead. Miranda was

impossible sometimes, but she was partly right. It *was* pure speculation that Kevin was following her based upon her posts. Sighing deeply, he said, "Fine, Miranda. Have it your way. Keep all your followers and tell them exactly where you are every minute of the day." His voice became even more sarcastic as he added, "Maybe we can set a trap for Kevin and catch him that way."

"Nice, Jackson." Miranda's eyes narrowed. "I came here so you could help me figure out what to do, not so you could insult me."

"What do you think I'm trying to do?" he exploded, flinging his arms wide. "I'm trying to help you, but you don't want to take my suggestions!"

She opened her mouth but snapped it shut again and clenched her jaw, still glaring at him. Finally, she responded, "Okay, fine. Let's do this. Show me how to keep my social media safe." Her voice dripped with sarcasm.

Jackson was more tempted to throw her out of his room and go back to sleep, but he knew he'd regret it later when he was more level-headed. Drawing a deep breath, he handed her phone back to her. "Let's start with your followers," he said in a tight voice as she snatched it away from him with an indignant sniff.

The two spent the next twenty minutes combing through her social media accounts to make her less accessible to the general public. Miranda gradually resigned herself to the task and stopped giving him the cold shoulder as they worked, and by the time they were done, Jackson wasn't upset with her anymore either. Arching his back in a stretch, he said, "That's a great start. But we need to do more. Let's go file a police report."

"Jackson!" she scoffed. "There's nothing to go on! What are

we going to say? That there's a guy I've seen on campus a few times? It's a free country. There's no crime in that."

"No, we'll tell them *why* he's on campus. Tell them that he got you drunk at that party with the intention of taking advantage of you. And now he's stalking you."

"Stalking is a pretty big word," she said, shifting uncomfortably.

"I know. And maybe he's not a stalker and it really is a big coincidence, but I'd rather be safe than sorry. I mean, maybe we get to the police station and they send us away and tell us there's nothing there. But we have to at least try, for your sake and for the sake of any future victims. Silence only guarantees he won't get caught."

Miranda nodded slowly. "You'll come in with me?"

"Of course. If they'll let me, that is. They may want to take our statements separately. I have no clue how they do it in real life. I'm only going by what I see on *CSI*."

She giggled. "That's about the extent of my knowledge too. Okay. Let's do this before I chicken out."

"Thatta girl! Just give me one minute. I have to comb my hair."

A few hours later, an inwardly reluctant Faith ushered Miranda and Jackson into the Youngs' apartment. Griffin was practically jumping up and down for joy, and Hope was toddling right next to her brother, mimicking his excitement, although she had no idea what was going on.

When Jackson had called earlier, he'd asked if Miranda could stay with them for a while in case Kevin really was stalking her and knew where she lived. Faith knew she couldn't refuse her brother's request, but she was less than thrilled about having another woman stay there for an undetermined length of time. Not only was their two-bedroom apartment far too small for an extra adult, she didn't want the hassle of dealing with a houseguest she barely knew.

"Mommy said you get to stay with us for a few days!" Griffin's enthusiasm made up for Faith's lack thereof. "You can sleep in their room and they'll pull out the couch! Daddy said maybe you can read me stories or play Candyland with me. And I'm in kindergarten, you know. I can show you how I write my letters!"

"You certainly have everything planned out, don't you?" Miranda laughed, then turned to Faith. "I don't want to take your room. The couch will do for me."

"No, it's fine," insisted Faith. "You need a door to close and lock or else Griffin and Hope will be all over you as soon as they wake up. At least Spencer and I are used to their early morning tackles, right, hon?" She elbowed her husband, not voicing the real reason she wanted Miranda in her own room. The last thing she needed was for Griffin to walk out in the morning and find Miranda wearing a skimpy tank top and boy shorts for pajamas. Nor did she want Spencer to see that. Not that she didn't trust her husband, but it never hurt to steer clear of temptation.

"Griffin, sweetie, why don't you take Miranda's bag back to her room? You can put in on the bed, okay?" she suggested. The bag was practically big enough to pack half of Faith's clothes in it. Good grief, had she brought her entire dorm room with her? And Faith sincerely hoped that Miranda wasn't going to hog the bathroom mirror every morning to get ready. It was bad enough to share one bathroom with four people. Five was getting ridiculous.

Griffin lugged the cumbersome bag to the room, his little sister following, and Faith turned to Jackson and Miranda to ask quietly, "So you filed a police report, huh? How'd it go?"

"Okay, I guess," Miranda answered. "I've never done one before, so I have nothing to compare it to. But Officer Washington was really nice. I showed him the pictures and told him what happened, and he said my story sounds a lot like one from another female who came in to report a date rape a few months ago. She gave a description of him to the sketch artist, and he does look sort of like Kevin."

"That's good news, right?" Faith asked hopefully. Maybe they'd catch this creep and Miranda would be back to her dorm in a jiffy.

"Kind of," Jackson said. "He'll contact the other victim and do some kind of line-up thing to see if she recognizes Kevin from Miranda's picture. But he also said they've had numerous complaints of attempted date rape over the last six months, all of them following the same pattern. What did he call it, Miranda? MO?"

"Yeah, 'method of operation,'" she answered with a giggle. "I feel so official using a technical term like that."

Faith resisted rolling her eyes as Jackson continued. "Basically, guy meets girl at party, maybe slips something into her drink, gets her drunk, and you know what happens next. The police department has had a number of complaints filed along those lines, but Officer Washington said that doesn't necessarily mean it's the same guy. It's a fairly common pattern."

"He also said each girl gives a different first name for the guy, and never a last name," Miranda added.

"That's true," said Jackson. "So if it *is* the guy we know as Kevin, he's trying not to get caught."

"What a scumbag," Spencer said. "Hopefully they catch him sooner than later. But in the meantime, you're safe here," he told Miranda. Faith did not miss the admiring look Miranda bestowed upon Spencer, and she wondered if it was too late to offer to pay for a hotel room for Miranda instead. Goodness, why hadn't she thought of that before? It would be so much better for everyone involved.

Griffin came back into the room then, heaving a dramatic sigh. "That bag is heavy, Miranda," he said reproachfully. "It took me four tries to get it onto the bed."

Spencer tried unsuccessfully to cover a snort with a cough, and Faith hid a smile.

"But I got it," Griffin assured the assembly at large. "I'm strong like Uncle Jackson." He smiled proudly, then switched gears. "Tomorrow is church! Are you gonna come with me?" he asked Miranda.

"Now how can I refuse such an offer from such a handsome little man?" she said sweetly, bending over to tweak Griffin's nose. "Sure, I'll go."

Jackson looked at her in astonishment.

"What?" she asked innocently.

"Nothing," he grumbled.

"What?" she cajoled.

"He stole my pick-up line," he pouted.

"And?"

"It worked for him."

CHAPTER

34

"So how's college life treating you?"

Grace chuckled at her sister's question. Her version of "college life" was drastically different from Jackson's. She considered herself a wannabe college student. Not many women her age were pursuing degrees, unless it was a graduate degree. Her AA was nothing impressive.

"I'm attempting three classes this semester," she answered as she nibbled the banana bread Olivia had set out. It was good to spend one-on-one time with her sister again. It had been far too long.

"And?" Olivia prompted.

"I'll probably fail at least two of them."

"That's the spirit!"

"You should see the syllabus for psych. If I would have known it would be this tough I only would have taken one other class."

"You did pretty well in both of your classes last semester, right?" Olivia peered at her over the top of her mug as she took a sip of tea.

"I got a B in each, thanks to David. Otherwise my papers would have pulled my grade down a lot."

"Don't be too hard on yourself. I give you credit for doing this at all. The last thing I'd want to do at this stage of my life is write papers or go back to school."

"Well, you *are* eight years older," teased Grace. "I'm still in my forties. I don't think I'd do this in my fifties."

"Careful," warned Olivia, wagging her finger playfully at Grace. "Your husband is in his fifties too."

"This is true. But getting back to your question, I'm overwhelmed by all the work this semester. I thought psychology would be easy, but it's the hardest class I'm taking. The workload is pretty daunting. And we also have to do this huge project that counts for a lot of our grade. The instructions are kind of vague too. I don't do vague. Give me a topic to write about and I'll do it. Well, with David's help, I'll do it," she amended with a laugh. "But this is a 'make-your-own-project' sort of thing, and I don't know what to do."

"Did the prof at least give you some guidelines?" Olivia snagged another piece of banana bread as she asked the question.

"We're supposed to observe and/or interview people in a setting of our choosing to do a case study on their behavior."

Olivia's eyebrows raised. "What does that mean?"

"I haven't the faintest!"

Both women laughed, and Grace continued. "She gave us a few examples. One student a few years ago observed groups of people at a restaurant and wrote about how their orders were influenced by the people they were with. Like, if one woman in the group said she didn't want dessert, the other women would follow suit. Another student watched teenagers in a high school cafeteria to see how often they used their phones and how that affected the way they interacted with friends, which groups of kids seemed to have the best friendships, stuff like that."

"So what are you thinking?"

"At first I was considering doing something at a hospital. When Jackson broke his leg, it really hit me that some of those kids would never go home." Her voice faltered as she thought of the man on the elevator and wondered whether his daughter was still alive or not. She cleared her throat to continue. "I'm sure that reality affects the way families deal with one another, when they know they have limited time."

"True," murmured Olivia. "That's a good thought, Gracie."

"But I'm not really sure I want to do that. It's too depressing. I don't want to get that deep. Besides, with all the privacy laws, I doubt I could observe much anyhow, unless I do a stakeout at the cafeteria and interview people. That seems too invasive, to have a stranger swooping in to ask how they're dealing with their child's terminal illness. It's insensitive."

"You're probably right."

Grace took a swallow of coffee before she went on. "I was also thinking about volunteering somewhere to see how people respond to 'handouts.' Maybe that food pantry in Forest Springs. You know, see if the people are just there to take advantage of free food, or if they're embarrassed to go, or genuinely appreciative of the service provided."

"That's a good idea too! See, you're coming up with this stuff on your own!"

"But I still don't have a clear idea. I'm not sure I want to do a food pantry either." She wasn't about to admit that it hit too close to home. Years ago when Katie was a baby and she was struggling to put food on the table, she'd gone to the food pantry herself. She didn't want to take the chance that the volunteers would recognize her from so long ago, and she remembered how self-conscious she'd been, wondering if the volunteers were judging her or speculating about whether or not she really needed the help. She didn't want to put that kind of pressure on others who walked in the doors.

"How about the crisis pregnancy center?" Olivia's voice broke into her thoughts. "You've talked about volunteering there before. This might give you the opportunity to do so."

Grace cocked her head as she turned the idea over in her mind. "Hmm… I could maybe do that. I could interview the volunteers to see how their clients use or abuse the system. If a client gives her permission, maybe I could also interview a few women who come for help. That's a good idea. Thanks, Liv."

"Always glad to help," responded Olivia smartly. "That's why I'm older and wiser." She popped a bite of banana bread into her mouth with a smug smile.

The sisters sat in silence for a few moments until Olivia sighed. "I'm jealous of you, Gracie," she confessed, lowering her eyes to stare into her tea.

"Jealous of *me*?" she asked in astonishment. "What on earth for?"

"You have so much potential ahead of you. So many possibilities. You're going back to college and opening up a whole new set of opportunities."

"I don't even know what I want to do for a degree yet," she reminded her sister.

"But that's part of the fun!" Olivia insisted. "Who knows what you'll end up doing? The sky's the limit. It's exciting. Me, on the other hand?" She gave a despondent shrug. "I'm stuck in a rut. I'm bored. So is Andy. He's been the pharmacist of this little town for thirty years. And now with the kids out of the house… I don't know. We're ready for a change."

"What kind of change?" Grace asked with a fair bit of trepidation. She didn't like her sister's tone. "You guys aren't talking about divorce, are you?"

"Oh, goodness, no," dismissed Olivia with a wave of her hand. "Nothing like that."

"Then, *what*?" Grace pressed. "Liv, just tell me."

"We're talking about moving," Olivia confessed, looking at her sister with tears in her eyes.

Grace's hand flew to her mouth. "Moving?! Where? Liv, are you serious?"

Olivia nodded sadly. "Gracie, you know I love you to pieces. You're my best friend, and I'd miss you like crazy, but we both know *you* aren't guaranteed to stay here forever either. Gracious, you almost moved to St. Louis a few years ago!"

"But we didn't!" argued Grace. "We're still here now! Wait until we move, and then you can move with us!" She was starting to sound desperate.

"No, Gracie, it's time," said Olivia, breathing out a laugh. "We both feel the itch. We've talked about it, argued about it, and prayed about it, in no particular order, and we both think this is a good time to move on."

"Where would you go?" A heavy feeling settled in the pit of Grace's stomach.

"Andy has already sent some applications and his resumé to a few hospitals in Milwaukee."

"*What*? And you're just now telling me this? Liv!" Grace was simultaneously furious and broken-hearted.

"He just sent them out. He hasn't heard back yet. And I want to start doing something more meaningful than high school boosters. I don't want to go back to work, but I'd kind of like to volunteer at a hospital myself, or maybe a nursing home—something that gets me working with people who need some cheer. And Milwaukee has more options than Mapleport. Besides, Justin and Jason are both near there, and with Justin and Amber expecting their first baby… I don't want to be that far away from my granddaughter when she's born."

"Faith and Spencer are three hours away with *my* grandkids!" cried Grace. "And she's expecting too!"

"Yes, but it's a lot easier to make that trip than a six-hour trip through Chicago."

"But once Spencer graduates from medical school, they could move anywhere at all! Liv, there are plane tickets for a reason!"

Olivia shook her head. "I'd much rather be close by. Justin and Amber are pretty much set where they are, and Jason's happy with his job, so at least we'd be near two of our kids. Maybe in time Claire will be persuaded to find a job closer than Toledo."

"So you're pretty serious about this?" Grace asked, blinking back tears.

"Pretty serious, yes."

She looked away, biting her lip as she fought for control. Finally she whispered, "Oh, Liv, I don't want you to go. For as long as I can remember, you've been here for me. What will I do without you?"

Her sister leaned over to engulf her in a fierce hug. "I feel the same way, Gracie. You're the one I'll miss the most. Yes, we need a change, and there's a lot of good reasons to make this move, but leaving you will be one of the hardest things I've ever had to do. Sisters like you don't come along every day. Honestly, I'm scared to death at the thought of moving away."

"Moving is always hard," Grace said bravely, attempting to be strong for Olivia's sake. "It's daunting to start over. But you'll do just fine. You'll blossom in a vibrant city like

Milwaukee. Besides, this just gives us an excuse to come visit. Sally and Trevor are in Wisconsin too. I'm thinking David and I need to plan a road trip that way each summer. Maybe I'll even convince him to take the ferry across Lake Michigan sometime! You're giving us a great excuse to expand our travel repertoire!"

Olivia giggled. "Gracie, you're the best. Even if you are my younger sister, I've always looked up to you. I want to be just like you when I grow up."

Tears sprang to her eyes at her sister's words, and despite the fact that she was devastated by the news, Olivia's sincere compliment stayed with Grace the rest of the day.

CHAPTER

35

David met her at the door when she arrived home from her afternoon class at four fifteen.

"I have bad news for you," he began apologetically.

"I know," she wailed, bursting into tears. She'd tried to put Olivia's news out of her mind while she endured her class, but at David's sympathetic tone, her tears started anew. She threw herself into his arms and cried on his shoulder.

"It's not *that* bad," he said, frowning slightly.

"Yes, it is!" she sobbed. "Things will never be the same again!"

"And here I thought Katie was our drama queen," he teased gently. "In a few months you won't even remember this. It *will* grow back, you know."

She pulled out of the hug and looked at his face. "What are you talking about?"

"What are *you* talking about?"

Before either of them could answer, Charlotte and Evelyn ran into the kitchen.

"Look, Mommy!" Evelyn exclaimed. "We played beauty

shop today!"

Grace gasped as she looked at her daughters. Evelyn's beautiful dark hair was hacked off crudely, now resembling the rough equivalent of straw. Charlotte's curly locks, thankfully not as tightly wound as were Grace's, were chopped to various lengths, some clumps so short her scalp was visible underneath. Both of them looked dreadful.

"Girls! You are not supposed to use scissors without supervision!" Grace chastised, aghast.

"We needed haircuts," Evelyn said, scrunching her nose as she looked at her mother.

"And now you'll need another haircut to fix the first one," she shot back. "If it *can* be salvaged." She turned to her husband and threw her hands in the air. "David, they can't go to school like that tomorrow! But I can't fix their hair myself. We'll need to take them to the walk-in place at the mall. I think they're open until seven."

Before he could respond, Katie stormed into the room, her eyes flashing. "Dad took my phone!" she accused, looking to her mother for support. "And I need it to record my band assignment!"

Grace looked at David, trying to process the sudden change of subject. He sighed wearily. "I was dealing with that while the twins were upstairs cutting their hair," he confessed. "I had no idea they were doing it."

"So what's going on with the phone?" Grace asked, looking from David to Katie for an explanation.

"He's all uptight because of a picture I posted," said Katie defensively, one hand on her hip. "And it's not even a big deal!"

"Oh, it *is* a big deal, young lady," David contradicted. "Let's see what Mom thinks." He pulled up a picture on his own phone and handed it to Grace.

"Katie!" Grace sucked in a sharp breath when she saw the photo. Her daughter was wearing too much makeup and glancing over her shoulder with a deliberately flirtatious look on her face. The sleeve of her shirt was pulled down to expose her shoulder. She looked like a teenager posing for a dating website. "When did you take this? Did you actually *post* this thing? And why in the world are you wearing makeup? And your shirt…!"

"Mother! It's no big deal! At Alyssa's slumber party over the weekend, we used her older sister's makeup and took pictures of each other. We all posted our pictures on Snapchat for a short time. Who even notices a picture posted for a few minutes?"

"Obviously *someone* did, or we wouldn't be having this conversation!" exclaimed Grace, exasperated. She turned to David. "How did you find it?" She felt a twinge of guilt that she hadn't noticed it herself. Despite starting a Snapchat account to follow Katie, she wasn't nearly as vigilant about keeping up with her daughter's posts as she should be.

"A parent stopped by my office today," explained David. "Her son is in seventh grade and saw it when it was posted. She took a screenshot so she could bring it to my attention. She was embarrassed to show me, but I'm glad she did." He looked at Katie and continued sternly. "You can't be posting pictures like this, Katie. You look like you're four years older, and it gives the wrong impression of you to your friends and classmates. This kind of attention is inappropriate for a young Christian woman."

"Agreed," Grace seconded, unable to say more at the moment.

"Snapchat pictures are erased once the time limit is up," protested Katie. "So no one can find it anymore anyhow!"

"Nothing is ever truly gone once it's out there," David said. "Case in point—the screenshot right here. Say you posted something like this—or worse—in high school as a dare, and one of the boys saw it and took a screenshot. He'd have it on his phone as long as he wanted it. He could even send it around to all his friends. Future employers might come across it someday. People have been blackmailed because of indecent pictures, Katie. You have to be very careful of what you post, what you say, the comments you make online—everything."

"Jackson theorizes the guy who found Miranda used her social media accounts to track her schedule," Grace reminded her daughter. "You can't be too careful in this day and age. I'm even leery of posting pictures of you guys on my own Facebook account, and practically the only people who see my posts are family! There are all sorts of crazy people out there who can learn an awful lot about a person from the internet, and I don't want to mess with that."

"Yeah, yeah," Katie said, rolling her eyes. "I *know* all that. But my picture is nothing to freak out about! I don't have that many followers, and I'm not giving out personal information. We all did pictures like that. It was just a silly thing to do at the slumber party, more like a joke. And I'm not going to post anything inappropriate. You can trust me!"

David spoke next. "I admit, in the grand scheme of life, this one picture isn't a huge deal. It's fairly tame compared to what some people post. But it's the principle of the thing. What happens if you get into high school and go to a slumber party where they want to do the same thing, only wearing bikinis? Or going completely topless? It's certainly happened before. Don't compromise yourself just to fit in. You may have your phone back on Sunday. Tonight, you can record your band assignment on my phone. Go practice now while your mom and I figure out what to do about the girls' hair. And if you argue back, I'll take the phone away until Wednesday. Go!"

Katie glared at her father a moment, as if deciding whether or not to press the issue, but all the kids knew from experience that he meant what he said. David was not one to back down on his word. While that came in useful for discipline at school, none of the children found it to be a particularly endearing trait at home. Katie sighed melodramatically and flounced out of the room, muttering to herself under her breath as she went.

Just then the front door opened and Fred entered. Zep's mother often drove him home from jazz band practice after school, a fact for which Grace was extremely grateful. It was one less thing to coordinate.

"Hey, everyone, guess what?" Fred asked in excitement. "I got—*whoa*! What happened to you guys?" he interrupted himself as he caught sight of his sisters' hair. "You look terrible! Like something you'd see in a horror movie or something!"

"Fred!" admonished Grace.

"We did beauty shop!" Evelyn insisted, sticking out her lower lip.

"You didn't do a very good job. So much for 'beauty' shop. More like 'ugly' shop."

"Fred!" It was David this time, his voice carrying a strong note of warning.

"Okay, so who wants to take the girls to the mall and who wants to stay here and make dinner?" Grace asked brightly, trying to steer the conversation away from an all-out fight.

"You pick," said David, massaging his temples.

"I'll take them to get their haircut," Grace decided. "You can throw something together for dinner while I'm gone. Even pasta. At this point I just don't care."

"Fair enough," David agreed.

"Go get your shoes, girls," she instructed. "We'll go do beauty shop for real."

The girls cheered and ran to retrieve their shoes, and Grace turned to Fred. "What were you saying when you came in?"

"Oh! I got a solo for our jazz band concert! In the middle of one of our songs, there's a trumpet improv section, and Mr. Schultz picked me to do it, even over a junior!"

"Fred, that's wonderful!"

"Great job!" seconded David. "Can't wait to hear it!"

Fred grinned proudly and turned to go upstairs to his room as the girls came running back into the kitchen, ready for their mall adventure. Grace gave David a quick kiss and walked out to the car with the girls. She was awfully proud of Fred, and after everything else that had happened that day, she was grateful for at least *one* piece of good news. She'd had about all the bad news she could handle.

Later that evening when they were in bed, Grace finally got around to sharing Olivia's announcement with David. When she finished breaking the news, he remained silent so long she thought perhaps he'd fallen asleep.

"David?"

He sighed next to her in the darkness. "I don't know what to say."

"Neither do I."

"I guess I always assumed *we'd* be the ones to move first, if anyone did," he said. "Andy has a steady job here. So do I, but he doesn't get calls like I do. I figured one of these years maybe I'd get another call we'd decide to take. It never even crossed my mind that they'd be the ones to leave."

"Same here. He grew up in the area, even though the rest of his family has moved away by now. But *her* family is still here, and she's going to leave us all!"

"It's harder to be the one left," David said quietly. "My mom told me that when I went to college, but I didn't get it until I experienced it myself."

"What do you mean?"

"It's harder for the person left behind to deal with a major change like this," he replied. "When Faith got married and moved out, for example, it was more of an adjustment for us than for her. Well, a more difficult one, anyhow. She was a starry-eyed newlywed. I'm sure she didn't miss living in our basement. But for us, it was hard to see her officially gone."

"Hmm, that's true," Grace murmured. "I've never thought about it like that before."

"Same thing with Jackson," David continued. Grace felt a familiar lump in her throat, remembering how it had gotten to the point where she cried just *looking* at Jackson before he left. "It was harder for us to say goodbye to him than it was for him to leave. He was off to new and exciting things, but we're the ones to feel his absence here. His room is empty, his spot at the table is unoccupied… We're reminded of his absence even in little things. So it's harder to be the one left behind."

"You're right," said Grace. "And I don't want Olivia to leave me behind. Jackson's away at college, and now Olivia and Andy are off to Wisconsin. I can't handle all this!"

She burrowed her head into her pillow and let her tears fall again. David rubbed her back in an attempt to comfort her, and she appreciated the gesture, but at the same time, there was nothing he could do to ease the pain of loss.

CHAPTER

36

Faith struggled into the apartment with two bags of groceries on each arm. She hoped Spencer had started dinner but quickly realized that was not the case. Rather, she found Miranda sitting at the table with him, her chair scooted way too close to his as he helped her with biology. Her scoop neck top was dangerously low too, which further put Faith in a foul mood. Good grief, could that girl leave anything to the imagination?

It hadn't been a great day as it was. She'd gotten a lower grade than she'd hoped for on a test, and had more homework than usual tonight. Then she'd gotten stuck in traffic, and the grocery store was ridiculously busy. Faith had a headache, and the last thing she wanted to do upon coming home was figure out dinner. Or deal with Miranda.

Sure, Faith felt sorry for her, and she knew Miranda was terrified Kevin would track her down, but at the same time, it was really wearing on Faith to have a constant houseguest. Since Miranda didn't have her own car, that meant either Jackson had to pick her up or Faith or Spencer had to drop her off. Coordinating schedules each morning was a nightmare. It was difficult enough just between her and Spencer and the kids, and this was not helping the cause. Yes, Miranda was good with the children, and Griffin absolutely adored her, but having her around set Faith on edge.

The other day, Miranda had innocently asked if she could pick up skim milk for her at the store rather than the two percent the rest of the family used. Faith had no intention whatsoever of complying with such a silly request, but that evening, she opened the fridge to find a half gallon of skim milk inside. When she asked Spencer about it, he shrugged and said, "It's the least I could do."

Now here she was, this perky and pretty blond, sitting at *her* table and flirting with *her* husband. Faith slammed the cabinet doors shut as she put away the groceries and started a simple pot of pasta for dinner. She was well past the point of trying to impress Miranda with her cooking. Pasta and canned sauce was as much as she could handle tonight.

While she waited for the water to boil, Faith overheard Miranda sigh, "You're so smart, Spencer. I should hire you as my personal tutor." Faith rolled her eyes and gritted her teeth even as her husband chuckled in the other room. Clearly Miranda was overstaying her welcome.

"She has to go," Faith whispered fiercely to Spencer.

They were in bed, trying to get comfortable on the lumpy pull-out couch in the living room. The kids were sleeping, and Miranda had retired to their room that had now become hers.

"We can't very well kick her out," Spencer objected in a whisper of his own.

"Spencer Young, it has been *two weeks!*" she hissed back angrily. "I don't want another woman living in this apartment with us! We've been gracious enough, but I don't know how much longer I can handle this!"

"You know Jackson would never forgive us if we sent her back to live on campus and Kevin found her. We wouldn't forgive ourselves either."

"Then let her stay with Jackson! He'll protect her!"

"Try explaining *that* one to your mom," Spencer shot back sarcastically. "A pretty girl staying in his room with him 'just' for protection? And we're all supposed to assume nothing else would happen?"

"*We* slept in the same room for three months before we were married," she pointed out. "It was completely platonic."

"Yes, and it was a hospital room and you were on what very nearly became your death bed," he argued back. "Even if we'd wanted to do something, we couldn't have. Jackson and Miranda hardly have that limitation."

"They aren't even dating!" Her voice was louder than she'd intended. She needed to keep it down so Miranda wouldn't hear them.

"The temptation is there regardless. She's very attractive, and Jackson isn't blind. And truthfully, he's a good-looking guy himself."

"Thanks for reminding me," she groused.

"What? That your brother is handsome?"

"That Miranda is pretty! She flirts with you, you know."

"No, she doesn't. That's just how she is. She's like that with everyone."

"Oh, Spencer, you're sooo smart!" she mocked in an airy voice. "Can you help me with my homework all the time? I need a man with brains to make up for the fact that I don't have any."

"Come on, honey, it's not that bad," chuckled Spencer.

"And the clothes she wears! I've seen women more covered up at the pool! I'm seriously considering buying her a bunch of turtlenecks. Size extra large." Faith was unabashedly pouting now.

"Oh, sweetheart, come here," Spencer said, pulling her into a hug. "Honey, you know me. I only have eyes for you. You're the one I love. You're the one I sleep with every night."

"Sleep *next to*, not *with*," she said pointedly. Their intimacy had become non-existent given their current circumstances.

"Don't worry," he soothed. "She'll be gone soon enough, and everything will be back to normal. Faith, you know I'm madly in love with you. You are my wife, and you are the mother of my children, including this little blessing." He placed a hand gently on her rounded belly.

She didn't dare admit that was another sore subject. Miranda waltzed around with her tiny waist while Faith's own stomach grew bigger by the day. By her third pregnancy, her body assumed the position that much sooner. She felt old, fat, and undesirable next to Miranda.

"We should never have taken her in," Faith complained, irritated that Spencer was touching her swollen abdomen. She pushed his hand away and continued. "Why didn't we get her a hotel room instead? She could have her own space and we could have ours."

"It's a little late for that now, isn't it?" Spencer sounded irritated as well. He was probably annoyed she'd pushed him away. "The least you could do is *try* to be a gracious host. Do you think we couldn't hear you slamming doors in the kitchen when you got home today?"

"And do you think I'm blind?" she shot back. "You were sitting so close to Miranda at the table she may as well have been in your lap! I'm sure you snuck a few peeks down her blouse while you were at it. It was so low she was practically inviting you to look!"

"What do you take me for, Faith?" Spencer was mad now. "You think I'm the kind of guy to look down another woman's shirt? Come on! I hope you trust me more than that!" He turned away in a huff so he was facing away from her.

"I'm just saying it's almost impossible *not* to look," she argued. "Especially with how close she was sitting."

"You've already pointed that out," he said shortly. "I get it."

"Then why didn't you *do* something about it? Would it kill you to scoot your chair away a foot so you don't have such a great vantage point?" She breathed out a snort and mumbled, "Now I know what Rachel and Leah must have felt like vying for Jacob's attention."

She felt Spencer stiffen beside her, and he asked, "Exactly *what* are you accusing me of?" His voice was menacing, and she could tell he was speaking through clenched teeth.

"I don't know, Spencer! You tell me! I don't know what goes on between you two while I'm not here. All I know is that I don't like walking in to find my husband slobbering over another woman!"

She knew she'd gone too far with that one. Immediately she was remorseful. "I'm sorry," she hastened. "I didn't mean—"

"You know what? Forget it. I don't need this." Spencer sat up angrily and swung his legs off the pull-out couch, stuffing his feet into his shoes. "I can't have my insecure wife accusing me of cheating on her."

Faith sat up as well. "Spencer—"

"Everything's always been this huge drama with you," he interrupted. "I can't deal with such high maintenance. You're right. This apartment is too crowded for all of us. *I'll* go to a hotel."

He'd walked into the kitchen as he spoke and now grabbed

his wallet and keys off the counter. Before Faith had a chance to say anything, he stormed out the door and was gone. She stared after him in disbelief. He wasn't serious, was he? Surely he'd take a walk and blow off some steam, but he'd be back. Wouldn't he?

She sank back against the pillow, desperately blinking back tears. It wasn't the first time he'd accused her of making everything more dramatic than it needed to be. She remembered something he'd told her before they were married. *I love you, but I swear, sometimes you drive me crazy.*

The tears she'd been trying to hold back now slid down her cheeks. Spencer was right. She'd blown everything out of proportion, even accusing him of slobbering over Miranda. Heat flooded her cheeks. Had she actually *said* that to him? Shame coursed through her entire body.

Faith turned onto her side and tried to find a comfortable position with her growing belly, but there was no way she could relax. The doors in their apartment weren't soundproof by any means, and unless Miranda was in a deep sleep, there was a good chance she'd heard at least part of their fight. Although they'd started out in angry whispers, they'd both gotten louder as the argument progressed. The thought of Miranda hearing the accusations she'd made against Spencer made her cheeks burn even more.

Sighing, Faith rolled onto her other side. Spencer had about the highest moral standards of anyone she'd ever met. He was right—he only had eyes for *her*. Why hadn't she left it at that and snuggled closer to him to go to sleep? Why had she insisted on picking a fight?

Although she stayed awake well into the night, Spencer did not return.

CHAPTER

37

"Jackson Williams! You open this door *right now!*"

The pounding on his door and Miranda's angry voice on the other side woke him once again, and he groaned as he checked his phone. It was eight thirty. What was wrong this time? He hadn't realized how needy Miranda was. This was getting ridiculous.

"Jackson! Open up!" She was going to wake the entire floor at this rate.

"Coming! Chill out!" He pulled on a shirt and ran his fingers through his hair before opening the door. "What's—"

Miranda shoved him forcefully in the chest, and he stumbled backward, nearly falling down. "What the—? Miranda! What was that for?"

She shoved him again, forcing him to take yet another step backward. She entered his room and slammed the door, her eyes shooting daggers at him. "You *pig!*" she yelled. "You jerk! To think I ever trusted you!" She angrily swiped at her eyes, wiping away tears.

"What are you talking about?"

She thrust a plastic object into his face. "*This!*"

"What is that thing?" It looked like a thermometer to him.

Miranda yanked a folded-up box out of her back pocket and pushed it into his hand. He held it up to read the words on the label. "A pregnancy test?" he asked. "Ohh... You're pregnant?"

She only glared at him accusingly. "What, you—you think *I* did it?" Jackson's eyebrows shot up. What on earth would make her believe such a thing?

"Golden opportunity, wasn't it? Kevin did the dirty work for you. He got me drunk, and then your part was easy! You swoop in like a knight in shining armor to rescue me, only to have me to yourself!" Tears spilled freely down her cheeks.

"Miranda, I would *never* do that to you! You know that!"

"Everyone there saw you dragging me out to your car! And your whereabouts are unaccounted for until much later that night!"

"I took you to my *sister's* place!" he shouted. Now he was mad. How dare she come in and make such an outlandish accusation? "She and Spencer can both verify that! Come on, Miranda. This is nonsense."

"But you could have done *anything* in the time between leaving the party and getting to your sister's apartment! And apparently, you did! Men are such pigs. Every single one of you. You see a pretty girl and you can only think about one thing!" She turned away in disgust and crossed her arms over her chest, wiping her cheeks with the heel of her hand.

"Miranda, you *know* I wouldn't do anything to you. I've been trying to protect you all along."

"But can you protect me from yourself?" She turned and met his gaze, her chin wobbling. Then she whirled around and flounced out the door, leaving him speechless.

From the top bunk, his roommate chuckled. "Smooth,

Williams. I wouldn't think you'd do something like that, but she *is* pretty hot."

"I *didn't* do anything to her!"

Connor chuckled again, and Jackson heard the covers rustling as his roommate rolled over. Apparently he was going to catch some more shut eye. "Hey, it's none of my concern," he said with a lazy yawn. "That's between you and her."

Jackson clenched his jaw so hard it hurt. Was there no decency anymore? Would his roommate really be okay with him taking advantage of a woman? Would he dismiss it just like that, saying it was none of his business?

He grabbed a jacket and his shoes and stormed outside, mad at the world. He sure wasn't going back to sleep, so he might as well blow off some steam at the gym. The punching bag sounded like a fabulous idea.

Jackson didn't see Miranda the rest of the morning, despite the fact that he looked for her. He waited for her outside her morning classes, but she didn't show up. She wasn't answering his calls or texts either.

Since he couldn't concentrate on his own classes anyhow, he swung by Faith's apartment after lunch to see if Miranda was there. The place was empty, and he decided to wait it out. He figured Miranda would have to come get her stuff at some point, if she hadn't already. Jackson even went so far as to park his car on another street in case Miranda spotted it and decided not to go inside.

By three o'clock, Jackson was about to give up, knowing Faith would be home soon with Hope and Griffin. He'd just wasted an entire day for nothing, and now he'd have to catch up on homework too. But as he rose from the couch, a key scraped at the door and Miranda walked in, peeking around to make sure no one else was there. In a heartbeat, Jackson was off the couch and across the room, closing the door behind her so she couldn't escape. Miranda screamed and cowered away from him.

"Jackson, you scared me half to death! What are you doing here?"

"Waiting for you." Her eyes widened in fear, as if he would attack her then and there. "When did you find out you were pregnant?"

She dropped her gaze to the floor. "This morning. I suspected it before then, but I didn't take the test until today."

"And you honestly think it was me?"

Miranda's shoulders drooped, and she walked over to sink onto the couch. "Oh, probably not," she moaned. "I'm so mixed up right now."

"Miranda, I didn't do *anything* to you. I swear. I didn't even *touch* you beyond helping you to the car and into this apartment."

She leaned her head back and closed her eyes. "I know, Jackson. I realized that later. I knew deep down it wasn't you. It's just that the party was the perfect answer to how I got pregnant, and since everyone there witnessed you dragging me away drunk..." She raised one palm and let it fall again. "I guess it made sense when I first thought of it."

Jackson lowered himself into the chair facing the couch as she continued. "See, the thing is that I *know* how not to get pregnant. I've slept with so many guys I've lost count. In high school I slept with half the football team. My mom was totally cool with me having guys over to spend the night. She had a revolving door of guys herself. But I never got pregnant before. I know how to be careful, and if there's ever any doubt in my mind, I take the morning-after pill to cover my bases. So this..."

this isn't right."

He was astonished that she'd be so frank with him about
such personal matters. He didn't need to know any of what
she'd just shared. In fact, he wished he *didn't* know. While he
could have surmised as much, he didn't want her to confirm it
for him so blatantly.

Miranda opened one eye to look at him. "My life is such a
joke. You were right not to want to date me. I'm just a floozy.
You can do so much better than me. Jackson, I don't even
know who got me pregnant. How pathetic is that?" She
squeezed her eyes shut, and a lone tear traced a path down one
cheek.

He walked to sit next to her and pulled her into a hug from
the side. "Want me to come with you to the doctor?" he
offered. "Maybe they can give you a good estimate for when
the baby's due. Then you can figure out about when you... uh,
when... you know..."

"When I got pregnant?"

"Yeah."

"No, I don't want to do that." She pushed him away.
"Jackson, I don't want to have a baby! I am nineteen years old!"

"Faith was in high school when she had Griffin."

"And your family is completely different from mine. Your
parents actually helped her raise him. My mom would just tell
me to get an abortion. She's had a number of them herself.
She'd understand. It's not the right time in my life for me to
raise a child. I'd make a terrible mother anyway."

He had to admit he couldn't picture her as a mother. "Then
don't raise the baby. You can give it up for adoption."

She sneered. "Jackson, you're a complete idiot sometimes."

"Thanks."

"You want to help?" She looked at him, a challenge in her

eyes. "You can drive me to the abortion clinic."

"I won't do that. Miranda, don't get an abortion. Please. There are other options."

"Yes, there are! If *you* won't drive me to the clinic, I'll find someone else who will!"

"That's not what I mean, and you know it. There are pregnancy centers that can help you with medical care and expenses, and you can opt for adoption when the baby is born."

"You are *so* naïve." She did an exaggerated eye roll. "Maybe you don't get this, but I don't *want* to have this baby. I don't want to go through nine months of pregnancy. I don't want to give birth. It's a huge inconvenience."

"It's a *baby*, Miranda, not an inconvenience." Man, did that line sound cheesy coming from his mouth.

"That's easy for you to say, now isn't it?" she scoffed. "It's easy for you to tell me to keep it, because you aren't the one dealing with it!"

"But I'll help you through it. So will my sister. She's pregnant herself. She can help you in ways I can't. And if you're worried about cost, Spencer's family has plenty of money. They can help you financially." Given the circumstances, he didn't think either Faith or Spencer would mind him making the offer without consulting them first.

"You know, it's great that your family is so amazing, Jackson." Her voice dripped with sarcasm. "It's wonderful that you all support each other and pay for other people's medical expenses and host random friends off the street, but not every family is like that. Mine sure isn't. I never even knew my dad. I'm not sure my mom knows who my dad is." She laughed harshly. "Sound familiar?"

"And what if your mom had chosen to abort *you*?"

"Excuse me?"

"You just told me she doesn't know who your dad is and that she's had a number of abortions. So why didn't she abort you?"

"I... I don't know," she faltered. "I've never thought about it before."

"Think about it now. If she hadn't kept you, you wouldn't even be alive right now."

"No big loss." She carelessly waved her hand in his general direction.

"You don't mean that," he said softly. "Your life is a gift, Miranda. Not only to you, but to your family and friends. Every life is a gift, even if the circumstances are less than ideal."

Miranda whipped her head around to look at him, her eyes snapping. "I'm glad you have such lofty ideals, but you know next to nothing about me or my family. Not everyone has a perfect life or a perfect family like you."

"You think my life is perfect?" He was quickly tiring of her sarcastic barbs. "You think you're the only one who's ever experienced pain and hardship? My dad ran off with another woman while Mom was pregnant."

"But your mom got remarried and now everyone's happy. That will *never* be me, Jackson. The best I can hope for is to end up like my mom, just going from one guy to another, looking for Mr. Right but never finding him."

"That's not true, Miranda. You're worth so much more than that."

Her lip curled in another sneer. "Says who?"

"God."

She rolled her eyes. "Jackson, don't even *start* with religion. Going to church with Griffin has been enough exposure to know it's not for me."

"Jesus is for everyone." He stifled a grimace at how cliché

that sounded.

"Not for me," insisted Miranda.

"That's your fault, not His. If you're going to reject Him, that's on you."

"Do you seriously believe in God?"

"Yes."

"Then you really are naïve. Don't worry, it's endearing in you." She patted him on the knee. "But you're still naïve. Even if there is a God, He wouldn't want the likes of me."

"Why not?"

"Because I'm trash, that's why! I have nothing to offer God."

"No one does! We can't offer Him anything other than a dirty, sinful heart! He doesn't choose you because you're good. He *makes* you good by choosing you." He was parroting back exactly what he'd heard Pastor Lixon preach, hoping he remembered the words accurately.

"Sure. Nice thought. I've heard enough Bible stories to know that the people in the Bible are good people. Not like me."

"Jesus forgave a woman caught in the very act of adultery once. She was blatantly guilty, and they brought her to Jesus hoping He would condemn her to stoning, which was the penalty in their day. But instead, He forgave her." Despite Miranda's weary sigh, Jackson continued the story. "He told them that whoever was without sin could cast the first stone. Jesus was the only one there who could have thrown a stone, but He chose not to, and when they all left, He sent her away with forgiveness, telling her to leave her life of sin."

"That's great, Jackson. That's one woman in the entire Bible—"

"Rahab was a prostitute," he interrupted. "But she became a

believer and ended up as one of Jesus' ancestors. And Bathsheba committed adultery with King David, and she's listed in Jesus' genealogy too. Miranda, no one is beyond hope. No sin is too big for God to forgive."

She shook her head at him and stood up. "I don't have time for this. Ashley is waiting outside for me. I told her I'd only be five minutes. I've gotta go." She hurried to "her" room and grabbed a few things before heading back out the door.

Jackson watched her go, knowing full well the conversation hadn't accomplished anything at all. Why on earth had he brought up Rahab? Miranda might have loose morals when it came to guys, but she was no prostitute. Of all the biblical accounts, why had he singled out prostitutes and adulteresses? He punched the couch in frustration. Despite his best intentions, he felt like he'd completely failed in the way he'd handled that exchange.

CHAPTER

38

For the umpteenth time, Faith checked her phone. No new texts. Sighing deeply, she tossed the phone next to her on the couch. Well, she'd gotten her wish for space. In the span of twenty-four hours, both Spencer and Miranda had left to stay elsewhere.

When she'd arrived home from class that afternoon, she'd been surprised to find Jackson in the living room, but when he'd explained Miranda's situation, she'd felt an overwhelming sense of guilt about her resentment toward Miranda. Coupled with the still-unresolved fight with Spencer, Faith was an emotional mess.

She'd been wary of Miranda intruding on their personal space, not realizing God may have sent her there for a reason. She should have known better, especially after Spencer's dad had passed away. At the time, she'd been so enthusiastic to be a better witness, but in the entire time Miranda had been there, the only witnessing she'd done was taking Miranda to church with them and praying together before meals. From what Jackson had revealed about his conversation with Miranda, her younger brother had been a better witness in ten minutes than she had in two weeks.

Faith peeked at her phone again. Still nothing from Spencer. Her own unanswered texts to him seemed to mock her. One read simply, *I'm sorry.* Another requested, *Please call me.* A few hours later she'd sent, *Are you okay?* The most recent was two hours old and begged, *Please come home.*

Her emotions were all over the place. She cycled through guilt, anger, and anxiety. Where *was* he, anyhow? They'd had arguments before, but they'd never gone this long without at least trying to resolve things. She was upset that he hadn't responded to her calls or texts, but her anger was just as easily replaced with worry about his well-being. Was he okay? She'd feel terrible if he'd been in an accident. But then again, if he *was* okay, why wasn't he calling? Just like that, she was back to her anger.

"Ugh!" she grunted in frustration, flopping down on the couch. The kids were in bed. Should she try to get some sleep too? She'd had a headache all day and desperately needed sleep. But what about Spencer? Should she call the police? Local hospitals? Her stomach twisted. She hated not knowing what was going on or where he was, but the worst thing was how powerless she felt. There was nothing she could do to change the situation.

"God, please..." Faith trailed off. Please, *what*? She wasn't even sure what to pray for. Wasn't there a Bible verse to that effect? Something about the Holy Spirit interceding with groans words cannot express? Well, she could certainly use some interceding right about now. "Please do that for me, Lord," she whispered into the semi-darkness of the living room. "I don't even know where to begin."

She squeezed her eyes shut and allowed the tears to fall.

She'd kept them in while the kids were awake. They'd had enough questions about where Daddy was. She didn't want to cry in front of them and make things worse. But now, completely alone in the living room, she could cry.

Eventually, Faith felt herself drifting into a fitful sleep, but she didn't get the chance to sleep long. The front door opened, and she sat straight up, her heart pounding. As her foggy mind cleared, her eyes focused on the person standing there. Spencer.

Faith quickly stood and studied his face, trying to decide what sort of mood he was in. Was he still mad at her? Or was he ready to make up like she was? The two stared at one another a long moment, but when Spencer opened his arms, she flew into them.

For a minute, she was unable to speak, and simply wept into his chest, a wave of relief washing over her. He'd come back. Things were going to be okay. *Thank You, Lord,* she prayed.

"Spencer, I'm so sorry about the other night," she began, tipping her tear-stained face to look into his own. Her voice sounded squeaky in her own ears. "I totally overreacted, and I've been ashamed ever since. I made a big deal out of nothing and made inappropriate accusations against you. You're right that I make everything more dramatic than it needs to be. Forgive me?"

"Oh, sweetie, of course I forgive you," he said, tenderly wiping a tear from her cheek as he cradled her face in his palm. "I owe you an apology too. I overreacted as well. I had no right to storm out and stay elsewhere. I should have manned up and apologized first. I only made the situation worse. Will you forgive me?"

"I forgive you," she said, reaching up to hug him around the neck.

"And I swear, Faith, I wasn't looking down Miranda's shirt.

I'm sorry if I ever gave you the impression that I—"

She cut him off by giving him a long kiss. When she pulled back, she said, "I know, Spencer. I trust you completely. But you weren't wrong about me. I *am* insecure. And I am kind of high maintenance because of my limitations from my transplant. Sometimes I worry that it gets tiresome for you, that I always have to be so careful or that you're the one changing diapers most of the time." She swallowed hard and looked away, lowering her voice to a whisper. "I'm afraid sometimes you want someone normal."

"Oh, Faith..." Spencer gently pulled her face back toward him. "Don't ever think that. On bad days, sure, I might complain about having to change diapers, but every time I have to do something for you or wash my hands *again* so you won't get sick, I'm reminded of the incredible miracle that you're alive at all. Neither of us thought you'd make it. I thank God every day that you did."

He was giving her his *look*, and Faith felt a shiver go up her spine as he pulled her closer to kiss her. It was nice to know her husband still loved and desired her, growing abdomen and transplant limitations notwithstanding.

After the kiss, the two remained standing a long while, Spencer's arms around her as she rested her cheek on his chest. She was content, but there was one thing still nagging at her. While she didn't want to ruin the moment or get into another fight, she had to know. Working up her courage, she ventured, "Why didn't you answer my calls or texts today?"

Spencer breathed out a chuckle. "I left my phone here."

"You did?" She peeked into his face.

"Yeah. I took my wallet and keys, but left the phone charging in the wall socket by the couch there."

She looked in the direction he was pointing and groaned as

she saw the phone on the ground, plugged in. "So that whole time I was getting more and more upset with you for ignoring me, the stupid thing was right next to me?" She laughed as he nodded.

"I'd turned off the sound for the night, so you wouldn't have heard the ringtone or any notifications," he explained. "I thought about coming back for it, but decided I could live a day without it. It was kind of nice, actually. Like that day you were in the hospital and we both put our phones aside and turned off the TV and read the Bible. I went to church and spent a few hours praying in the sanctuary and searching the Scriptures. It was neat to be there alone and take in the stillness of it."

Faith was simultaneously impressed and ashamed. How vastly she had misjudged her husband. He had been doing what she should have been doing all along: praying. He'd prayed for a few hours, and all she could muster was asking the Holy Spirit to intercede for her? Gracious, she had a long way to go.

"So were you there this late?" she asked. It was nearly ten.

"No," he admitted sheepishly. "I, uh…" He cleared his throat. "I went out to eat and took my time. I was hoping to avoid the kids and Miranda so you and I could talk. I know that's a cowardly thing to do, but I wasn't up to facing any of them."

She laughed at the expression on his face. "It's okay. I'm not mad about it," she assured. At least, she wasn't mad *anymore*. "I was just getting worried. I thought maybe you'd been in an accident or had decided not to come back at all."

"I wouldn't do that," he assured her. "Remember, we're in this for life. I'm afraid you're stuck with me."

She giggled as he swept her into his arms as if he were

carrying her over a threshold. He gave her another kiss and walked over to the couch, depositing her on the cushions before sitting next to her. "So I knew the kids would be in bed already, but I wasn't sure about Miranda," he said. "I guess she already retired for the night, huh?"

A wave of sadness washed over her as she thought about Miranda. She'd nearly forgotten the new development. "Actually, she's not here," Faith answered.

Spencer glanced at her sharply. "Please tell me she didn't hear our fight and leave."

"Oh, I haven't the faintest idea if she heard our fight or not. I dropped her off at school early this morning and haven't seen her since. Jackson was the one who told me what's going on. She… She's pregnant."

"Seriously?" Spencer gaped at her, his mouth hanging open.

Faith could only nod. Now that she and Spencer had made their peace, she was able to more fully grasp the enormity of Miranda's situation. She bit her lip and looked at her hands, twisting her wedding ring around her finger.

"Oh, man," Spencer groaned, plopping his head back against the couch.

"I know."

Abruptly, Spencer sat upright and turned to her. "Please don't tell me you think I'm the one who—"

"Oh, goodness, no, Spencer! Just—no." She waved away the ridiculous thought. "According to Jackson, she doesn't even know who the father is. She's… um, she has a number of possibilities, I guess." Faith was trying her best to be charitable.

Spencer put his elbows on his knees and dropped his head into his hands, blowing out a long, slow breath. "And you haven't seen or talked to her since you found out?"

"No. At first she accused Jackson of taking advantage of her after he dragged her away from that party. That's how he found out in the first place."

"Jackson wouldn't do something like that," Spencer said through gritted teeth. "She should know better than that." His head shot up and he looked at Faith. "You—you don't think Kevin somehow…?"

"I wondered that too," she said. "Like, maybe he'd already gotten to her before Jackson pulled her away?"

"Or what if he *did* track her down later and… I don't know. That doesn't make sense either. She would have known it was him, unless he somehow drugged her." He shook his head in frustration and put his chin on his clasped hands.

"I think she just sleeps around enough that she isn't sure which guy is the father," Faith said. "She was pretty frank about her love life with Jackson. She's made the rounds." Okay, so maybe that wasn't entirely charitable.

Spencer shook his head sadly. "I don't even know what to say." There were a few moments of silence until Spencer asked, "Do you think she'll keep it?"

Tears pricked Faith's eyelids. "Jackson said she asked him to take her to an abortion clinic."

"We have to stop her from doing that."

"But how? She didn't answer my calls or texts today either." Faith winced slightly at the way she'd phrased that. She didn't mean to be accusatory or put Spencer on the defensive. Thankfully, her husband didn't seem to notice.

"Is her stuff still here?" he asked.

"Most of it," Faith said. She'd at least been nosy enough to snoop around and find out what Miranda had taken and what she'd left.

"Then that means she'll have to come back to get it at some point," Spencer mused. "So one of us should do a stakeout tomorrow and see if she returns. Eventually one of us will run into her. Right? I mean, if we can't get her on the phone, we'll have to get her in person."

"But what can we say to convince her not to get an abortion? Jackson tried talking to her about God and she completely tuned out."

Spencer remained silent for so long Faith thought he wasn't going to answer. She looked at him and discovered that his eyes were closed. Perhaps he was praying? She allowed him the time and space he needed. Eventually, he opened his eyes and straightened up to look at her fully.

"We could adopt her baby," he suggested quietly.

Faith's eyes widened. Was he joking? Miranda's baby would only be a few months younger than *their* baby. She wasn't at all sure she wanted the responsibility of two more babies at once. One more would be hard enough. Taking on two would double the number of their children. She began to perceive how her mother must have felt when Grace had realized she was pregnant with twins, on top of Faith's unexpected teenage pregnancy.

"Spencer, there's no way we can handle another baby!" she protested. Visions of both herself and Miranda strutting around the apartment with pregnant bellies made her close her eyes. They really *were* starting to look like Jacob, Rachel, and Leah. To outsiders, it certainly would appear they had that sort of arrangement going.

"We'll be moving into a house in another few months," he argued. "And my mom will be moving to Ann Arbor too. We'll have an extra adult to help with childcare. Maybe Mom would even be willing to have Miranda's baby live with her."

Faith rested her head against the couch, trying to process Spencer's sudden proposition. "Oh, I don't know, Spencer. It's going to be enough of a challenge with three kids with both of us still in school. Couldn't we just encourage her to give the baby up for adoption without making the offer ourselves?" She looked at him hopefully.

"We could," he conceded, "but I don't think that would be as effective an answer. It's too open-ended, and it still places the burden on her. *She* has to contact an adoption agency and be the one to make the arrangements. If we offer to take the baby, she already has a plan in place. Plus this way we know the baby will be raised in the faith. With adoption, that's never a guarantee."

It was Faith's turn to be silent for a long minute. He made a good point, but at the same time, it almost felt like he was guilting her into it with that logic. She closed her eyes and prayed. *Is that what you want us to do, God? Or is this just Spencer trying to solve things on his own? I'm already overwhelmed at the thought of three kids. Parenting requires so much effort, and I don't want to stretch myself so thin I'm not a good parent to any of the kids. I need Your wisdom, Lord.*

Although she remained silent, her eyes still shut, she didn't hear an answer or get a feeling one way or the other. Sighing, she opened her eyes and looked at Spencer. "Let's pray about it and sleep on it," she proposed. "That's a huge commitment, and not one I'm willing to agree to without serious consideration."

"That's fine. We should get to bed anyhow. Let's pray together and get some sleep and see what the morning brings."

It was a fabulous suggestion, and the two did exactly that. But for the second night in a row, sleep eluded Faith until the wee hours of the morning.

CHAPTER

39

The next morning didn't bring any sudden answers or new insights, but Faith still hoped to get the chance to talk to Miranda, so she offered to wait at the apartment that day. She wasn't thrilled about skipping her classes, but this was too important. A life was at stake. She spent the time alternately praying and napping. Her two previous nights of little sleep were taking a toll on her.

When Miranda walked in around lunchtime, Faith rose to greet her with a hug.

Miranda was clearly taken aback by the physical contact. She and Faith didn't have a close enough relationship to hug one another, but Faith didn't let go. Eventually, she felt Miranda relax and accept the embrace, sagging weakly against her as she started sniffling. Faith just hugged her and allowed her to cry.

When Miranda pulled away, she said in a dull voice, "Jackson told you."

"He did." Faith pulled her gently toward the couch and sat down next to her.

"Pretty pathetic, aren't I?"

"Not at all. Spencer and I had Griffin when we were in high school. It happens."

"But you knew the baby was Spencer's. I don't even know who got me pregnant."

"It's okay. Whoever it was, he probably wouldn't be very supportive anyhow. Spencer wasn't at first. He wanted me to get an abortion. But eventually he came around, and now we couldn't imagine life without Griffin. Even though he was an accident, we wouldn't have it any other way now. He's a huge blessing, even if it took us awhile to see that."

"Yeah." Her voice was still flat.

"Miranda, I know you don't want this baby. I don't blame you. But Spencer and I will adopt him or her." She still wasn't one hundred percent sure about it, but knew she had to make the offer. "We want—"

"I already got an abortion," interrupted Miranda.

"I... you... you did?"

"This morning."

Faith's heart shattered into a million pieces, and she felt a crushing sense of guilt. She was too late. "Did... are you okay?"

"I don't know. It hurt a lot more than I thought it would."

Faith shut her eyes tightly, trying desperately not to cry. Of course it had hurt. A life had been ripped from her womb. "Oh, Miranda, I'm so sorry." She leaned over to hug her again, her heart aching with loss. She was also filled with indignation at the injustice of the situation. Miranda had been able to get a same-day appointment for an abortion, probably even a walk-in, but to make a real appointment with an OB would have required a wait of at least a couple weeks. How was that fair?

"It'll pass. I'll get over it." Miranda pulled away from the hug.

Faith didn't voice her thoughts. She remembered a conversation she'd once had with her mother when *she'd* gotten pregnant in high school and Grace was afraid she'd run out and get an abortion. Grace confided that she'd had an abortion years ago, and that not a day went by without her thinking about it. She knew God had forgiven her, but she still struggled with guilt, even two decades later. Would the same hold true for Miranda?

"What can we do?" Faith asked. "What do you need from us?"

"Nothing. I'm fine. I've already been mooching off you guys too long anyhow. I'm gonna stay with a friend in her dorm room for awhile. I'll try to make it to the end of the semester. It was a mistake to come here anyway. I don't belong in college."

Deciding to ignore Miranda's comment about college, she addressed instead the more immediate issue of housing. "Don't leave, Miranda," she pleaded. She knew Miranda needed emotional support now more than ever. "Please stay with us, at least until you've healed."

"I've already been here too long, and we both know it."

Faith flushed. She wasn't wrong, but circumstances had changed drastically. "Give yourself through the weekend here at least," she suggested. "Take a few days off from classes. You can sleep and allow yourself time to heal. We'll take care of you."

Miranda wavered, and Faith seized upon her moment of weakness. "Come on back to your room now," she said, standing and offering Miranda her hand. "I've got a heating pad you can use on your abdomen. It'll help relax your sore muscles and ease the pain. I'll make you some soup for lunch and bring it back to you in a few minutes. I've got some sleeping pills around here too. You've got at least three hours of silence until Spencer gets home with the kids. Take a long nap and let your body recuperate."

Miranda allowed herself to be led to the bedroom without further protest, and gratefully curled up on the bed. Faith found the heating pad and a sleeping pill, covered Miranda with a blanket, and went out to start the soup. Her heart still ached, but not just for the lost baby. Abortion had two victims, and Miranda was the second one in this case.

When Spencer walked in the door with Griffin and Hope a few hours later, Faith swooped her children into a hug on the floor and started crying again. She'd called Spencer to tell him about Miranda, and she knew her husband was devastated about the situation as well. He knelt right down next to her and joined the family hug.

Griffin squirmed away. "Mom, you're squishing me!" he protested.

"Sorry, honey. I just want you to know how much I love you." She gave him a kiss before he scurried off to play. Hope toddled after him, always ready to copy anything her older brother did. Spencer scooted closer to Faith and wrapped his arms around her.

"Spencer, that could have been us," she whispered hoarsely. "That could have been Griffin!"

"I know." His own voice sounded strained. "If you'd have listened to me, it *would* have been us."

"If it hadn't been for my family, that's entirely possible. I don't think anyone realizes how close I was to going to Planned Parenthood. I was thinking so short-term that it was a really tempting option. But when David and my mom found out, I knew I couldn't go through with it. They would have been even more disappointed in me than they already were. It was a weird kind of peer pressure."

"Thank the Lord for that."

The floor wasn't a particularly comfortable place to be, but Faith welcomed her husband's strong arms around her and made no move to get up.

"I've been thinking about this all afternoon, Spencer. If my mom hadn't married David, and I'd gotten pregnant, I never would have been going to church, which means I wouldn't have had a reason to go practice music with Aaron, so I wouldn't have told him I was pregnant. Then he wouldn't have told David, and David wouldn't have confronted me, and I probably *would* have gotten an abortion."

She looked into his face to make sure he was following her train of thought. "You wouldn't have had any reason to come back to meet your baby, so we wouldn't have gotten back together. Griffin wouldn't be here, Hope wouldn't be here, this baby wouldn't be here"—she patted her stomach—"you and I wouldn't be together right now, and I wouldn't even know what I was missing! That's a scary thought."

Spencer cupped her face in his hands. "But that *didn't* happen, Faith. We *are* together, our kids are alive, and God has brought good out of what otherwise could have been a really bad situation."

"I just hope He'll do the same for Miranda." Her voice broke as she said it.

"Me too," he whispered, placing his arms around her once again. She simply buried her head in his chest and wept. There was nothing more to say.

Jackson stood at Faith's apartment door and took a deep breath. His sister had informed him about Miranda's abortion, and he felt the loss deeply. It was almost as if it *had* been his baby. He'd certainly cared more about the child than whoever the father was. And more about Miranda. She was worth so much more than a one-night stand, and it made him angry that so many guys apparently didn't believe that about her.

Although Jackson wanted to be a good friend for Miranda, the truth was, he was scared to death. Empathy did not come naturally to him, and he didn't know what to say to her. Other than Sam, he didn't have conversations with anyone about personal matters like feelings. It made him break out in a cold sweat just thinking about it, but he knew he had to be there for Miranda now when she needed support the most.

Shaking his head to clear his thoughts, he knocked softly on the door and peeked inside. "It's me," he said quietly. "Can I come in?"

Faith rose from her kneeling position on the floor and threw her arms around him, crying against his shoulder. "I'm so glad Mom met David," she said.

Jackson was taken aback. "Um… okay…?" he responded, not knowing what else to say. What did their stepfather have to do with any of the events of the last few days? Besides, he and his sister generally didn't show a lot of affection to each other. The last time they'd hugged was… Jackson didn't even know for sure. An obligatory hug at Faith and Spencer's wedding? Maybe?

Awkwardly, he patted her on the back and snuck a glance at his brother-in-law, who was still kneeling on the floor. What in the world was going on? They were seriously freaking him out. He hoped they weren't having a mental breakdown of some type.

"Miranda…?" he asked, and Faith motioned with her head toward the master bedroom.

"She's been sleeping for a few hours," his sister said. "She needs to heal."

"Should... Can I... Do you think she'd mind if I go check on her?" he stammered.

Spencer spoke up. "Go ahead. She probably needs a friend right now." He peeled himself off the floor and twisted from one side to the other in a stretch.

Jackson took the opportunity to slip back to the master bedroom. He knocked and waited for a response from Miranda. Hearing none, he opened the door a crack and saw her curled up on the bed. Compassion flooded his heart, and a fierce desire to protect her overwhelmed him. She looked so small and vulnerable. He'd do whatever he could to help her, even if that meant talking about feelings.

Pulling over the rocking chair from the corner, he settled himself next to the bed and placed a hand gently on her shoulder. "I'm here, Miranda," he whispered.

For a long moment, she didn't answer, and Jackson figured she was still asleep. But then she took his hand and gave it a little squeeze. His throat burned. She knew what he meant with those three simple words. He squeezed her hand in return and didn't let go.

CHAPTER

40

Dipping his roller brush in the paint, Jackson started spreading it on the wall, grateful he didn't need to concentrate too hard on the task at hand. He barely even paid attention to the conversations between his fellow pledges. All he could think about was Miranda, back at Spencer and Faith's apartment, where she'd been hiding out for the last few days, rarely venturing out of her room.

Jackson spent a fair amount of time at the apartment himself, usually with Miranda in the master bedroom. They didn't talk much, but he knew Miranda appreciated his presence. He'd bought flowers for her once, often took food back to her, and ran errands for her when she asked. He knew his sister was surprised to see this side of him, but he was determined to be Miranda's biggest supporter.

The few times Miranda did venture out of her room, she was much more subdued than she used to be. She wore sweatshirts instead of low-cut tops, she didn't bother with makeup, and she usually just pulled her hair into a ponytail. But the biggest change by far was her attitude. She no longer flirted with either Jackson or Spencer, and she seemed much less confident than she used to be.

Absent-mindedly, Jackson dipped his brush again and kept rolling, still pondering Miranda's new attitude. He didn't know if this was a temporary thing, like a short-term depression, or if she really was trying to change the way she'd been living. His heart ached for her, because her life seemed so empty. As far as he could tell, she didn't have any close relationships, not even with her family. Not that he wanted to be egotistical about it, but he might well be the best friend she had.

Faith and Spencer had stepped up and become a type of surrogate family in her own mother's absence, and Jackson was astonished to see how much Faith now cared for Miranda. He could read between the lines enough to know that Faith hadn't been thrilled to take her in, but something had changed. Jackson grinned, thinking that Faith seemed like a mother hen, hovering over Miranda to make sure she took care of herself.

"Williams!"

With a start, Jackson snapped out of his reverie to turn toward the voice. Alex, another pledge, was staring at him with a strange expression on his face. "What's going on with you today, man?" he asked. "Your head is in the clouds. You've barely said three words all morning. And you've been painting the same section of that wall for the past fifteen minutes. I think you got it."

"Oh, right," Jackson mumbled, embarrassed. He dropped the brush into the pan and stretched his arms over his head. Honestly, he could have done without this service event today. Normally he enjoyed the camaraderie and friendly banter, but today he had little to no patience for the lame jokes and superficial conversations floating around. He really just wanted to be with Miranda. She could have used his company more than these guys.

Alex was still looking at him suspiciously. "You okay, Williams?"

"Yeah, yeah, fine. Just tired, I guess. Late night." He tried to pull off a careless laugh, but it fell flat even to his own ears. Quickly, he said, "Hey, I think these fumes are getting to me. I'm gonna go get some air."

Without waiting for a response, he left the fraternity house. *What am I doing here today, anyhow?* he asked himself irritably. He took a few deep breaths and rolled his shoulders, trying to relieve some tension. It was true that he hadn't been sleeping well the last few nights. He could turn off the light, but he couldn't turn off his thoughts. Despite Faith's assurances that he had done all he could, Jackson still felt that he'd failed Miranda. His mind wouldn't let it rest, replaying the conversations he'd had with her before her abortion, thinking of things he could have—*should have*—said and done.

But it was too late.

Ultimately the choice had been Miranda's, but that knowledge didn't ease his conscience. And despite the fact that he couldn't picture Miranda as a mother, he was still crushed that she'd so quickly and effectively put an end to the possibility. Would her decision come back to haunt her later, or would she even care? He wasn't sure which would be worse.

Sighing deeply, Jackson turned to go back inside. As he re-entered the living room, he tried to be casual as he walked back to his wall and picked up the roller again. There was a conspicuous silence, and Jackson suspected his fellow pledges had been talking about him in his absence, speculating on his present state of mind.

The noise of footsteps on the stairs provided a welcome distraction, and people glanced over to see who was coming down. A sophomore fraternity member emerged with his girlfriend, and the guys in the living room exchanged knowing glances as the two kissed each other goodbye before she left.

"She spend the night again, Kastner?" Alex teased, wiggling his eyebrows.

The goofy grin on Eric Kastner's face confirmed the answer, and the guys hooted.

Alex let out a low whistle. "Dang, Kastner, you are one lucky guy. She's pretty hot."

"Oh, please," objected Bryce from across the room. "Like you have anything to complain about. Your girl spends the night with you all the time." He tossed a stained painting rag in Alex's general direction, which fell a good three feet short of Alex.

"Aw, you're just jealous, Bryce," Eric said, leaning against the unpainted door frame. "Ever since your girlfriend dumped you, you've been lonely."

"I'm not lonely. I just widened the playing field, that's all. I'm keeping my options open."

Jackson rolled his eyes as the inane conversation continued. This was no different than the stupid locker room talk in high school.

"C'mon, Williams, you're being awfully quiet over there," ribbed Alex. "Who are you thinking about?"

"Betcha he's thinking about Miranda," Pete Jennings offered from the lone couch left in the center of the room, covered with an old bedsheet. As a full-fledged brother and not a pledge, Pete was immune from the laborious task of repainting the house, but didn't mind lounging around telling the pledges how to do the job.

Jackson's face went hot at the comment, which the guys took as a sign of affirmation.

"No way! Miranda Russo?" Bryce asked, his jaw hanging open.

"Who else?" asked Alex. "They went to high school together."

"How did I not know this? You're sleeping with Miranda?" The expression on Bryce's face was one of awe.

"We aren't sleeping together," Jackson said shortly, barely concealing his disgust at the question.

"Oh, sure," smirked Alex. "I've seen her sneaking out of your room in the morning before."

Jackson glared at him. "We *aren't* sleeping together," he replied more forcefully.

Alex held up his hands in a surrender motion. "Okay, okay. Easy, man. Hey, it's no skin off my back if you are or aren't." He turned and dipped his roller into the paint bin before calling over his shoulder, "But if you aren't, that means she's fair game, right, fellas? I bet she's amazing."

A sudden rage filled Jackson with an intensity that frightened even him. He'd dealt with fits of anger all his life, but the fury he felt now was new. Miranda's sorority did a lot of joint events and parties with his fraternity. She was familiar with a lot of the guys in this room. It dawned on him that any one of his fellow pledges could have been the father of that baby, completely oblivious to the situation as they joked blithely about sleeping around.

Throwing his roller brush down so hard it splattered paint all over, Jackson crossed the room in three steps and grabbed Alex's shoulder roughly, spinning him around. Alex's eyes widened as Jackson leaned in close and growled in a menacing voice, "You leave Miranda out of this, understand?"

"Whoa, dude, chill." Alex shook Jackson's hand off his shoulder and stepped back, glaring at him. "Whatever's going on with you today you need to pull yourself together, Williams. We're just joking around."

"Yeah, man. Seriously, not cool." Pete had stood and was frowning across the room at him, his arms crossed.

"No, I'll tell you what's not cool," Jackson retorted. "Talking about girls like this. How would you like it if some guys were talking about your sister this way?" He wondered if the high school football team had ever discussed Faith so crudely, or if someday guys would do the same for Katie or the twins. The thought made his stomach turn.

"Or someday when you guys have families, how would you feel if you knew guys were talking about getting your daughter in bed? Have some respect, is all I'm saying."

"Oh, like you don't think girls talk about us like this?" Bryce scoffed.

"And that makes it okay for us to do the same?" asked Jackson. "When women accuse men of being pigs, *this* is what they're talking about." He never thought he'd be making the same accusation Miranda had made of him not so long ago. Turning to Eric, he asked, "What would your girlfriend think if she was listening to this conversation on the doorstep, Kastner? Huh? Think she'd be impressed?"

There was a moment of uncomfortable silence as everyone else in the room avoided Jackson's challenging stare. He let the question hang for a moment, then softened his tone to take on a more conciliatory nature.

"All I'm saying is that our fraternity is all about honor, respect, and integrity, right? Isn't that what our motto means? To become men of character? So what if we started acting like we actually mean all that?"

Pete spoke up in an obvious effort to ease the tension of the last few minutes. "Yeah, Williams, you're right. But you're taking this way too seriously. Is everything okay? You having a rough time with something?"

Jackson blew out a long breath and a mirthless laugh. "You could say that. It's been a tough week." He rubbed his temples in a vain attempt to massage away his headache. He rarely even drank it, but he could really use a strong cup of coffee right about now.

"Look, man, we're here for you, okay?" Pete crossed to him and slapped him on the shoulder in a friendly gesture. "But we've got to know you're on our side too. You can't just blow your top over an innocent conversation about girls."

Just like that, the tension returned. "Is that what you call this?" Jackson shot back. "An 'innocent conversation'? About which girls you want to sleep with?"

"Williams, chill. Let's not get into that again. Whatever's bugging you, I promise, it will pass. Soon you'll be back to your normal self. Right, guys?"

"I get it," Alex said, snapping his fingers as if he'd gotten an idea. "You and Miranda broke up, didn't you? That's why you're not sleeping together, and that's why you're all bent out of shape today."

Desperately fighting the urge to punch Alex, Jackson crossed his arms and drew himself to his full height, knowing he looked intimidating with his broad shoulders and large biceps. Alex had a small build, and Jackson could snap him in half like a twig if he wanted to. Suddenly it was very important to him that Alex was well aware of this fact also.

"As a matter of fact, Miranda and I were never dating in the first place, and we've never slept together. But I know her better than any of you, and I love her like a sister, and if any one of you ever hurts her, so help me, I will make you regret it."

Everyone's eyes were wide as they stared at him, and Bryce muttered, "Note to self: Stay away from Miranda."

A nervous ripple of chuckles followed Bryce's comment, and Jackson responded, "What you don't realize is that you're playing with fire. My sister fooled around with her boyfriend in high school and ended up pregnant at sixteen. What happens if you get your girlfriend pregnant? Would you step up and be a man and help her with the responsibility? Or would you dump her or tell her to get an abortion?"

He knew he was talking too much, making more of the conversation than he should have, but Jackson couldn't stop the words from coming. It was as if all the emotions he'd tried so hard to bottle up over the past week were now spilling out, and he was taking his frustrations out on his friends.

"My sister decided to keep her baby when she got pregnant in high school, but I know other people who chose *not* to go through with an unplanned pregnancy." His voice cracked, and Jackson cleared his throat before going on. "Either way, it's hard. So it's best to avoid the chance of getting pregnant altogether."

Eric rolled his eyes. "Are you seriously talking about 'chastity'?" He did air quotes as he asked the question in a mocking voice.

"Yes, I am. Until marriage."

The room erupted in laughter, and Bryce said, "I never had you pegged as that kind of guy. That's pretty old-fashioned, isn't it?"

"So are the commandments not to steal or murder, but they still apply, don't they?" retorted Jackson.

"Oh, no, don't tell me this is about religion," groaned Eric. "You're one of *those* guys?"

"I'm a Christian, yes, not some religious wingnut. God's

commandment for chastity makes all kinds of sense. Think about this—would you want your wife sleeping with someone else someday? So what's different about sleeping around before marriage? Every woman you sleep with could be someone's wife someday, and maybe not your own. Respect that fact."

"Are you going to be preaching to us like this all the time?" asked Bryce. "I don't think I can handle that. I like to have fun in life." He wiggled his eyebrows, and the rest of the guys laughed.

Jackson sighed wearily. Apparently, being a Christian was synonymous with having no fun. And why had he spoken up in the first place? Heaven knew he wasn't usually one to speak up about anything remotely religious.

"Look, if that works for you, Williams, that's fine," Pete said diplomatically. "Just remember that not all of us believe what you believe, okay?" He clapped his hands together, signaling the end of the discussion. "Now, you pledges need to clean up. Tony just got back with the pizzas."

A rowdy cheer rose from the assembly at large, and the pledges quickly put lids on top of paint cans and took brushes to the bathroom to rinse them off. Jackson moved slowly, pouring his leftover paint into the can and taking great pains to make sure the lid was secure. He didn't feel like talking to anyone and decided he'd just leave. After the conversation they'd just had, he highly doubted anyone would miss his presence.

Straightening at last, Jackson was surprised to see Brandon hanging around the otherwise-empty living room. Brandon was another pledge, one Jackson didn't know well. He was a quiet guy, and the two didn't have any classes together.

"Hey, I just wanted to let you know that I admire you for standing up like that earlier," Brandon said, shifting from one foot to the other.

"Oh… um… thanks," Jackson mumbled.

"It's hard to be in the minority, but I agree with you about… you know… like, waiting until marriage and all that." Brandon's cheeks were bright pink.

Then why didn't you say something? wondered Jackson angrily. At the very least, the guys would know he wasn't the only one with such "old-fashioned" views.

"Well… good. Thanks for letting me know," he said, faking a smile at Brandon.

Brandon flashed a quick smile in return and left to go to the kitchen for lunch. Jackson watched his retreating back, wondering at the short exchange. He should feel some sort of connection, he supposed, with someone who shared similar values, but Jackson felt only frustration. Was it really so hard to speak up?

The thought was immediately followed by guilt. Yes, it *was* that hard to speak up. Today was a first for Jackson. Normally, he'd just ignore the crass conversation or even join in. It's not as if he hadn't heard that kind of talk before. But bringing Miranda into it had crossed a line for him.

The thought of Miranda jolted him into action. Grabbing his jacket, he slipped out the back door and walked quickly to his car. He'd grab something for Miranda and eat back at Faith's apartment with her, and he'd deal with the fraternity guys another day when he was in a better frame of mind. Yes, he'd ruffled feathers today, but Jackson knew he could patch things up. The other pledges and brothers in the fraternity were all good guys, friends who would do anything to help one another. Even when they disagreed, he knew they all had each other's backs.

Now he needed Miranda to know he had her back too.

CHAPTER

41

Faith set out a bowl of chips, which Jackson normally would have scarfed down, but tonight he only nibbled at a few of them. "So are you and Miranda dating?" she asked.

He narrowly avoided spitting his mouthful of Coke across the room, forcing himself to swallow it instead, which prompted a fit of coughing. Pounding himself on the chest, Jackson choked out, "No, we aren't. Why would you ask that?"

"You're spending a lot of time together lately. I just thought maybe..."

It was true he'd spent the afternoon with Miranda, who by now was already in bed. Now here he was, dreading going back to his dorm room to face his roommate, who had likely heard about his erratic behavior that morning.

Jackson had almost gotten his voice back to answer, "No, I don't have *those* kind of feelings for her. I feel more like her older brother, looking out for her. And I think she sort of sees me the same way, like a brother. I know she used to like me, but I don't think she does anymore. Just as a friend."

"We were just wondering. How do you think she's doing?"

He sighed deeply. "I don't know. I've never seen her like this before, so contemplative. She won't even really talk about it. It could either be a good change or a bad one. I don't know yet."

"Yeah." They fell into silence again before Jackson voiced a question he'd been mulling over in his mind for some time. "Why does life have to be so hard? It seems like the lives of my good friends are crumbling in front of me."

"You mean Miranda?" asked Faith.

"Yeah, her. And Sam too." He found it strange to realize his two closest friends were females. "Guys, you have no idea what kind of upbringing Miranda had, but it's bad. Her mom was more like a peer than a mother. She didn't do Miranda any favors. Faith, you know things were rough for Mom after Dad left, but at least she kept being a mom to us. In Miranda's case, it's like her mom didn't even try. She just went from guy to guy, as Miranda says, and sort of let Miranda and her sister raise themselves. Can you honestly expect either of them to turn out any better?"

He fell silent for a moment, pondering Miranda's life. She'd spent so many years looking to superficial relationships with guys to give her a sense of self worth when the only thing that would make a lasting change was the transforming, redeeming love of God.

"And then there's Sam," he continued, "on the completely opposite spectrum. Her dad was the DCE at their church, they went to church together every Sunday, and they were a picture-perfect family from all appearances. But then her brother developed schizophrenia and got off his meds and killed someone, and now he's in jail. Sam's parents couldn't deal with it, so they're divorced. Her family has completely fallen apart."

"I didn't know any of that," confessed Faith. "But then

again, I don't know her very well."

Shoot, he hadn't meant to let the part about her brother slip. "I actually shouldn't have told you," he said. "Even Mom doesn't know, so keep it to yourselves, okay? But my point is that she didn't do anything to deserve that. Her family did all the 'right' things, and it's like they're being punished for something. It's just not fair."

"It's really not," agreed Spencer.

"She's mad at God, and frankly, I don't blame her! I would be too, in her situation. What can I say to convince her that God still cares when from all outward appearances, He doesn't?"

His sister was silent a long moment before responding slowly. "That's the funny thing about faith. Believing God is for us when it doesn't seem like it. We can't use visible circumstances to determine how we think God views us. Otherwise, we'd think that in good times He's happy with us and in bad times He's punishing us. That's simply not true. In a lot of cases, God uses hard times to mold and shape our character. It's not fun going through them, but in retrospect, we can see that those rough times were a gift from God."

Spencer leaned over to grab a chip from the bowl and spoke quietly. "Maybe this rough patch Miranda is going through is God's way of getting her attention. You've been really great with her, and I think God is using you in her life more than you might realize." Jackson felt himself flush at the praise as Spencer continued. "Faith getting pregnant with Griffin was the wake-up call God used for me, even if it took me a long time to see that."

"Even though that time was very painful, God used it for the good of *both* of us," Faith added. "Same thing with my liver a few years ago. I honestly thought I was going to die, and at the time I couldn't see any possible good coming out of it. But if it hadn't been for that time, Dad and I wouldn't have made up. We'd still be mostly estranged, and I wouldn't have had the chance to forgive him."

Jackson felt a strange mixture of emotions at his sister's comment. Guilt, resentment, and—inexplicably—longing washed over him as he thought about his father.

"Plus my sickness really cemented *our* relationship," Faith continued with a tender smile at her husband. "I think I fell more in love with Spencer while I was in the hospital than I ever would have under 'normal' circumstances. And that brings us back to what I was talking about earlier—having faith when we can't see God's plan. Trusting that even though life is hard and things won't always turn out the way we want them to, God is still working."

"I can see that," said Jackson. "I know it's not on the same level, but breaking my leg was sort of like that. Before then, I was pretty confident in myself and my own abilities. But then I realized how quickly things could change, with no advance warning. It was kind of sobering. It made me realize how powerless I really am in the grand scheme of life. How little I can rely on my own strength and how much I need to rely instead on God's. Plus it gave me a whole new understanding of my confirmation verse." He grinned, and after a moment of thought, Faith burst out laughing.

Spencer wasn't in the know. "What verse is that?"

"Ephesians 6:13. Check it out," Jackson answered.

Spencer pulled up his Bible app on his phone and typed in the reference, then chuckled as he read it. "'Therefore take up the whole armor of God, that you may be able to withstand in the evil day, and having done all, to stand firm.' Nice. Very apropos."

"Mom reminded me of it when I was laid up on the couch. She thought it was pretty funny. I was not amused at the time, but now I can see the humor in it."

"That's a great verse, though," Faith said. "It's a perfect reminder of what we have to do as opposed to what God has already done. Pastor Lixon talked about this once in a sermon, and I've always remembered it. He said God doesn't instruct us to advance. He tells us to stand. We're already where we need to be because of what Jesus has done for us. We only need to rely on God's armor to stand firm in our faith."

"It's hard to do that when you feel like you're standing alone," Jackson said. "Do you ever feel like everyone around you thinks you're an idiot for believing in God? Miranda thinks I'm hopelessly naïve, and Sam doesn't know if she even believes in God anymore. My roommate teases me about going to church. My science classes talk about evolution as fact and creationists as morons. The other guys in my fraternity think I have old-fashioned morals. It's easy to think you're all alone."

"For sure. Even my own brother refuses to talk to me about religion," said Spencer. "I'm the only one in my family who believes. It's very isolating."

"The world will do everything it can to fight against the truth," Faith said. "That makes it all the more important to be in church on a regular basis, gathering with other believers so you know you *aren't* alone."

"Honestly, if you guys weren't here in the same town, I may have stopped going to church in college myself," admitted Jackson. "Without someone to keep me accountable, it's easier to just skip church and sleep in. You guys are way more holy than I am."

"Oh, trust me, we aren't! You've seen how distracting Hope and Griffin can be in church. Some days I feel like I don't get a thing out of the service," Faith protested. "I totally get that it would be easier to stay home and forget about it. We've been tempted many times not to bother. Some weeks we only drag them there because we know *you'll* be waiting for us! So you keep us accountable too."

The three fell into silence for a few moments until Faith spoke again. "I never thought I'd be telling you this, but I'm glad you're here. In Ann Arbor, that is. It's nice being able to see you so often now that we're both out on our own. Growing up together, we were never very close, but now... I feel like we've both changed and learned to appreciate each other. I actually *like* spending time with you now. You're not just my annoying little brother anymore. You've become a true friend."

His sister's words meant more to him than he wanted to admit. "Thanks, sis. I feel the same way." He stood and stretched. That was as sentimental as he wanted to get for the night. "Well, guys, I should be getting back. Thanks for everything. I'll text you before I come tomorrow to check on Miranda."

"Sounds good. Drive safely."

"You sound more and more like Mom every day."

Faith rolled her eyes. "Well, I *am* a mom myself now, so I guess I should sound like one."

"Want me to pull your bed out before I leave?" he teased.

"How about you stay on the couch tonight and Faith and I will go to a hotel so we can sleep in a real bed for once?" Spencer asked with a sly grin. Jackson wasn't sure how serious his brother-in-law was, but he wasn't going to take any chances. No way did he want to be awakened at the crack of dawn by his exuberant nephew leaping on top of him.

"Tempting as that is, I'll pass. That's one surefire way to chase a guest out."

Spencer laughed and stood to shake Jackson's hand. "It was good talking with you tonight," he said. "Thanks for coming."

Faith stood as well and gave him a hug. "Yes, thank you for coming. I enjoyed our talk too."

Jackson took his leave, marveling to himself that his sister had hugged him twice in less than a week. She'd better be careful. At this rate, she was going to make a habit of it.

CHAPTER

42

The following Sunday found the Youngs, Jackson, and Miranda gathered around the small table in the apartment for Sunday brunch after church. Miranda had been making baby steps in her recovery, and had moved out of their apartment earlier that week to stay in a friend's dorm room. Faith was exceedingly glad to have their apartment to themselves again, but she missed Miranda more than she'd thought she would. She felt a need to take care of her, given the events of the past number of days.

"So, G, what was your Sunday school lesson today?" Jackson asked his nephew. It was their own tradition, and Griffin took his assignment seriously as he reported back to his uncle what they learned each week.

"We did the Transformers on the mountain."

"Transfiguration," supplied Spencer with a chuckle.

"Yeah, that."

"Okay," Jackson encouraged. "So what happened?"

"Four guys went up on a mountain. I don't remember any of them except the important one."

The adults laughed. "And that was…?" Faith prompted.

"Jesus!" exclaimed Griffin, as if surprised his mother didn't know this simple fact.

Just then, Miranda's phone rang, causing her to jump. She glanced at the screen and went white. "It's the detective from my case," she announced. "I'd better take this."

Hurriedly she ran to the kids' room and accepted the call as the others sat around the table, exchanging uneasy glances and wondering what was going on. No one was sure what to think of the fact that he was calling on a Sunday.

Six minutes later, Miranda emerged from the room, tears streaming down her face. Jackson jumped up from his spot at the table and crossed the distance between them to engulf her in a hug.

"Is everything okay?" he asked.

Wiping her face, she took a shuddering breath and said the three words they'd all been waiting to hear.

"They caught him."

Dinner that night was a festive affair, everyone relieved to hear about the arrest. "Kevin," aka Gary Schubert, had been caught attending a party at Eastern Michigan University. A quick-thinking female had noticed suspicious behavior on his part as he was hitting on a friend. She'd snapped a picture of him and sent it to her boyfriend, a campus security employee, who passed it along to the police. Only after he was in police custody did anyone realize the full extent of his crimes.

Gary Schubert was not a student anywhere. The twenty-four-year old had never even graduated high school. He couldn't hold a job and drifted from one fast food restaurant job to another, staying with friends and relatives until they got sick of him and kicked him out to the next place. Over the past five years he had made the rounds of campuses across the state. Complaints and reports of date rape from East Lansing to Mount Pleasant had been traced back to Gary, and two DNA samples from victims provided enough evidence that it was unlikely to go to trial. He wouldn't stand a chance. More than likely, he would plead guilty in the hopes of getting a lesser sentence for cooperating. But at any rate, he wouldn't bother any women for a long, long time.

To celebrate the happy turn of events, Faith hosted dinner for Miranda and Jackson and made the fanciest meal she knew how to make, Chicken Marsala. Everyone chatted happily, relief evident in their faces and their easy conversation. Faith was glad to see that Miranda seemed much less tense than she'd been in a long time. Her eyes held a look of peace that hadn't been there before, and Faith offered up a silent prayer of thanks that her would-be attacker was safely locked away. She was certain this was a step in the right direction for her healing process. When Miranda left with Jackson, Faith gave her a warm hug and wished her the best, assuring her that if she ever needed anything, she was there to help.

Spencer did the dishes while she put the kids to bed, and when all was quiet at last, she walked over to her husband and wrapped her arms around his neck.

"Thanks for cleaning up, hon. You're the best husband a gal could ask for."

"I am, aren't I?" he grinned.

"Spencer Young!" She punched him playfully on the arm. "This is the part where you're supposed to tell me I'm the best wife a guy could ask for!"

He put his arms around her waist. "And so you are," he said. "I don't deserve you."

"No, you don't," she teased.

"That's it! Come here, you!" He dragged her over to the couch and pulled her down next to him, tickling her as she begged for mercy and tried to wriggle out of his grasp, giggling the whole time.

When he finally let up, she curled up next to him, trying to catch her breath. He put his arm around her, and she leaned her head against his shoulder contentedly. "That was the best evening we've had in a long time," she sighed. "It was good to see Miranda so relaxed. I think this was exactly what she needed to put that part of her life behind her and start to move on."

"Absolutely. After everything that's happened recently, it was good to be able to celebrate something. You blew it out of the park with that chicken dish, by the way. That was amazing."

"Thanks, sweetie."

Spencer rested his cheek on the top of her head. "I've changed a lot, haven't I?"

"Changed since when?"

"High school."

"Oh, gosh, *yes*. And thank goodness for that."

He laughed good-naturedly. "I was really kind of a jerk then, wasn't I?"

"More than 'kind of.'"

"But now…?"

"You're a wonderful husband and a great daddy and the man I love and respect more than anyone else."

He squeezed her shoulder gently. "That was sweet."

"It's true. But why are you asking about how much you've changed?"

"Because it gives me hope that Miranda can turn things around in her own life."

Faith's throat burned. "Same here."

Just two weeks ago, she'd been yearning for the day Miranda would be out of their home and they'd be free of her. But now Faith found she cared very much about what happened to her. In a short amount of time, Miranda had gone from an unwanted house guest to an honorary member of the family.

CHAPTER

43

Knocking on the door, Jackson waited with an expectant grin. When Sam answered, he held out a bouquet of daisies and exclaimed, "Happy Birthday!"

"Jackson!" she laughed in disbelief, giving him a hug. "What are you doing here? We just saw each other over spring break!"

"You don't think I'd pass up the opportunity to see you again, do you? Especially on your birthday! I'm taking you out to dinner."

"How do you know I don't have plans already?" she asked, raising an eyebrow.

"I asked your roommate."

"Since when do you talk to Megan?"

"Since I dropped you off on Monday. I asked her about it when you were in the bathroom and told her not to let you make plans."

"Oh, Jackson!" She shook her head, obviously very happy he'd come. "I should have known something was up with you. You texted to wish me happy birthday, but that was it. I would think you at least would have called or asked about my plans or *something.* This is the best gift I could have asked for!"

As they drove to the restaurant and placed their orders, Jackson dared to hope that this would be a normal get-together for them. That disastrous dinner when he'd made the team was still seared into the back of his mind, and for the life of him, he couldn't understand why Sam refused to try dating. He knew she liked him, so what was the hangup?

Since that evening, their texts had been more careful than usual, almost strained. They'd gotten together a few times over spring break, but neither had mentioned anything about dating or their conversation about it. It was as if they were both pretending it had never happened. Jackson was even nervous about the flowers he'd given her, afraid she'd take it the wrong way and think he was trying to be romantic. Good grief, and she thought dating would complicate things? Their relationship was more complicated now than ever.

"Chris wants me to visit him." Sam's voice brought him back to the present, and he swallowed his mouthful of food to answer her.

"In jail?" Jackson kicked himself for such a stupid question.

"Mm-hmm."

"I didn't think the two of you were in contact."

"We aren't. He told my dad to pass along the message."

"Oh. Well, do you *want* to visit him?"

"Honestly, no. I don't even know if I want to *write* him, let alone visit. I just… I can't bring myself to do it, Jackson. Not knowing what he did. It's… It's too much."

"Yeah." He didn't blame her. If one of his siblings had killed someone, he very much doubted he'd want to be in contact either.

"The thing is, my dad is totally after me to do it," she continued. "He says Chris is doing really well under gentle medical supervision. Dad even arranged for a pastor to visit him, and he says Chris is secure in the knowledge that he's forgiven." She said this last part scornfully.

"And you don't think he deserves to be forgiven?"

She looked at him in surprise, as if she was startled he'd read between the lines. "Well... I guess... No, I don't. There, I said it. I mean, he kills someone and just like that he's forgiven? No consequences? How is that fair?"

"He *does* have consequences. He's in jail, isn't he?"

"But I mean, like... I don't know..."

"Like maybe he needs to earn back God's favor or something?"

"Something like that."

Jackson chewed a bite of food before answering. "I can see where you're coming from. But that's a human way of thinking. To God, all of us are sinners and none of us deserve His forgiveness. Even if we tried, we couldn't earn His favor. But Jesus died for even the worst sinners in the world."

"Oh, really? Well, what would you say about Kevin or Gary or whatever his name is? Should God forgive *him*?" Sam threw the question at him spitefully.

Jackson felt white-hot anger well up inside him all over again. Sam hit a nerve with that question. He still got mad thinking about what Gary had done to all those women, and what he would have done to Miranda given a few more minutes. "Truthfully? I don't want him to be forgiven. You're right. It's too personal. But that's sinful human resentment talking. As much as I hate to say it, yes, Jesus died for his sins too. I may not *want* him to be forgiven, but ultimately, if he repents and believes in Jesus, he would be forgiven and saved as well."

"Does the same hold true for your dad?" She peeked at him

out of the corner of her eye, and Jackson sighed wearily. Would Sam ever let this drop? "Never mind. I'm sorry, Jackson. I shouldn't have brought him up. I told you before I wouldn't." She pushed the last few bites of her food around her plate, not looking at him.

Taking a deep breath, Jackson said, "No, it's okay. You're right. I *am* setting a double standard, telling you one thing but doing another. I guess I'm sort of thinking the same way as you with Chris, that my dad needs to earn God's favor, or at least mine. Like he needs to experience consequences for his actions; to be hurt like he hurt us. But yes, if he was to repent, God would forgive him, just like He forgives Chris. And if God would do it, I should too."

He took a drink before continuing. "I've been thinking a lot about our conversation at Homecoming, and I think we *can* forgive people even if they haven't asked or aren't sorry. Jesus forgave those who crucified Him, and they weren't asking to be forgiven. So we *should* forgive other people, but… I don't know if I'm strong enough to do that," he finished in a near whisper, feeling very foolish to admit it.

Sam reached out and gave his hand a small squeeze. "I know exactly how you feel," she said. "I know I *should*, but I don't think I *can*."

They lapsed into silence for a few more bites until Jackson had an idea. "What if we work up to it?" he suggested. "It's obvious you don't want to visit Chris, so don't—at least, not yet. Send a message through your dad sometime to let Chris know you're thinking of him. Then when you're ready, maybe write a short letter. Baby steps, as my mom would say. But don't force yourself to do anything before you're ready. What do you think?"

She nodded slowly. "I like it. That's a good idea. So… what

would that mean for you?" she asked tentatively.

"I… I have no clue," he confessed sheepishly. "I'm open to ideas."

She bit her lip in concentration, then said, "You could maybe do the same thing. Like, have Faith give your dad a message for you. Have her tell him you made the football team and it would be nice for him to come to a game next season or something. Then if he comes, shake his hand. You don't have to be best buds. Just start by being cordial."

"Yeah." He blew out a frustrated sigh. "You know this is going to be one of the hardest things I'll ever have to do, right?"

"Same here. Even worse than breaking your leg?"

"For sure. That was painful when it happened, but it healed."

"And so will your relationship with your dad, given time. But only if you let it."

"Maybe." He still wasn't convinced.

"You're not the only one who's been thinking about our conversation at Homecoming," Sam said. "But I've been focusing more on forgiving God." She drew in a deep breath and straightened her shoulders. "You know I haven't been going to church in college. I've been struggling with my feelings and beliefs about God, wondering why He would let something like this hit my family. But the more I think about it, the more I come to the same conclusion: what's the alternative?"

She stopped and looked at him, and Jackson nodded, encouraging her to explain herself. "Like when Jesus asks the disciples if they want to leave Him too, and Peter says, 'Lord, to whom shall we go? You have the words of eternal life.' We sang that verse as part of the liturgy every week growing up, and it's been stuck in my mind lately. So I went back and checked the Bible reference."

"And...?" Jackson prompted.

She looked a bit flustered. "My dad always said we should know the context of a single Bible verse for better understanding, so that's what I did. Jesus had just finished talking about how He was the bread of life, and the people listening started to grumble and say, 'This is a hard saying; who can listen to it?' And a bunch of people left and quit following Jesus. So that's when Jesus asks His disciples if they're going to leave, and Peter answers by asking, in effect, 'Where else can we go?' He's saying that Jesus is the only way to eternal life, so if they're going to believe that, they have to accept the hard teachings along with the easy ones."

"Huh." Jackson had read the account before but never really thought too much about it. The way Sam explained it made perfect sense.

She went on. "I... I realized the same thing has to be true in my own life. If I can accept the good things from God, I have to trust Him in the bad times too. I don't want to be like those people who turned away when things got hard."

"That's a good connection, Sam."

She shrugged one shoulder uncomfortably. "Thanks."

"So does that mean you'll start going to church again?"

"I guess so."

"That's great!"

"It'll make my dad happy too," she said with a half smile.

Jackson smiled as well. He knew her father had been displeased at her church absences. "Will you be spending the summer in Mapleport, then?"

"I haven't even thought about that yet," she answered. "It's too far away."

"It's, like, six weeks, Sam."

"That's too far," she insisted stubbornly. Jackson laughed as she continued. "Mom wants me to visit her part of the time. I just don't know. Not that we were living in Mapleport for long, but it's more 'home' to me than Indianapolis. I'm half tempted to just stay in Lansing and find a job so I don't have to deal with both parents pestering me to stay with them."

"Don't do that," he begged. "Then when would I see you?"

"Oh, please! You'll be spending your entire summer at football camp and practice. You won't be lounging around sleeping in back home."

"Hmm. Good point. On second thought, stay in Lansing. It's closer than Mapleport. Or maybe I can find you a job in Ann Arbor?"

Sam giggled. "I wouldn't do something *that* drastic," she teased.

They paused as their waitress stopped to refill drinks and ask about the food. When she left, Sam said, "So I have to ask. Are you and Miranda dating?"

Jackson was surprised she'd asked. Sam should know he'd tell her if he was dating someone. "No, of course not. Why? Are you jealous?" He asked this with a sly grin. Maybe he'd get his wish and she'd agree to date him after all.

Sam flushed and hastened to explain. "No, I mean… I'm not… I was just wondering. You guys were… different together over spring break. More comfortable around each other. She seemed different too. Less flighty and a little more serious. I thought maybe she wasn't trying as hard because you guys were already going out. Plus, you certainly swooped in to save her, and then you helped her a lot through the whole mess with Kevin."

"Gary."

"Whatever. But women tend to fall for men who save them, like the damsel in distress. And Miranda liked you in high school as it was."

"There wasn't anything there," Jackson explained. "She just isn't my type. But you're right—she has changed. She's starting to take herself more seriously and she's not relying on her looks like she used to." Although Jackson didn't keep secrets from Sam, he hadn't told her about Miranda's abortion, nor did he intend to. That wasn't his secret to tell.

"I noticed that. Her makeup was way more subdued. Her clothes too. It's a nice change."

"Yeah, it is." After a moment of silence, Jackson pressed, "So *were* you jealous?"

"Jackson! We're best friends, for Pete's sake. I'm the one who encouraged you to date other people in the first place."

"But...?" Jackson knew there was something she wasn't telling him.

Sam heaved a heavy sigh. "You really are impossible, you know that? You can read me too well. Fine. I don't mind if you're dating someone so long as it's not Miranda."

She blushed furiously at the confession, but Jackson leaned back in his seat and grinned away. "You know, if you'd taken me up on my offer to go out with me, we wouldn't be having this discussion right now. Just saying..."

"Yeah, yeah, yeah. Don't even go there. You know how well it went last time."

They weren't given the chance to dwell on the subject, because just then a group of employees surrounded their table to chant a birthday song in monotone but loud voices, clapping enthusiastically to the beat as they shouted incomprehensible words. The other patrons turned to see whose birthday it was, and Sam turned deep red at the sudden attention. When they were done, a waiter set down a small cake with a flourish, bowing and wishing her a happy birthday.

Still blushing, Sam looked at Jackson, who was immensely pleased with himself. "I suppose I have *you* to thank for that lovely serenade?"

"Of course! I told our waitress about it when you went to wash your hands. I just did it for the free dessert. You *are* gonna share with me, aren't you?"

She grinned smugly and took a large bite. "Maybe, maybe not."

He grabbed his fork and reached across the table for a bite of his own. Sam laughed. "Okay, okay," she said. "Here." She pushed the plate to the middle of the table so they could share the chocolate cake peacefully.

When Jackson dropped her off at her dorm later that evening, Sam gave him a tight hug and thanked him profusely for making the trip to see her. Although it was late and he had an hour drive ahead of him, Jackson didn't mind in the least. It had been worth every minute.

CHAPTER

44

Jackson glanced covertly at Faith, trying to read the expression on her face and decide what sort of mood she was in. His sister had asked if he'd take a walk with her after dinner at her place, which was something she'd never done before. He wondered what merited a private conversation like this.

The two made idle small talk for a few minutes before Faith got around to the reason for the discussion. "So…. my birthday is next week."

Jackson slightly frowned. "I know." She wouldn't invite him on a walk to tell him that.

"It's also the four-year anniversary of my liver transplant."

"Yeah, that's right! Congrats!" Then a chilling thought occurred to him and he glanced at her quickly. "Are… is everything going okay with that? You aren't having any complications or health problems, are you?"

"No, no. I'm feeling fine, don't worry. But I…um… "

"Look, sis. I know you brought me out here to talk to me in private either to give me bad news or to tell me something you don't think I want to hear. So just get it over with so I'm not worried about it, will you?"

She smiled ever so slightly. "Okay. So I want you to come for my birthday dinner, but you won't be the only one. It's a tradition that Dad comes up for the evening to celebrate the anniversary of the transplant." She pinched her lips together and it seemed to Jackson she was holding her breath waiting for his response.

Jackson shook his head and breathed out a disbelieving laugh. Since his talk with Sam over a week ago, he'd not acted upon his tenuous agreement to take baby steps toward restoring a relationship with his father. "Pretty subtle, God. Pretty subtle," he mumbled. Of *course* God would force the issue so soon. Jackson shouldn't be surprised one bit.

"Huh?" Faith squinted at him in confusion.

"Oh, nothing." They walked in silence a few moments. "So you want me to be civil to Dad at your birthday dinner? That's basically what you're saying?"

"Something like that."

He mulled that over in his mind. "Okay."

"I don't even expect you to—what?"

"Okay. I'll be civil to him."

"You... you will? Just like that?"

"Yeah."

"But you... I mean... you, like, hate him," she objected. "And now you're going to be nice to him without even arguing about it first with me?"

"You *want* me to argue with you?"

"No, but I expected as much."

Jackson gave her a sad smile. He'd built up quite a reputation for himself. "I've been struggling with my resentment toward him for a long time," he admitted. "Sam called me out on it. So you can take comfort in knowing I argued with *her* instead of you."

"Oh, that's a relief," teased Faith.

"Right?" he chuckled. "But it's hard, Faith. It's really hard. How do you forgive someone who's caused so much pain? How were *you* able to do it? Although I guess him giving you his liver took care of that, huh?"

"The liver had nothing to do with it. We had the forgiveness discussion before he even told me he had the right blood type."

"Seriously?" Jackson had a hard time believing that.

"Yes. He came in to visit me in the hospital, and at first I was mad at him, coming in at almost the final hour when he'd been gone all those years. I vented my frustration and yelled at him a bit, and he apologized."

"And that's it? You got mad at him, he said he was sorry, and you forgave him? Just like that?"

"It wasn't easy."

"You sure make it sound easy! 'I know you've been a total jerk, Dad, but what's that? You're sorry? Oh, in that case, no big deal. I forgive you.' You're a far better person than I am, sis. I couldn't do that."

"I'm not a better person. But being sick in a hospital bed thinking I was going to die gave me a different perspective. If he'd shown up any other time, it would have been completely different. But while I was in the hospital, God knew it wasn't just my liver that needed help. I needed a heart transplant too. Like that verse in the Old Testament where God says He will remove their hearts of stone and give them hearts of flesh. That's what I needed too."

Jackson's conscience was pricked. He could use a heart transplant himself.

"Pastor Lixon and Pastor Chris had both come to visit

recently," Faith went on, "and I was spending a lot of time reading the Bible as I was confined to the hospital bed. One of the passages I'd read the morning Dad came was the one about how we're supposed to forgive one another as God has forgiven us. When Dad told me he was sorry, that verse was the first one that came to my mind, and I couldn't push it out. Plus I knew that if I didn't forgive him then, I may not have another chance. I didn't want to die with an unforgiving heart."

"But I'm hardly in such dire circumstances."

"That makes it all the more important."

"You lost me there," he confessed.

"If you think you have all the time in the world, like you can deal with it later, that day may never come," explained Faith. "Spencer's dad had a heart attack and died immediately. No one was expecting that. Spencer carries all this guilt that he didn't make more of an effort to witness to his dad or build a better relationship with him. None of us would have thought his dad would die so abruptly, but the truth is that any of us could die at any time. Dad could have an accident on the worksite, you could get in a car crash on the way home… We aren't guaranteed tomorrow. So act now, before it's too late."

Jackson followed his sister's lead as she turned the corner to go around the block. "You're probably right, but it's not as easy for me to forgive and forget as it apparently is for you."

She glanced sideways at him as they continued to walk. "Forgiveness isn't easy for any of us. It's not our natural inclination. And don't think that you can ever really 'forget.' Forgiveness usually isn't a one-time deal. I've had to work through my own resentment even after our hospital discussion. Dad will make a comment about being a bachelor for years, and I'll get mad and think it's his own fault. Stuff like that. So in some ways I've had to forgive him again and again."

"That's hardly encouraging right now. It will be hard enough for me to forgive him *once*, let alone multiple times."

"I know. But the first time is the hardest. I'm not asking you to have a deep heart-to-heart with him next week. I just want to know you aren't going to blow up at him."

"I won't blow up at him. But..." Now it was his turn to trail off, embarrassed to voice his question.

"But what?"

"Can I maybe... um, could I invite Sam to come too? I think her presence would... uh, help me be nice." His face burned at his admission of weakness.

Faith smiled. "I'd love to have Sam come too. I think that's a great idea."

He breathed a sigh of relief. Having Sam there would be good for him. Maybe with enough support around him, he could actually be civil to his father this time. Maybe.

CHAPTER

45

A week later, Jackson sat in Spencer and Faith's living room, his stomach churning. Sam sat next to him on the couch as Griffin talked a mile a minute, excited to have visitors. Thankfully, Sam was listening and responding to his incessant chatter. Jackson couldn't for the life of him concentrate on what his nephew was saying.

When a knock sounded on the door, Jackson's stomach tightened even more. Sam reached over and gave his hand an encouraging squeeze. "You can do this," she whispered. "Baby steps."

He nodded and tried to swallow, but his mouth was as dry as cotton. He stood woodenly and watched his sister answer the door.

"Hi, baby girl!" exclaimed Bob. "Happy Anniversary!" He gave Faith a kiss on the cheek and a long hug. When he released her, he gave her a gentle pat on the stomach. "And how's my latest grandbaby? Still cooking in there?"

Jackson barely managed to suppress a snort. His dad was hardly qualified to be a doting grandfather. Faith didn't seem to mind the question, though, and answered easily, "Baby Young is doing just fine. Only three months to go!"

"And you're doing okay?" he asked, concern in his eyes.

"I'm fine, Dad. They're watching me like a hawk during this pregnancy too."

"Good." He handed her a gift bag and she peeked inside and giggled, giving him another quick hug.

"Grandpa Bob, what about me?" Griffin tugged at Bob's pant leg. Jackson was surprised by the title. He hadn't expected Griffin to call him "Grandpa," but then again, what else would he call him? "Mr. Coleman" seemed too formal, and "Bob" was too familiar.

Bob easily swung Griffin into the air as Griffin shrieked with glee. "Hi, little buddy! I've missed you! How ya been?"

"Gah-pah!" Hope was mimicking Griffin now, pulling on his other pant leg.

Bob smiled and reached down to scoop her into his other arm. "Hiya, princess. You get prettier and prettier every day. You look just like your mommy when she was this old."

Jackson fought back a wave of resentment. His dad made it sound like he looked back with fondness on those days. But if that was true, why had he left? Yes, he'd been around for Faith's infancy and early childhood, but he hadn't bothered to meet his other daughter when Katie was born. He wasn't a parent who could claim he'd "loved every single minute" with his kids.

Putting the kids down, Bob shook Spencer's hand. "Hey, Doc, how's it going? Keeping this family in line?"

Spencer chuckled. "I try."

Bob smiled and slapped him on the shoulder before walking into the living room. Jackson knew he ought to meet his dad halfway, but his feet felt rooted to the spot. He could only stare as his father came closer and closer. Sam nudged him discreetly with her shoulder as Bob held out his hand.

"Hi, son."

Again, Jackson struggled to keep his composure. Dang it all, why did his father insist on calling him "son" when he knew he didn't like it? Was he just determined to make this as difficult as possible?

Jackson felt like everyone in the small apartment was watching him, holding their breath as they waited for his response. He slowly let out his own breath as he extended his hand toward his dad. It was a seemingly small gesture, but it was a huge step for both Jackson and Bob, and everyone in the room seemed to breathe a little easier as the two shook hands.

Next, Bob turned to Sam to shake her hand as well. "Sammie, great to see you again." Jackson nearly gagged. Who did he think he was, calling her "Sammie"? He must have picked that up from her aunt, but he was hardly on familiar enough terms with her for such a nickname.

"That's one of Uncle Jackson's girlfriends," announced Griffin importantly.

The blood drained from Jackson's face while Sam, by contrast, turned bright red. Bob didn't miss a beat. "*One* of them, huh?" he chuckled. "How many does he have?"

"Two."

Bob lowered his voice and bent closer to Griffin. "Do his girlfriends know about each other?" He smirked at Jackson.

"Oh, yeah," Griffin assured. "They both went to high school with him."

"Griffin just means Jackson has two good friends who are girls," Faith explained, rescuing Jackson from his uncomfortable predicament. "Now, dinner's just about ready, so let's come sit at the table. Drinks, anyone? We have Coke, sweet tea, and lemonade. And water and milk, of course."

"Coke sounds great, sweetheart," answered Bob. "Thanks."

"I'll get it," assured Spencer. "Faith, you take it easy. Jackson, Sam, need a refill?"

"I'll take some more water, if you don't mind," Sam replied.

Spencer took her glass with him into the kitchen, and Faith assigned seats around the table. She'd had the foresight to place Jackson between Griffin and Sam so he wouldn't have to be next to Bob. As they settled into their seats, Spencer brought their drinks out and disappeared back into the kitchen to get the food. He reappeared with a covered skillet and set it on the table before returning to the kitchen for more.

"That smells wonderful!" exclaimed Sam. "Did you make this, Faith, or did Spencer?"

"I did, thank you very much," answered Spencer, returning with a bowl of buttered noodles and a basket of rolls. "My own secret recipe."

Faith giggled. "It's a Campbell's skillet sauce," she said in a stage whisper.

"Hey! Don't give away my secret!" he protested. "This is the first dinner I ever made for you. It's special."

"It is," she agreed, beaming at him. "And I love it. Thanks for cooking tonight, hon."

"Shall we pray?" asked Spencer as he sat down and extended his hands to Faith on one side and Hope on the other. "Lord God, thank You for gathering us together tonight to celebrate. We thank you for Faith as she celebrates her birthday, and also for Bob, whose donation allowed her more years on this earth. We ask that You bless this food tonight, and bless our conversation as well. Thank You, Lord, for Your blessings on our lives. Amen."

As everyone passed around the food, Bob said, "So your

mom tells me you made the football team, Jackson."

"I did."

"As a walk-on, huh?"

"Yep."

"That's a pretty big deal, son. They don't take just anyone off the street. You must be as good as your mom brags. I always thought she was just biased, but to make a Big Ten college football team... Whoa. Pretty impressive."

A sharp retort rose to Jackson's lips, but Sam jumped in before he could say anything. "He's amazing. You should see his highlight reel from high school. The way he cuts through the other team's defense is incredible. And he's made some catches that look impossible. You'll have to come see him play next season."

"Maybe I will," mused Bob, taking a bite of chicken. Jackson silently thanked Sam for her response, which had been far better than his own would have been.

"I'm jealous, man," Spencer said. "It's gonna be awesome to play in the Big House. I didn't think I missed football until I found out you'd made the team."

"Oh, you played too, Doc?" asked Bob.

"In high school. I wasn't nearly as good as Jackson."

"But you were the best player on the team that year," Faith said.

"You even gave me a few pointers, remember?" asked Jackson, grinning at the memory of Spencer's first dinner with their family.

"I remember that!" Faith said. "And then we played a game in the backyard. Boys against girls. Katie just stood there jumping up and down. It was basically you guys against me. How fair is that?" She looked to Sam for sympathy, who shook her head.

Jackson and Spencer both laughed. "Ah, come on, you had fun," argued Spencer, elbowing her playfully. "You just wanted to be around *me*." He wiggled his eyebrows at her, and she rolled her eyes back at him.

"He's right," Jackson said. "You let him tackle you every time."

Bob guffawed as Faith blushed. "Ah, the truth comes out," he said knowingly. "How is Katie, by the way? And Freddie?"

"Katie's fine," answered Jackson. "And it's just *Fred* now. He dropped *Freddie* when he started high school." There was a trace of scorn in his voice. How little Bob knew about his own children.

"But it's hard to remember that," Faith said diplomatically. "We knew him as Freddie for so long, it's hard to make the change."

"How about your mom? How's she doing?" Bob asked.

Faith answered again. "Mom's doing great. Almost done with her first year of college."

"How about that, huh?" Bob chuckled with a little shake of his head. "After all these years. I'm proud of her for going back to get her degree."

Sam nudged Jackson's elbow before he could say anything, her way of reminding him not to make any mean comebacks.

"And you, son? Still thinking of teaching?" Bob looked at him over a forkful of noodles.

"Yes. And coaching."

"But mainly coaching," Sam added teasingly.

"Coaching I can see," Bob responded. "But I never would have imagined you'd go into teaching. As a kid, that seemed like the last thing you'd end up doing."

Jackson's face went hot at his father's comment. His dad barely knew anything about him, and a six-year-old kid was hardly a litmus test for the type of adult he would one day be. He opened his mouth to respond, but Sam discreetly reached under the table and squeezed his knee.

"That's what his siblings said too, isn't it, Jackson?" she answered hastily. "But he'll be great at it. He's got the right temperament to make kids behave in the classroom and on the field."

She shot Jackson a pleading look, and he nodded briefly at her, playing along. "Sam was the one who was most encouraging about it when I decided to be a teacher. She's been my biggest fan for a long time."

Sam flushed slightly at the praise and changed the subject. "So, Faith, are you going to tell us what your dad's gift was earlier? Or is that a secret?"

Faith laughed. "He gave me an assortment of hand sanitizer."

Sam looked confused. "Oh. Interesting gift."

"It's sort of an inside joke," Spencer explained. "Faith has to be really careful about germs because of her transplant. The anti-rejection medications she takes are immunosuppressant, so she has to take extra precautions not to expose herself to germs and sickness."

"I use hand sanitizer religiously," Faith continued. "I have some with me at all times."

Realization dawned on Sam's face. "That explains why Jackson made me squirt some on my hands when we got here."

"Yeah. It's kind of embarrassing to ask visitors to do that, but I can't take any chances."

"No, I totally understand now," said Sam. "So how do you avoid getting sick from the kids?"

"That's a challenge," admitted Faith. "I'm always making them wash their hands, especially during flu season. But at school and day care they're exposed to so many germs it's insane. And kids are *supposed* to get sick. It builds their immune systems. So when they do get sick, I wear a mask around the house and sanitize everything and make Spencer deal with the invalids."

Spencer chimed in with a sad shake of his head. "It's my cross to bear in life."

Jackson chuckled as Faith hit her husband's arm. "Oh, stop!" she protested. "You knew all this before you asked me to marry you!"

"So that's why Jackson has to change poopy diapers for you?" asked Sam slyly, with a sideways glance in his direction.

Jackson felt his face redden again as Bob snorted across the table. "Atta boy, son! It takes a real man to change a diaper."

"It does," Spencer agreed, jokingly swelling with pride. "Although I have to admit, I'm not complaining that Jackson's willing to help share that duty when he visits. And it was nice when Miranda was here and she could help."

"Miranda is Uncle Jackson's other girlfriend," Griffin told Bob.

Sam choked on her bite of food and took a swallow of water, and Faith spoke quickly. "It's not that I *can't* change diapers, but they want me to wear a full hazmat suit if I do."

"Do you seriously do that?" asked Sam, her voice nearly recovered. "Wear a hazmat suit?"

"Usually not. I did at first, but it's a ridiculous hassle. I wear a mask and gloves and scrub my hands and arms when I'm done."

"But that's only if I'm not around," Spencer said. "I won't let her change diapers when I'm here. I don't want her taking chances."

Jackson spoke next. "Faith has all sorts of restrictions since her transplant, don't you, sis?"

"I really do. It's not an exaggeration to say it was life-changing. I have to get bloodwork on a regular basis, especially now that I'm pregnant. Right after my surgery, they had to do it twice a week as they figured out the right dosage for my medications. I felt like a guinea pig. They'd test me, adjust my dosage, and test me again until they got it right. It was pretty frustrating."

"I can only imagine," Sam murmured.

"I also take anti-rejection meds twice a day," Faith continued. "I have an alarm set on my phone to remind me. Plus I have to be really careful what I eat. I can't eat certain foods because they mess with my meds or carry a risk of contamination. Eating out is something I do sparingly, because I don't know how it was prepared and who touched the plates, and buffets are totally out. Who knows how many people coughed or sneezed near the food?"

"Being in public is challenging because germs are everywhere," Spencer added. "She's supposed to wear a mask in public, but she only does that on occasion."

"It depends where I go," Faith said. "Whenever I go to the doctor, I wear a mask, because sick people come to the doctor's office all the time. And sometimes if I'm in a crowded place like the mall or the grocery store, or even church, I'll put one on. I also wear it during flu season in my classes."

"It seems like that kind of restricts what you can do and where you can go. Like, are you allowed to travel?" Sam asked.

"Yes and no. Travel *is* complicated. Originally Spencer wanted to take me on a European cruise for our honeymoon, but that was out of the question, especially less than a year after my transplant. They were still monitoring me pretty closely with regular bloodwork and appointments. They weren't about to let me out of the country and on a crowded boat with all those strangers, eating from buffets and restaurants the entire time."

"So what did you do instead?"

"We went to Breckenridge, Colorado," answered Spencer. "I tried to teach Faith how to ski."

Faith laughed. "I was pretty bad, wasn't I? By the end I could make it down the bunny hill about half the time without falling down. But then again, our family didn't go skiing every winter like yours did."

"That's true. You did great, all things considered. We stayed in a nice little chalet and I hired a housekeeper to cook for us while we were there. Trust me, I wasn't about to subject Faith to *my* cooking for our honeymoon. I didn't want to get on her bad side already!"

Sam smiled. "Aww, that was sweet!"

"But don't let him fool you," said Jackson. "It was no 'little' chalet. You should see the pictures they texted us. It had four bedrooms! Our whole family could have stayed there!"

Sam nudged him with a giggle. "He's just jealous because he's never been out of Michigan."

"That was the first time *I'd* been out of state," Faith said. "And I don't think Mom left Michigan until her honeymoon with David, other than Chicago."

"You're always welcome to come visit me," offered Bob, surprising Jackson. He'd been enjoying the conversation so much he'd almost forgotten his father was there. "To get to Chicago, you have to drive through part of Indiana too, so you get two new states!"

Jackson didn't respond, but his sister answered, "That would be fun, actually. I'd love to tour the Windy City. Maybe a summer trip sometime?" She peeked at Spencer, who shrugged agreeably.

"Not this summer, though," he answered. "With the move and the new baby, we've got enough on our plates. And this time, please, no wine?"

Bob and Faith both laughed, and Faith turned to Jackson and Sam to explain. "When we got together for my twenty-first birthday, he brought me a bottle of expensive wine as a gift, but I'm not allowed to drink alcohol after my liver transplant."

"I had to force myself to drink it in her stead." Spencer said with a wink.

"Big sacrifice on your part," said Faith teasingly.

"Hey, I'm looking out for your well-being!"

"You are. You're actually very good about that. You pamper me. In fact, I feel like sometimes the people around me are more considerate of me than I am of myself! Like, Jackson will text and tell me he's coming down with a cold and shouldn't come over for dinner. Or Spencer will bring along a plate of food from home if we're going to a party. It's great to have such supportive family surrounding me, watching out for my health."

"That all seems really complicated," Sam said. "I'd have a hard time keeping track of everything you're supposed to do and not do."

"It was really overwhelming at first, but it's not so bad once you get used to it. It's just part of life for me now. But I married a future doctor, so I know I'm in good hands." Faith beamed at her husband. "Spencer is the one who figured out how sick I was in the first place."

Spencer shrugged modestly. "When your girlfriend is as yellow as a highlighter, it's not too hard to deduce there's something wrong."

"Spencer Young!" Faith protested. "I was not! Slightly

jaundiced is all."

Sam laughed as Spencer shook his head and muttered under his breath, "Highlighter."

"That must have been a crazy time for everyone," Sam said. "And tense while you were waiting for a transplant."

"It was," agreed Spencer. "But thankfully her dad was a match."

Faith spoke next. "Had the situation been reversed, though, it wouldn't have worked. Dad's liver was plenty big enough to give part of his, but I couldn't have donated part of mine to him because he would have needed a bigger portion than I could give."

"It worked out exactly the way it was supposed to," Bob insisted. "And I got the better end of the deal. Being the donor, my surgery was free for me, and I don't have the hassle of anti-rejection meds. I still have my own liver, and it regenerated itself."

"You know, a century ago no one would have dreamed a living donor transplant would be possible," Spencer said, "but now they're fairly common."

"And thank goodness for that!" exclaimed Faith. "It saved my life! Thanks again, Daddy," she said as she turned to Bob.

"For you, baby girl, anything," he replied with a smile.

Jackson had the sudden realization that his father was sincere in his affection toward Faith. The two obviously shared a special bond, not just from the transplant, but from the effort both of them had put into rebuilding trust between one another. He'd always been suspicious of his dad's motives, but watching him interact with Faith made Jackson believe that perhaps Bob really did love his daughter. It made Jackson wonder what his dad felt toward *him*. It was an uncomfortable thought, and Jackson quickly pushed it aside.

"Cake, anyone?" Spencer asked.

Faith's birthday cake was a hit with the kids and adults alike, and shortly after finishing dessert, Bob stood. "I've got a long drive ahead of me, and I have to work tomorrow. I hate to eat and run, but..."

Faith stood and gave him a hug. "Thanks for coming, Daddy."

Jackson stood as well and extended his hand. "Yeah, thanks for coming." He couldn't quite bring himself to call him "Dad" yet.

Bob shook his hand with a smile in his eyes, and Jackson noted that Faith's eyes were shining as well. He had a feeling he'd just given his sister the best birthday gift possible.

CHAPTER

46

"Do you have a minute?"

David looked up in surprise at Grace's question. He was in their room changing his clothes after school, and this wasn't normally a time to have a deep discussion. Fleetingly, he wondered if he was in trouble. He hadn't missed any birthdays or anniversaries, had he?

"Sure," he said. "What's on your mind?"

Grace perched on the edge of the bed, toying with a loose thread on the comforter. "I… um… I was wondering if you could proofread my psych paper for me."

David's brow creased in confusion. This was hardly an unusual request, but she seemed nervous asking it this time. "I'd be happy to," he assured. "You know that."

"But this is different," she explained, her eyes still focused on the comforter. "This is for the project I had to do for my case study. The one I was volunteering for at the crisis pregnancy center."

"Okay." He still wasn't following where she was leading this conversation.

"I wrote about how people use the free services there. Some people are genuinely looking for help or advice, while others just come in for a free pregnancy test or ultrasound. And I've been there long enough now that they're starting to let me be an advocate, following a script as I ask the clients questions when they come in. It's been really interesting."

"So you've mentioned," he replied, sitting down next to her on the bed. "You've told me about the interviews you do. That's neat."

"Yeah, well…" She still avoided eye contact and looked instead at the wall. "The last few times I've gone I asked if I could sit in on a few ultrasounds, with the client's permission. I want to know how it affects the pregnant moms, seeing the images of their babies on the screen as opposed to just talking to a counselor. And today I got to talk to the ultrasound technician during a lull. She's a volunteer from a local OB-GYN office, but she's pretty swamped. They could use another tech." Taking a deep breath as if to gather her courage, she finally looked him in the eye. "I want to be that other tech."

David blinked in surprise, not completely sure he understood. "I mean, get a degree in sonography, David," she clarified. "It would take me probably two, maybe three more years at this rate."

He merely stared at her in astonishment, and she hurried on, concentrating on the loose thread again. "I know finances are tight, and I know you want me to get a job to help out, but I really feel like God is pushing me in this direction. Yes, it would be pro bono, but I feel like I'd really be making a difference—maybe even impacting life or death decisions. It's a completely different type of paycheck."

She looked at him then, her eyes pleading, and all David could do was pull her into a hug, unable to speak over the lump in his throat. He'd never been so proud of his wife as he was at that moment.

Grace handed her final exam to the professor nervously. It was her last psychology class of the semester, and although she'd studied for it, her mind tended to go blank when she got flustered.

"Do you have a second?" Dr. Benson asked quietly as Grace handed in the test.

Her heart plummeted. This could not be good. Managing a weak nod, she braced herself for bad news.

Dr. Benson pulled out Grace's paper from her project and handed it back to her. She'd gotten an A. Grace looked questioningly at the professor, who smiled. "I wanted to tell you that your paper was one of the most interesting and most original ideas I've seen in quite awhile," she said, still keeping her voice low so as not to disturb the handful of students still working on the exam. "I enjoyed reading it, and I can tell the experience of volunteering at the pregnancy center really made an impression on you. I like that you made it into a double case study. Not only did you get the chance to see how the clients responded to the free services offered, you also evaluated how the experience affected *you*. I'm glad this class prompted you to volunteer there so you could realize your desire to do sonography. Congratulations on deciding on a major, and I'll selfishly take credit for planting the idea in your head." She winked, and Grace laughed in return, giddy with relief.

"Thank you, Dr. Benson. You're right—if it hadn't been for your class and this project, I wouldn't have volunteered there. It worked out really well. And thank you for your work with our class. It was far more challenging than I thought it would be, but it was good for me to be stretched like that. I learned a lot."

"Excellent! It's been a pleasure to have you join us for class. I enjoyed your questions. It's refreshing to have an adult in class to offer a different perspective than the typical college-aged students. I can tell you took the class seriously."

"It was fascinating," she replied. "I wasn't expecting that." She blushed at the way she'd phrased the thought, but Dr. Benson laughed it off.

"I take that as an even greater compliment, then," she assured her. "Best of luck to you in the future." She shook Grace's hand, and Grace walked out of the classroom with the paper grasped proudly in her hands, grinning from ear to ear. As soon as she was out of the building, she pulled out her phone and called David.

"How'd it go?" he asked in greeting. He knew how nervous she was about this exam.

"I got an A!" she informed him excitedly.

There was a pause on the other end. "She... graded the exams already?" he asked in confusion.

"No, I mean on my paper! She told me it was one of the more interesting case studies she's read, and she really liked how I tied in the way it affected me too, and not just the clients."

She could hear his smile in his voice as he responded. "That's wonderful, sweetie! I'm so proud of you! You put a lot of work into that paper, and it paid off. Aren't you glad you didn't quit last semester after all?"

Grace laughed. "Thanks for forcing me to stick with it," she teased.

"Just doing my part. So how do you want to celebrate?"

"It's hardly worth celebrating passing a class," she objected.

"I disagree. This is a huge deal for you, Grace. I'll think of something. Leave it to me. I'll see you when I get home. Love you!" He hung up without giving her a chance to respond, and she shook her head with a smile.

David arrived home later than usual with the girls that afternoon, and the twins ran into the house excitedly to give their mother a hug.

"Daddy bought something for you!" Evelyn exclaimed.

"Two things!" added Charlotte.

David entered then with Katie, holding out a huge bouquet of flowers. Grace's eyes clouded with tears. Her husband generally looked upon cut flowers as a waste of money. The fact that he'd bought her such a pretty bouquet meant a lot to her.

"They were on sale at Kroger," Evelyn explained.

Grace laughed as David sighed. "You really don't need to point that out, Evy," he said wearily.

"It's okay," Grace assured him with a kiss. "I'd do the exact same thing. They're just as beautiful whether they're on sale or not."

"The flowers were my idea," Charlotte bragged.

"But *this* was my idea!" exclaimed Evelyn, holding out a bag of chocolates. "Daddy promised you'd share."

Again Grace giggled as she looked at her husband. "You both certainly know what makes me happy. Flowers and chocolate—who could ask for anything more? Thank you all!"

The sound of the front door opening signaled Fred's arrival. He raced into the kitchen and burst out, "I won the poster contest! They picked my design!"

"Fred! That's wonderful!" Grace engulfed her son in a hug. His class had sponsored a contest to design a logo for the class, open to any freshman who wanted to enter. Contestants had submitted entries two weeks earlier, and the class had voted on them to choose which would be their official logo for shirts and correspondence. Fred had worked hard on his submission, and while Grace was admittedly biased, she'd thought his finished product was pretty spectacular.

"Congrats, son," David seconded, grinning away. "We have all sorts of things to celebrate today!"

"Can we go out to eat since everyone's so happy?" asked Katie hopefully.

"Why not?" he answered with a chuckle. "Fred's choice. Unless you'd rather I buy you some flowers too," he teased the high schooler.

Fred made a face. "I'll take dinner out any day."

"Can we get dessert there?" Evelyn asked brightly.

"Don't push your luck, young lady," David warned with a twinkle in his eye. "Remember, you've got a few chocolates coming your way."

"Yes! And speaking of which, let's break into them now, shall we?" Grace offered, ripping open the bag. Everyone clustered around her excitedly, like baby birds wishing to be fed. As they all savored their chocolates, Grace snuck a glance at Fred, who was obviously pleased that his family was making a big deal out of his news. He'd come a long way since the beginning of the school year. So had she.

It looked like their morning prayers had been answered after all.

EPILOGUE

Four months later

Running onto the field with the rest of the team was every bit as exhilarating as Jackson hoped it would be. The roar of the crowd in Michigan stadium reverberated so loudly Jackson could almost feel it in his bones. It was the first home game of the season, and the crowd was excited to be back in the swing of football again.

Jackson scanned the section where his family had gotten seats, close to the fifty-yard line behind the home sideline. Yes, there they were, proudly sporting his jersey and taking pictures and videos of him. He tried to be nonchalant as he waved in their direction, but the truth was he had never been so excited.

He looked down the row, mentally taking stock of everyone who was there. His mom, David, Uncle Andy and Aunt Olivia, Fred, and Katie had all come from Mapleport. Sam had driven over from Lansing to join them, and Spencer and Faith were there as well. It meant a lot that his sister had made the effort to be there. In this crowd, germs were everywhere, but Faith was there with her mask on, armed with plenty of hand sanitizer.

Faith and Spencer had had a busy summer with the move into their new house and the addition of their third baby, Preston Leo, in July. Jackson knew Faith was physically and emotionally drained, but she was here to support him. What a sister.

Because the seats were so close together, it was difficult to tell for sure, but Jackson was pretty sure there was still one empty seat at the end of their row. He swallowed over the lump of disappointment in his throat, surprised that he cared as much as he did. He hadn't even been certain the final person of their party would make it, but seeing the empty seat felt very final. He shouldn't have gotten his hopes up.

Shrugging it off, Jackson turned his mind back to the warm ups on the field, trying to get into his zone for the game ahead, where all he focused on was football. As they finished their warm ups and the team trotted off the field, however, he couldn't resist one last look at the section where his family was. The final seat remained empty.

But wait. Someone was jogging down the steps, getting close to that row... Jackson smiled as that someone slipped into the final seat of the row next to Spencer. He turned his attention back to the coach, who was giving final reminders to the team before the kickoff. Now he could put his full concentration into the game.

Three and a half hours later, Jackson fought his way through the crowd to his family in the bleachers. Miranda had joined them by now, coming from her spot in the student section. Everyone surrounded him with hugs and congratulations on Michigan's victory. He grinned proudly and posed with them for pictures. One member of the party stood off to the side, clearly not wanting to intrude, but Jackson walked over to address him.

"Hey, Dad. Thanks for coming."

Bob smiled. "I told you I'd come see you play. Glad I was able to make this game."

"Me too," Jackson replied, surprised that somehow over the past number of months he was able to make the comment in all sincerity.

Bob shook his hand and turned to walk away. The rest of Jackson's family was discussing plans to get together at Spencer and Faith's new house, but Jackson knew they wouldn't mind if he was a little late. "Hey, Dad?" he called.

Bob turned, and Jackson asked, "Want to grab some pizza at Cottage Inn before you head back?"

A slow smile spread across Bob's face.

"You got it, son."

AUTHOR'S NOTE

Every book has its own backstory, but this particular manuscript has a few personal connections for me. Like Jackson, my son really did break his femur playing football, although it was a backyard game rather than organized football. The first chapter is nearly an exact retelling of our own experiences, complete with Dr. Kahn and the father and daughter on the elevator. I pray that wherever that father is, he and his family have the peace that passes understanding, the peace that only God can give His children.

Likewise, Sam's brother Chris is inspired by a real-life friend who graciously agreed to allow me to share his story. His mental illness caused him to commit a crime for which he is now serving time in prison. However, God has even used this experience to further His kingdom. The Lutheran pastor who visits him has started a prison ministry which now includes five inmates, one of whom is on death row. Never underestimate the power and work of the Holy Spirit!

ACKNOWLEDGMENTS

As always, I am humbled by the number of people and amount of support that helped to make this book a reality. God has truly blessed me with wonderful friends, family, and fans.

To my husband Jonathan and children Benjamin, Timothy, Miriam, Sarah, and Samuel, thank you for always rooting me on. Benjamin, I know it's not the claim to fame you would have chosen, but thanks for allowing me to use your own experience of a broken femur to lend credibility to Jackson's story.

Mom and Dad, thank you for bringing us up in a Christian home and for encouraging and challenging us to stand up for what's right. Marty and Anthony, you're the best brothers I could ask for, and I thank you for your advice and support along the way.

Anthony, I cannot thank you enough. Thanks for your formatting and design expertise, for sharing your knowledge of the U of M campus, and for the Chocolate Mocha coffee that accompanied much of the writing of this book, but most of all for your continued support and encouragement. You are one of my biggest fans.

My editor, Abi, deserves much of the credit for this book. Abi, your suggestions were instrumental, and I thank you for the care with which you handle my manuscripts. I think you love my characters nearly as much as I do!

To Suzie at Sunset Rose Books, thank you for yet another

fantastic cover design and for your flexibility. Blessings on your own writing!

For all my friends who encouraged me along the way and volunteered to read the manuscript, thank you. Thanks especially to Jenny, Michelle, Sandy, Kristen, Kathleen, Melissa, Sarah, Jane, Mary, Kendra, Kaethe, Esther, Shirley, Barb, and Deb.

To the real Dr. Kahn, thank you for taking such good care of Benjamin's broken leg. You are a fantastic doctor and a delightful person, but I hope we never have need of your services again.

And, of course, thank you, dear reader! Thank you for caring enough about my characters to welcome them into your hearts. I love to hear your feedback and reactions.

Above all, I thank my Lord and Savior Jesus for granting me saving faith in Him. With His strength, I pray I may always stand firm.

OTHER BOOKS BY RUTH MEYER

CHILDREN'S BOOK

SOLA SERIES

Read the first chapter of each of the Sola books at:
www.ruthmeyerbooks.com/books

Discussion questions for these books, including *Stand Alone*,
are available as well.

Book 5 of the Sola Series coming in 2020

CONNECT WITH RUTH

WEBSITES
www.ruthmeyerbooks.com
www.truthnotespress.com

NEWSLETTER
www.ruthmeyerbooks.com/newsletter

BLOG
www.TruthNotes.net

FACEBOOK
www.facebook.com/TruthNotes

AMAZON AUTHOR PAGE
www.amazon.com/Ruth-Meyer/e/B00E6QC2RI

CPSIA information can be obtained
at www.ICGtesting.com
Printed in the USA
BVHW071627071019
560429BV00005B/516/P